Glen Erik Hamilton is a Seattle native. His first Van Shaw novel, *Past Crimes* (2015) won a Strand Critics Circle Award and was nominated for all of the other major US crime writing awards – the Edgar, Nero, Anthony, Barry, Macavity and Shamus Awards.

Hard Cold Winter

A VAN SHAW NOVEL

GLEN ERIK HAMILTON

FABER & FABER

First published in 2016
by Faber & Faber Limited
Bloomsbury House, 74–77 Great Russell Street
London WC1B 3DA
This paperback edition first published in 2016

Printed in England by CPI Group (UK) Ltd, Croydon, CR0 4YY

The right of Glen Erik Hamilton to be identified as author of this work has
been asserted in accordance with Section 77 of the Copyright, Designs and
Patents Act 1988

This is a work of fiction. Names, characters, places, and incidents are
products of the author's imagination or are used fictitiously and are not to be
construed as real. Any resemblance to actual events, locales, organizations, or
persons, living or dead, is entirely coincidental.

*This book is sold subject to the condition that it shall not, by way of trade
or otherwise, be lent, resold, hired out or otherwise circulated without the
publisher's prior consent in any form of binding or cover other than that in
which it is published and without a similar condition including this condition
being imposed on the subsequent purchaser*

A CIP record for this book
is available from the British Library

ISBN 978–0–571–31805–6

2 4 6 8 10 9 7 5 3 1

For Mom and For Dad, with Love
They took me to the library and let me run

Hard Cold Winter

Chapter One

I stood on a dark road, on the north side of the ship canal that wound like a lazy snake off Puget Sound. Wind coming off the water stripped another twenty degrees from a night that was already below freezing. No homeless in the little park across the canal tonight. They knew better. Stay in one place too long, and this cold would kill you.

The road was empty. Normal for midnight on a Saturday, but the place might have been just as quiet at noon. Across the road from me was a row of small warehouses lining the canal. A few of the warehouses boasted unbroken windows and exterior lights, weak sixty-watt dots that barely cracked the gloom. Most of the business owners had given up, and boarded up. A neighborhood on the final and fastest part of its downslope.

One feeble lamp dusted specks of light over black letters painted five feet high on the warehouse nearest me. After a decade or two of erosion by rain and wind, the words were barely visible on the cracked wood siding. LONERGAN REPAIR LLC.

Nobody in sight.

But lots of cars.

Not all grouped out in front of the Lonergan building.

Nothing that obvious. But parked here and there along the road and on the side streets were Camaros and Beemer 6 convertibles and higher-end Toyotas with aftermarket racing gear. I'd marked the cars when I'd circled around, getting a feel for the place. Cars for young guys, guys with money to burn. The resale value of my old blue Dodge pickup wouldn't buy a set of rims for most of them.

There was one guard, watching me from the driver's seat of a Ford Excursion thirty yards up the road. I couldn't see him, but I could hear the Ford's engine. So he could keep the heater going.

My cell phone showed no signal here. Not surprising. There would be no calling ahead to announce my arrival.

I walked across the road and up to the warehouse, and around the side of the building toward the water. My breath made visible puffs in the air. The leather of my hiking boots creaked. I'd bought them when I'd returned home to Seattle to stay, less than a month before, and they weren't completely broken in.

The back of the warehouse faced the canal. On the loading dock, six steps up from the pavement, the big metal rolling door was down. Light shone from underneath, where the rubber stripping was cracked with age. I could hear the faint sound of many voices inside, blended together.

At the far side of the dock was a human-sized door, also closed. A man leaned against it, smoking a cigarette, looking at me. With only the dim light coming across the water, neither of us could see each other clearly. He had a walkie-talkie to his ear. Maybe complaining about the cold to his partner, who was warm and cozy in the Excursion.

I walked up the steps and across the loading dock.

"Willard called me," I said.

He glanced down at the bleach-stained Mariners sweatshirt I was wearing. My grandfather's. Now mine. I'd inherited it along with almost all of Dono's other worldly goods ten months ago, the last time I was in Seattle. But I still tended to think of the house and everything inside of it as his.

"What's your name?" the guard asked. He was a beefy guy, about two bucks and change and taller than me. He'd weighed closer to one-ninety when he'd bought his black sport coat. His biceps and shoulders strained the fabric. Maybe it was intentional.

"Get Willard," I said, stepping a little closer. The guard's eyes caught the scars on my face, held there. His jaw went a little slack.

"O-kay, Chief," he said. "I know who you mean. Stay right here."

He knocked twice on the door, his eyes still on me, and it opened a crack. He went in. Light flooded out onto the dock, and I caught a glimpse of a slim girl lifting a tray of drinks from a bar, and another guard in another black sport coat, glowering at me before the door closed.

When it opened, light didn't come booming out again. There was no room for it, not around Will Willard.

3

Willard was one of the largest men I'd ever known. It wasn't just his height, or weight. He was massive. Like a granite block from a quarry, cut to man-shape and set loose.

"Get in here," he said. His voice had come from the same pit, pieces smashed to gravel and turned over and over in a concrete mixer.

I followed him into the bright interior of the warehouse, the light provided by dozens of work lamps and the occasional tiki torch. Half a dozen circular tables covered in green felt were set up around the broad room. Six or eight men sat at each, playing cards. Each table had a dealer, and a wooden shoe from which the dealers swept cards across the felt. All of the dealers were female, dressed in black blouses and short black skirts. All of them looked attractive from where I was standing. If it wasn't for the warehouse setting, it could have been the back room at any tribal casino in the state.

"Nice setup," I said.

"Portable," Willard said. "It all fits into a moving van."

I wondered if he counted the hot dealers as part of that truckload. "This a regular thing for you?"

"Regular enough."

Enough to mean he didn't have to set up other jobs, I guessed. Willard was in the same line of work as my grandfather had been. They had been partners, on occasion. Burglaries. Robbery. Whatever paid. With his giant size, Willard was way too memorable to work up front, but he could handle a steering wheel or a welding torch better than most. Reliable. And a bigger brain than anyone would expect, behind that Cro-Magnon brow.

"Is it yours?" I said.

Willard didn't reply. I waited, watching the tables. The card games were simple. Blackjack or Texas or variations of stud. The players were all male, and all under thirty. An even assortment of white and Asian and Indian, outfitted in Seattle Hip—laser-straight blue jeans and thick boots and plaid button-downs and logo T-shirts too expensive to look new. I guessed them for the sons of tech movers and venture capital shakers, or maybe they were rising stars themselves. Every once in a while, one of them would glance over at Willard. He had that effect.

I recognized one player. Reuben Kuznetsov. He hadn't spotted me yet. If I was lucky, he would stay focused on his cards.

"It's a partnership," Willard said finally. "I take it on the road. Kick a little up to whoever has the territory. Everybody wins."

"Way cool crowd."

He exhaled slowly. "It is what it is. Kids sick of online poker want a taste of the real thing."

And an underground game, staffed by thugs and dealt by babes, would make a hell of a lot cooler story for them than driving out to the Indian reservations to join the blue-hairs. Judging by the cars outside, I put the buy-in somewhere in the low five figures. With a third of it going to the house, for the privilege.

"You're using a jammer," I said, stating the obvious. No way any of this was winding up on some geek's Twitter feed.

Willard almost sighed. "It's not enough. We have to put all the gadgets into a box, just to keep the idiots from snapping pictures. It's like taking away a hype's syringe."

"So why am I seeing all this glory?" I said.

Willard walked slowly around to the back of the room. I followed him to the small bar. It was a real bar, with sinks and soda guns, with the whole thing on casters for easy transport. A petite girl with a waist-length fall of dark brown hair stood behind it. She gave us both a big smile.

"You want?" Willard said to me.

"If you mean a drink, I'll take whiskey. Neat."

"You got a brand, handsome?" asked the bartender.

"Anything Irish," I said.

"Faithful to your roots," said Willard.

"Dono would have enjoyed this." I nodded at the room. The bartender poured us both two fingers of Jameson 12 in crystal lowball glasses. Posh.

"Here's to him," said Willard, "I miss the son of a bitch."

We drank. I was enjoying the first icy touch of air in my throat chasing the liquor when someone put a hand on my shoulder.

"I know this fucking face," said Reuben K. "Well, half of it, anyway." He laughed at his own joke. So did the short guy standing behind him, on cue.

"Reuben," I said.

Reuben Kuznetsov was the eldest son of a Bratva crime boss, in the loosely affiliated Russian mob. His father, Old Lev, wasn't the only boss with a thumb on the North Pacific coast. He swung more weight and spent more time in Siberia than in Seattle. But connected was connected. And Reuben K lived his life in the decadent West, free from consequences.

"The fuck you doing in Seattle, Van?" he said. Reuben was all extremities. A big square head balanced on his neck, big hands and big feet stuck onto sinewy limbs. He stood close, leaning his high forehead down like an oily sunlamp. "I heard you went into the Army. Killing for your country."

"All good things," I said.

"My people could have told you to keep your ass out of Afghanistan. No way you win in that shithole." He looked me over. "You need work? I have work for somebody like you."

"Just visiting." I nodded at Willard, standing as expressive as a marble column behind me.

Reuben brushed some imaginary dust off the sleeve of his glossy blue 38-long jacket. "Too bad. Good money."

"RuKu," said Reuben's buddy, looking back at the table. "Game's back on." He was a fireplug. Short but wide as hell, with huge trapezius muscles in search of a neck, and stuffed into a silver Raiders jacket. A constellation of anabolic acne on his forehead.

Reuben ignored him. "Hey, Willard," he said. "I still want to get that cage match idea rolling, yes?" He mimed punching. "This crowd could go for a little blood."

"Next year," said Willard.

"How 'bout next weekend?" Reuben jabbed me on the shoulder. "You should get in on that, Van my man. I remember you. Fucking werewolf."

"Catch you later, Reuben," I said.

He grinned and smoothed his slick brown hair back in place. "Nobody fast enough for that, Shaw."

Back when I was a teenager, and Reuben not much older, he was running a whorehouse made up of Novosibirsk girls buying their way into the land of opportunity the only way they could. Reuben sampled the goods as much as he sold them. And he was prone to beating up customers who liked his favorites. The smart johns didn't fight back. Old Lev could make it much worse. The whole situation had given Reuben the idea he was a badass.

Reuben's silvery friend gave me what he thought was a hard stare as they drifted back to the table.

I looked at Willard. "Like I said. Way cool crowd."

"I told you. I kick up to whoever owns the area. Lev's reasonable."

Willard drained the last of his Jameson, put the glass down on the bar. He was looking out at the tables, but his focus was somewhere else.

"It's my niece," he said. "Elana."

I stopped in midsip. "I remember."

" 'Course you do."

"I thought she moved east somewhere."

"And back to Seattle and then south and back here again, for a couple of years now." He waved a shovel-blade hand. "None of that is the point. The point is that she's not here. Not tonight, and not last night, either. She was supposed to be working the tables."

"She's not checking in?"

"She left me a message last night to say she was sorry she didn't show up for work, but she was headed out to the Peninsula. To her boyfriend Kend's cabin, up in the Olympic Forest."

"And she said she'd be back for tonight?"

"Yeah. I got the impression the trip was a last-minute thing. Maybe a party. I didn't think much about it. But I couldn't reach her today. And she didn't show during setup. That's when I called you."

"Elana do that a lot? Blow off work to party?"

"She'd done it before."

"No cell phone towers in the mountains. If she decided to extend her weekend through tonight, she couldn't tell you."

"I know that," he said, exhaling heavily.

"But you called me."

"Elana's easy to read. There was something in her tone, I guess. Too calm. Too flat."

Not like the Elana Coll I remembered at all. A girl of fire, or ice, but not much in between.

"Anything wrong in her life right now?" I said.

Willard grunted. "She's her own person. She insists on it. You know that."

I watched the room for a minute. The games were slow. Inexperienced players, taking their time with every decision, trying hard to look like the guys they'd seen on TV.

"What do you know about Kend?" I said.

"I've met him. Here, in fact. Not this location, but Elana brought him to a couple of the card games we had during the past year. She was showing off a little, I think. Kend seemed all right. Less spoiled than most of these little shits."

"He's rich?" I said.

"He's Kendrick Haymes."

The curve balls just kept coming, low and inside. "Haymes as in . . . ?"

"Haymes as in," Willard confirmed. "Nobody starts a question with those words unless the family's fucking loaded, do they?"

The name Haymes was on a lot of buildings around Seattle. Hell, all around the western half of the state and a few beyond. Kend was a hell of a catch for any girl, especially one with Elana's jagged background.

Willard would have been the black sheep of most families. But Elena's parents, Willard's sister and her husband, had been aggressively committed burnouts. Stoned all day and calling it spiritual. Elana had lived with them in whatever mobile home or camper van they'd squatted in that year. If they were away dancing around some tree in some jungle, she might accept a little help from Willard. Somehow she had survived.

As hard-assed as my grandfather had been, I knew even back then that my home life could have been worse.

Willard tapped his knuckles on the bar. "Tomorrow night I got to have this whole damn room set up in Portland. In California the day after that. Besides, I don't know shit about finding things in the woods." He looked at me. "You do."

"Tell me you can narrow that down."

"The cabin's on private land in the east part of the national park. Inholder, they call it. I got the name of the road it's on."

"Some of those private tracts cover thousands of acres," I said. "But forget that for a minute. Is there some reason you're not calling the county sheriff about Elana? Besides the usual history with you and the cops."

"She's not in any trouble, far as I know."

"As far as you know."

Willard stared at the bustling room. "You're not Dono's kid anymore. I get that. I wouldn't ask you if I thought there would be problems."

Once upon a time, it wouldn't have mattered what Elana might be into. I could have matched her beat for beat in making trouble. B&E. GTA. Grand larceny. Dono had trained me very well.

But like Willard said, I wasn't that kid anymore.

He reached into his pocket and put a small roll of hundreds on the bar. "Just check in on her, all right? It's stupid of me to get wound around the axle on this. Elana probably just blew off work for a couple of nights. But she's family."

He didn't have to say I owed him. He was there during Dono's last days.

"I'll find her," I said.

He nodded. "I'll call you after the game breaks up tonight. Tell you what I know about the cabin."

Willard slipped me the bills as we shook hands. I wove through the tables full of designer hoodies to the exit.

I'd think of it as a weekend excursion. A paid vacation. I could use the thousand bucks. An honorable discharge and the thanks of a grateful nation hadn't bought me much in terms of job prospects.

Outside, Reuben K and his fireplug friend in the Raiders jacket were chatting with the guard at the door. Somebody had turned the exterior light back on. Reuben was smoking. Hand-rolled tobacco, laced with something stronger from the smell of it.

"You really work for the big man now, my friend? Willard's past his ex-pir-ation," he said to me, drawing out the syllables.

"Just dropping by."

"So you say, so you say. Still, you want something better, you know where."

"Not my idea of better," I said.

"What the fuck does that mean?" said Fireplug. "You

watch your mouth, asswipe." His pupils were pinpricks. The guard chuckled.

I looked at Reuben. "He one of yours?" I said.

"Hmm?" Reuben had a little trouble focusing. "Pauly? No, he's jus' hanging around."

"You wanna go?" Pauly said. He was up on his toes, hands already tightened into fists at his sides.

I put my hand on Pauly's face and shoved hard. He took a step back, right off the edge of the loading dock, and fell five feet backward onto the asphalt. The impact sounded like a sack of melons.

The guard hadn't moved. He just stared at me. Pauly moaned. And Reuben started cracking up.

"If he needs an ambulance," I said to the guard as I walked down the steps, "you wait until Willard's moved his stuff out."

"Hey, Shaw," Reuben yelled after me, still bent over with laughter. "You come back when we get the cage matches going. I swear I split any bets you win for me. Fucking beast."

Age Sixteen

Our Paladins were getting creamed. The football game was only one minute into the second half, and already looking like a rerun of the first, with Garfield High rolling over our defense like a threshing machine.

I sat in the stands with Rob and Luis Firmino, surrounded by cheering students and family members of the home team. Enemy territory. They waved their Go Bulldog flags. The Firmino brothers and I were the only crimson blemishes in the waving field of purple, the contrast uncomfortably obvious under the hard glare of the stadium lights.

I'd come to the game partly to watch my friend Davey Tolan play. Davey was small, but he could beat anybody on the field when it came to quick feet. Unfortunately one speed demon wasn't going to get the job done. Davey managed one touchdown until Garfield started crashing the line. So far those six points were the only thing keeping the game from being a shutout.

"Geez, Van," said Rob. "Coach is *pissed* at you."

I knew it. When we'd said hello to our friends at halftime, Coach Kray had ordered us off the field. No one else, just us. And Rob swore he had glared at me from the opposite side of the field during timeouts.

In my first year at Watson High I'd played running back, the same position Davey had now, but by the time I was a sophomore I'd gained enough meat on my bones for Coach to move me to defensive tackle. After a couple of games, he bumped me up to the starting line.

"See that?" he had bellowed after I'd knocked the opposing team's halfback out of bounds and upside down. "Shaw ain't huge. But that's how you mothers should hit somebody! Show some gee-damned aggression!"

14

But early last summer, things had changed for me. My granddad Dono had taken me on two trips, one to Portland, and one east to Billings, Montana. Both jobs were fun. More than that, both were profitable. I'd scored two grand. I wanted more. And that meant keeping my afternoons and weekends free. When practices had started up in July, I wasn't there. Coach Kray called the house. No matter how many times I told him I had taken an after-school job—close enough to the truth—he toasted my ear for ten minutes, telling me how much I was letting down my school, my teammates, and myself. He called once a night for a week, until Dono took the phone from me and quietly informed Coach that if he referred to me as a quitter one more time, Dono would teach him the difference between American football and what he called Belfast Rules Rugby. The phone calls stopped after that.

So now we were getting mauled, and Coach seemed to blame me for the whole mess.

"He'll get over it," I said.

"Whatever," said Luis. "But you better pray you don't pull him for Chem class next semester, Vannie."

Luis liked to call me Vannie. He called everybody by some nickname, even if it ticked them off. Luis didn't care. He also didn't care who knew he had a stone crush on one of the Garfield players. 'Phobes could go screw themselves sideways, he would say, sometimes right to the 'phobes' faces. Which was exactly why Rob had asked me to come to the game, in case Luis's attitude created a situation.

The Paladins fumbled the ball before they could get it to Davey. To look at something else, I scanned the crowd for girls.

I spotted one worth looking at, off our side of the bleachers by the concession stand. Dark hair in mini-braids, very long limbs in purple leggings and a white tank top. She was sitting up on the wheelchair ramp railing, legs tangled around the pipes, shoulders back, like she was posing for an invisible photographer.

Then she turned around. I laughed, mostly at myself.

Elana Coll. Big Will Willard's niece.

What was Elana doing here? She was fourteen, barely. Too young to go to Garfield. With her height she could pass. Maybe she was dating a guy who went here. I usually saw Elana with a flock of tween girls like Lucille Boylan and Tammi Feitz trailing after her.

I watched her. She kept her eyes on the concession stand. The long lines of customers from halftime had dwindled to a trickle of people, and only one skinny kid was left in the stand to take orders. He took the money from each customer and made change out of a little steel lockbox. Cash only, just like the games at Watson.

Boys tossed furtive glances at Elana as they walked past. Some made sure to walk past more than once. Her eyes stayed on the skinny kid, and the money.

"Hang here," I said to Rob. "I'll be back."

"Hustle up. No way I want to sit to the end of this horror movie," Rob said.

"Which one is she?" Luis teased.

Elana was so focused on the concession stand that I was sitting on the railing next to her before she turned. She had painted dark black eyeliner all around her green eyes, and her lips shone under a thick layer of caramel-colored gloss.

"Oh, hey," she said, recognition hitting her. "You're Van."

"I didn't know you were into Mathletes," I said, nodding toward the geeky counter boy.

"Huh?"

"You've been staring at him for like half an hour."

She looked back and forth between the kid and me. "What, are you *stalking* me?"

I grinned. "It's a really dumb idea. The cashbox, I mean."

Elana stiffened and hunched her shoulders. "I don't know *what* you mean. Or care."

"Okay."

I watched the game. She held out for one more Garfield first down.

"Why is it a bad idea?" she asked.

"I gotta guess at a couple of things," I said. "At the end of the third quarter, Computer Camper there will stop selling soda and popcorn and lock everything up, just like at football games at Watson. Maybe you've already got a way to get into the stand. But he'll probably lock the box in a cabinet inside the stand, too."

"Maybe that's not a problem. Maybe I can pick locks."

"Fine."

"You think I'm lying?"

"Like you said, I don't care. So it takes an extra minute or five for you to open the cabinet, and the box. Meanwhile that cop watching the crowd will probably come down here to keep an eye on people leaving the game."

She glanced up the bleachers. She'd known right where the cop was without looking around for him, which was one point in her favor.

"Maybe he comes down," she said. "Maybe not."

"Where you gonna hide the cash?" I said. "It's all small bills. You got no pockets. Unless you're wearing a much bigger bra than you need."

She flushed. "You're an asshole."

"But I'm not wrong."

I watched the game, and the cop, for another minute. He hadn't looked our way. Didn't mean he hadn't noticed Elana hanging around.

"You think you could open the cabinet?" she said.

I was sure I could steal the cop's police cruiser and disable its transponder before he noticed it was gone, but this wasn't a game of you-show-me-yours.

"I think it's too much risk for three or four hundred bucks," I said.

"Would you do it?" said Elana. She slid off the railing to stand almost in front of me, a little slantwise, head

18

tilted just so. Another pose for the unseen photographer. "It would really help me out."

"Nope."

"Please," she said. She moved close, touching my thigh with hers. Close enough for me to smell floral soap and hair spray. She tossed her head back and gave me a big green-eyed invitation.

"Try that on the kid at the counter," I said. "He'll probably hand over the box without even knowing it."

Garfield must have scored again, because the crowd in the bleachers behind us suddenly roared. Elana flinched. When the noise died down she pouted at me and folded her arms.

"Jackoff," she said, without any heat to it. "I need the money."

"We all need the money," I said. "That's why they put it in steel boxes with cops around."

"You go to Watson, right?"

"Yeah."

"I'll be at Roosevelt next year. Too bad." The enticing look was back. "Would have been cool to see you."

I was saying a silent thanks that Elana Coll wouldn't be lurking around during my senior year when she stepped in and kissed me hard on the mouth. I didn't immediately kiss back. I didn't move away. She broke it off an instant before I decided.

"See you," she said, smirking. She took off at a fast walk out the exit. The candy smell of her lip gloss lingered.

When I got back to where the Firminos were sitting, Luis was grinning so wide that the corners of his mouth almost touched his pointy sideburns.

"Ooooo, Vannie," he said.

"I don't know her, do I?" said Rob, frowning at the gate where Elana had left the stadium. "She's hot."

"She's like fourteen," I said.

Luis waved a hand, weary of the world and everyone in it. "If there's grass on the field, then you play, fool."

"Flag!" laughed Rob. "Ten yards at *least*."

I shook my head. Elana Coll had definitely scored some points off me. I just wasn't sure how.

Chapter Two

At six a.m. the next morning I joined the line of cars filing onto the early ferry to Bainbridge Island. My truck's cold engine clattered in protest as I gunned it up the steep ramp and onto the ferry's upper parking level. By the time the boat began its sluggish pull away from the pier, I'd bought a cup of coffee and was standing out on the deck.

I passed the hot paper cup between hands and looked at the black skyline still waiting for dawn. The city had changed radically in the ten years I had been away. Was still changing. Evolution seemed to be a constant. Even after the economy tanked, construction cranes kept sprouting up like skeletal sunflowers, transforming the old into new and the newer into bigger. Corporations took advantage of the slump to double down on foreclosed real estate.

Luce Boylan was making the same wager, hoping that the Morgen—the downtown bar she owned which had once belonged to my grandfather and Luce's uncle— would ride the wave of urban renewal and its lease would multiply in value.

Luce had been drifting off to sleep when I'd left. The two of us had tumbled into bed shortly after she'd closed up the bar around three and come upstairs to her small one-bedroom. She'd told me about her night and I'd told her about Willard and his niece. Luce and Elana had run in the same pack as young girls, but they had fallen out of touch when their group split into different high schools.

Somewhere in the middle Luce and I had stopped talking and started undressing each other. A lot of our conversations went that way. I'd only been home a month. The bloom was still on the rose, as Dono would have put it.

We'd been dozing when my phone pinged with a message from Willard, spelling out what little he knew about the location of Kendrick Haymes's cabin. I tucked Luce in, and made the short drive to Pier 52 and the ferry terminal.

The trip across Elliott Bay wasn't long. I was still thinking about how Luce's hair smelled like freshly sanded cherry wood when the big engines downshifted, and a cloud of acrid diesel fumes caught up to the slowing boat.

State highways traced an almost straight line across Bainbridge Island and the first part of the Peninsula, until the blacktop connected with the Hood Canal Bridge. The bridge took me over the canal, to the last piece of continental U.S. before the Pacific Ocean. It was a hell of a piece. More than half a million acres of wilderness, big enough to surround the Olympic Mountain range and the national park named for it.

Willard's text said Kend's cabin was on a private road off of Salismount Lane. Google Maps depicted the lane as a very crooked line, deep in the eastern peninsula. The GPS got me most of the way, following roads with names like Penny Creek and Buckhorn. But it still took me half an hour and two passes to find what must be Salismount, a narrow strip of asphalt with no signage.

Once I was off the charted roads, there was nothing but giant trees, any direction I looked. The pavement was shaded and wet, and the truck's tires slipped an inch or two every time I turned the wheel or tapped the brake.

For the first half mile it was easy going. But the farther I went, the thicker the white layer covering the ferns and mossy soil in the ditches became. The asphalt ended and my tires started crunching an uneven beat over frozen gravel. Another half inch of snow under the treads, and I'd have to stop and put on chains.

As it was, I ran out of road. Tire tracks led off Salismount. Multiple sets of tracks, recent enough to be clearly visible in the dirty snow. The tracks followed a short dirt lane, which curved for another twenty yards before it ran into a closed gate. I got out to take a look.

The gate was made of welded iron pipes and corrugated sheet metal, and chained with a heavy padlock. The padlock had a Day-Glo yellow foam cover to keep it from freezing solid in rain and cold. My breath made dragon plumes in the air.

I could have the padlock open in less than a minute. Dono's good set of lockpicks was hidden under the wheel well in the truck.

But I wanted to stretch my legs. It was half the reason I'd agreed to Willard's request. After leaving the big man's card game the night before, I'd swung by my house and packed a ruck. With my Army gear and what I'd found while sorting through Dono's stuff during the last few weeks, I had everything I might need for a couple of days in the wild.

Willard's thousand dollars filled in the other half of my motivation. The sizable nut I'd earned during my last short visit to Seattle had disappeared just as fast, sucked away by legal fees and repaying favors and especially Dono's astronomical hospital bills. Only the rich could afford to die slowly.

My ruck weighed about forty pounds, counting the two gallons of fresh water in the CamelBak. Less than half of what I was used to humping. It felt odd on my shoulders without the balancing weight of a combat kit and ammunition. Just another little adjustment to being a civilian.

There had been a lot of those discoveries recently. After ten years of taking orders on where to go and what to go, the bigger changes to my life were obvious, and welcome. But small things scratched at me. Choosing the shirt I was wearing had taken half an hour. The streets smelled unfamiliar late at night, after Luce's bar had closed, all damp and charged with electricity. Even the buildings seemed to lean toward me. I used to be a city kid.

So I'd go for a long walk. Check in on Elana Coll and

tell her that she owed her uncle a thousand bucks' worth
of bartending time. Enjoy the scenery. Not a bad deal.
And I was curious to lay eyes on Elana again, after more
than ten years.

I wasn't sure how far the Haymes road went. Willard
thought there might be a main house that the family used,
along with Kend's cabin, somewhere in all their family
acreage.

The road wound slowly upward. After an hour of hiking I guessed my elevation at about 1,500 feet. My breath
was steady and my lungs burned just a little from the
chill. It was easy hiking. The Olympics were an impressive range of mountains, but gentle. Afghan mountains
were like stone knives, slicing up from the earth to shatter
anyone foolish enough to underestimate them.

Eventually the road emerged from the trees. It curved
along the sunlit edge of the mountain, providing a stretch
with no snow on the ground and a view over the forest below. Countless trees blanketed the horizon and
crumpled into folds between the nearest peaks. I stopped
to open the ruck and eat some jerky and an apple I'd
grabbed off Luce's counter.

Overhead, a hawk was circling. Watching the road in
case some small animal dashed across, maybe. I drank
water until I'd had enough, and then drank a little more
as I hiked on. The road became steeper. Most of the thin
layer of snow here had frozen solid, and my progress
slowed as I picked my way around the icy patches.

25

I wasn't worried about missing the cabin. The multiple sets of tire tracks had been a constant companion since the locked gate. I tried to guess what they belonged to. One was a midsized car with tires that were nearly bald. The second might be a small sports car, front-wheel drive, with newer curving treads that looked like fishhooks. The third was the easiest to spot. A dually, a big truck with four wheels on the rear axle.

Willard had said it might have been a party that had tempted Elana to play hooky from work. There was only one set of tracks for the car with worn tires. The other two vehicles, the sports car and the dually, had gone up the road in my direction and come back down again. I'd have to hope the bald tires belonged to Elana.

Within another four miles the road had narrowed sharply, to where the big dually truck would have had barely a foot of clearance on either side. Low branches hung down over the road, and the shade was thick. All of the tire tracks overlapped now, making two long, straight indistinguishable channels. I hiked along one of them. There was less snow underfoot here, thanks to the canopy of the trees. But the ground was still frozen, and my boot soles made only soft thumps, like walking on concrete. In the quiet, I could hear individual branches moving above me in the mild wind.

Then I heard a distant sound that was not the trees, or the wind. A low animal snort of exhalation and effort, from somewhere out in front of me. I stopped.

26

When the sound didn't repeat, I took a few quiet steps forward. And a few more. Far out of my sight, in the thick of the woods, something like fabric or wings rustled. I moved off the road and into the trees.

The ground was twisted by roots and covered with leaves and moss and millions of evergreen needles. On every step I put my foot down softly. When I had gone about a hundred paces, I heard the snorting noise again.

Definitely an animal. A large animal.

The noise had come from my two-o'clock, off in the shaded depths of the forest. When I looked hard in that direction I could see a yard or so of angled rooftop, an unnaturally sharp edge among the branches. Kend's cabin, almost certainly. It was another fifty yards off.

The trees offered plenty of cover. I moved closer, taking my time. The road to my right turned sharply to lead in front of the cabin. A blue Volvo hatchback was parked off to the side.

I was looking at the back of the place through the trees. It was maybe fifteen by twenty, more of a tiny house with wood siding than a true cabin. More sounds of movement now, from around the front. I slowly walked a wide circle, keeping my distance.

There was another snort, and a tearing sound. My circle widened and the area in front of the cabin came into view.

And I stopped and held very, very still.

A black bear. It stood on all fours about ten feet in front of the cabin, its head bent low as it worked at something on the ground. It snorted again, and tugged, and moved around to get a better grip.

And I saw what the bear was dragging.

The half-eaten carcass of a human.

Chapter Three

By the size of it, the body was a man's. It had hiking shoes and jeans on, and its arms were still mostly covered by blue plaid sleeves. The torso, or what was left of the torso, was red where the bear had been feeding and grayish where it hadn't. I couldn't see the man's face, and considered that fact a small blessing.

Was he Kendrick Haymes? Where was Elana?

The bear huffed. It swung its big head around and looked out into the trees. Maybe it had caught my scent. I continued my imitation of a statue.

I didn't know a lot about bears. They weren't high on the list of probable engagements in Army training. I knew they preferred to avoid people, and that they had sharp ears and even better noses, like dogs. And they hibernated. What the hell was this one doing awake in February? Maybe bears didn't hibernate all the way until spring.

Or maybe it had smelled something worth waking up for.

The bear turned back to the body. After another moment, I could hear it chewing.

The smart thing for me to do would be to turn around, double-time it back to the truck or at least to where my cell phone could get a signal. I wasn't eager to challenge a three-hundred-pound animal eating what might be its first meal in weeks.

But I kept thinking of Elana. Was she trapped in the cabin by the bear? Was she hurt? The door was open. No lights on inside, from the narrow sliver I could see. No smoke coming out of the chimney, either.

The bear tugged at the corpse, tearing off strips of its plaid shirt and what might be a down vest.

I had to see what was in the cabin. Or who.

Hikers sometimes carried airhorns to scare off bears, or some kind of supercharged pepper sprays for really desperate situations. I didn't have either of those things. What I really wanted was a flashbang grenade. Something that would send the bear and every other creature nearby running for the next county.

I didn't have that, either, but the notion got me thinking about what was in my ruck.

Five paces behind me was a huge Douglas fir, with a trunk wide enough to conceal a whole squad. I faded back to it. Slowly, I took off the ruck and opened the pocket with the emergency kit, in a soft waterproof bag. In the kit I found three signal flares, yellow tubes about ten inches long with translucent caps, and a small roll of duct tape.

I'd also brought a couple of three-gallon trash bags. I wadded up the mouth of one of the bags and blew into it, until it was mostly inflated, like a balloon. When I stopped I was a little dizzy from hyperventilating. A cheap high.

It would have been funny, if it weren't for what was happening at the cabin.

I pushed a signal flare halfway into the closed mouth of the bag. With the bag inflated, its plastic was held away from the tip of the flare inside. I sealed the bag tightly around the middle of the flare's tube with duct tape.

When I finished my invention it looked something like a small sad beach ball. Ludicrous. But it was all I had.

Edging around the side, I looked for the bear. It was facing away from me, pawing at the thigh of the body. There were twenty yards between us. I'd have to get closer.

I moved slowly between trees, keeping my eyes on the animal. When I was forty feet away it snorted and lifted its head. I slipped behind the nearest tree, and heard the bear move again. It had heard me, or caught my scent. This was as close as I was going to get.

Through the plastic of the trash bag I popped the cap off the signal flare. Got the cap turned around, and struck the sandpapery end.

A flame bloomed instantly inside the bag, and without stopping to check it—the thing would work, or it wouldn't—I stepped out from behind the tree and threw the flare and the already swelling balloon of the trash bag toward the cabin. The bear saw me and rose up on its hind legs with a heavy grunt.

Both of us watched the trash bag as it landed and gently bounced. Its plastic stretched and strained rapidly.

It exploded. A shockingly loud bang that rang my eardrums and shook a torrent of needles off the nearest trees.

The bear wheeled and ran in the opposite direction, blowing a deep groan of what I guessed was fear. It crashed through the brush. In seconds the sound of its panicked flight faded into the distance.

I rushed forward, stomping on the flare and crushing the flame into the earth.

"Elana," I yelled at the dark cabin door.

There was nothing I could do for the man. I ran for the silent cabin. If Elana was in there, hiding, she'd be terrified. Maybe in shock.

But even before I crossed the threshold, I knew I was too late.

Chapter Four

The sudden reek of death at the cabin door made my throat close up in protest. Inside, I could feel the smell seep into my skin and clothes like water from a fog.

Her body was seated at a small rough pinewood table. She had fallen forward, facedown on the table, long, brown hair draped over the unfinished planks. The back of her head was misshapen and clotted with gore. The body had bloated at some point during the past day or two. Now it was deflated again, and the skin I could see was gray, like the remains of the man outside. Blowflies buzzed into tiny cyclones as I stepped closer.

On the drywall behind her, two wide splashes of black blood, like spread wings reaching almost to the ceiling.

I couldn't see her face under the shroud of hair. From the exit wounds on the back of her head, I knew I didn't want to. But her body was long and lean. Familiar.

The cabin was crowded with fake-rustic furniture, a table and chairs, and two double beds and a single dresser. All expensively designed to appear as though some hillbilly had chopped the pieces from raw trees, and joined them together with crude dovetails and dowels instead of

33

hidden screws. Only a potbellied stove and battered pine cabinets looked authentic.

A woman's shoulder bag was on top of the dresser. In the bag was a green bandanna. I fished it out and used it to keep from leaving fingerprints as I went through the bag's contents.

I found a pocketbook, opened it, and saw Elana's face, smiling up from a driver's license photo under a clear plastic window. It wasn't quite the face of my memory. The girlish softness had been sculpted in the past dozen years into something more defined, more striking. Strong Eastern European cheekbones framing bottle-green eyes. And vibrant. That indefinable something that makes one girl hold your eye among a hundred others just as beautiful.

Elana Michelle Coll. Twenty-seven years old. Five foot nine inches, 130 pounds, brown over green. And gone.

God damn it, Elana.

I edged my way around the table. Her suede blouse was heavy with crusted blood, but intact. There were two crude holes in the painted pink drywall four feet behind her chair. More blood on the chair, and the floor.

Two shots, straight and close. A high enough caliber to go through her head and take most of it along.

I suddenly needed to be out of the cabin. Away from the charnel-house smell.

At the instant my boot was about to cross the threshold, I saw a spattered purple line crossing the grain of the oak floor. I stopped so abruptly to keep from stepping on it that I had to catch my fall on the doorjamb.

It was just a thin dappling, as if from a flicked paintbrush. Blood, but not Elana's. She was on the other side of the table. There was another flaking patch of it, just under the base of the open door. And on the floor, pushed almost against the wall by the door, lay a Glock handgun.

I lay down to put my nose near it. The smell of burned powder in the barrel was strong enough to make out over the fog of decay.

9mm Parabellum, I was pretty sure. Easily enough punch to be the murder weapon. And from this new sprinkling of blood, I guessed that Elana wasn't the only victim.

No sign of the bear outside. I walked over to check the man's body, what there was of it. The animal had left his chest alone, finding the belly easier picking. There were no gunshot wounds on his front.

Birds or something else had been at his face and eyes. I knelt to try and get a look at the underside of his head, where his cheek lay against the earth. His right temple was blackened, in sharp contrast with the pallor of his skin. The thick red-brown curls over his ear were fried as black and stubby as candlewicks.

The shot had been so close, it had lit his hair on fire.

Was it self-inflicted? I could make that fit what was here. Kend standing at the open door. Elana sitting at the table. He shoots her twice, then puts the gun to his temple. Dead so fast that he barely bleeds at all. Unlike his woman, whose wings would still be spreading on the wall when his body hit the floor.

He had something in his front pocket. I took it out, very carefully avoiding the flecks of torn flesh. A money clip. Kendrick Haymes's driver license was at the top of a stack of credit cards, along with maybe three hundred in cash. The photo on his license was handsome in its awkwardness, from the mop of curls to the crooked smile. I put the clip back.

The wind kicked up a little, and the sudden icy prickle on my face and ears made me realize I was flushed. And sweating.

Come on, Shaw. I'd seen plenty of dead bodies, a lot of them worse looking than these two. I knew what to do. Take my memories of the girl, and put them in a box at the back of my mind. There would be time enough for her later.

Had they been alone? At least two other people had been at the cabin recently, in the sports car and the dually. Had they all left before the shooting started? Or fled after it happened?

I wondered how long Kend and Elana had been dead in the cabin, before the bear had picked up their rising scent on the wind. Long enough at least for smaller creatures to brave the interior, to get at their faces and fingers.

Willard. I'd have to tell him. I went back inside the cabin. Maybe Haymes had kept a satellite phone, for emergencies.

A backpack lay on the bed against the right wall, a big blue High Sierra with aluminum frame, for camping trips. It was open and half of its contents spread out messily on the bed. Men's boxers and shirts and thick books on sports history. A yellowed copy of *The Boys of Summer*, and a collection of essays on boxing from the fifties. Like stuff my grandfather might have read, if he had given a damn for American sports.

I looked under the bed. No other backpacks. Willard had said Elana only planned to be gone overnight. But there didn't seem to be so much as a toothbrush here. Maybe Elana's bag was still out in the Volvo.

Kend's cell phone lay on the bed. I picked it up with the bandanna. No signal here, of course. Before I set the phone back, I copied the numbers of the friends Kend called most often into my own phone. Somebody would have to tell them about Kend's and Elana's deaths. If Luce knew any of them, maybe the news would be better coming from her.

I found Elana's phone in her shoulder bag. Unlike Kend's, her phone had a security lock. I didn't want to risk finger-prints or breaking it to mess around with beating the code. Kend's friends would have to be enough. I put it back.

Then I looked at the table again. Elana's head, still at rest.

But nothing else on the table's surface. Huh.

I looked at the squat wood stove again. The powdery ashes fluttered into motion with a wave of my hand, imi-tating the panic of the blowflies. They were fresh.

37

So Kend and Elana were here and alive long enough to build a fire. Kend had unpacked. But Elana hadn't taken anything out of her shoulder bag. Not her cell phone or a book or even the bottle of water tucked neatly in the side?

A quick check of all the cabinets and drawers didn't turn up a satellite phone. I went outside to look at their car, and to think in the clean air.

The Volvo was unlocked. Its interior had the look of a lot of time spent driving and eating and maybe sleeping inside. Crumpled food wrappers and T-shirts crushed into the crevices. Some back issues of women's magazines with muddy footprints where they had slipped to the floor. In the glove compartment, under a pile of receipts and maps and paper scraps, I found the registration in Elana's name.

Something large had taken up all of the space in the back of the car. The rear seats were folded down, and a brown woolen blanket was shoved to one side of the trunk area, like it had been used to cover whatever had been inside. Large, and heavy, judging by the sharp rectangular dents in the nappy fabric of the trunk's floor.

No second backpack, though. They'd driven up here together. Kend had brought enough gear for a long weekend. Elana had only brought her shoulder bag. And left it alone.

Something didn't resonate. I couldn't tell what, or why. But I wasn't going to get any answers here. It would be dark in another hour. Already the deepening shadows around the glade made me uneasy, thinking about the bear. I had to get down the hill. And give Willard some very bad news.

Before I retrieved my ruck, I dragged what remained of Kend back inside the cabin. It was the least I could do for the son of a bitch.

Chapter Five

I ran down the mountain. Night had fallen so rapidly that it seemed to have skipped dusk altogether. I had duct-taped my Maglite to my shoulder. The stark white blaze showed me an oval-shaped fraction of the world ten feet in front me. My steps were short and choppy, but in a steady rhythm that let me coast for long sections. When the lower half of my quads started quivering threateningly, I let myself walk for a quarter-mile before starting again.

I reached the gate at the edge of the Haymes property just before midnight. My truck was where I had left it, on the opposite side. My phone had one signal bar. I wiped trickles of icy sweat from my face while waiting for Willard to pick up.

"That was fast," he said. "I'm not even to Portland yet."

"Are you driving now?" I didn't want him rolling his car in shock.

Willard must have caught something in my voice that was worth an instant of hesitation before he replied. "What is it? You found her?"

Sugarcoating the news wasn't going to comfort anybody.

"I found Elana. She was at the cabin. She and Kend. They're both dead, Willard."

"What?" he said, as if the line had stuttered, and he'd misheard.

"Elana is dead."

I heard him take a breath, almost a hum, low and under the digital static. "That—" he tried. "What. What happened?"

"I don't know. She was shot. Willard." It was my turn to take a breath. "There's something else. Kend may have killed her." When he didn't reply I continued. "I'm about to call the cops."

"Where are you?"

"Down the mountain from the cabin."

It might have been my imagination, but I thought I heard tires screeching in the background. I could picture Willard pulling a U-turn right over the highway divider.

"I'll be there in two hours," he said. "Find out where they're taking her. I'll meet you."

He was two hundred miles away. Set on covering the distance with the accelerator stomped to the floor.

"Willard, there's no fixing this."

He had hung up.

*

I didn't see Willard in two hours. It was close to seven o'clock in the morning when a sheriff's deputy named

Banks and I were waiting at the emergency entrance to the main hospital in Port Angeles. Willard would be coming there to identify Elana's body as soon as the sheriff was done talking to him.

I'd been interviewed three times. First by the deputies who'd responded to my 911 call. Then by the sheriff, before he and one of the deputies drove off in their green county SUV, headlights pointed up the mountain toward what awaited at the cabin. Then once again, in a conference room at the National Forest Service station in the nearby town of Quilcene, with a recorder running. They wanted to make very sure they had every detail.

Every cop I told, I could see the shock underneath their practiced poker faces. One of the deputies spoke to the other before he was completely out of earshot. *Maurice Haymes's kid, for God's own sake.*

What I told them was 98 percent facts, 2 percent omission. I left out only that Elana hadn't shown up to work—the cops sure as hell didn't need to know about Willard's card game—and I claimed that the idea to go hiking had been mine. When Willard had said his niece was in the area, I'd decided to start my weekend in the woods by dropping by Kend's cabin to say hello.

Just as the sun was starting to push its way into the sky, a black Escalade flew into the parking lot, barely slowing its speed from off the main street. It whipped to the right and stopped perfectly centered in a parking space.

Willard had arrived.

Banks stared as Willard got out of the SUV and managed to make it look smaller by comparison. Instead of one of his usual custom-made brown suits, he wore a red rain jacket over wool pants. His face, which always looked dour from his heavy brow and jaw, had sunk even lower, into mournful.

"Sheriff kept me all goddamn night," Willard said to me in his ground-glass voice. "I want you along when I go to—to see her." He glared at Deputy Banks. "Okay with you?"

It took Banks a second to find his words. "Sure thing."

The morgue was on the basement level of the hospital. It was the only room on its hall without a sign. The attendant, a stoop-shouldered woman with braided gray hair, unlocked the swinging doors.

We walked into a frigid wind. Vents and fans worked noisily to keep the temperature somewhere under forty degrees. I smelled the sharp tang of antiseptic cleaning products, over the heavier scent of something like old leaves. Yellow tiles covered the floor. Most of the opposite wall was dominated by the faces of large stainless steel drawers, in two rows of four.

"Normally we could do this with a photograph," the attendant said, "but I'm afraid in this case—" She tilted her head sympathetically and checked a whiteboard—*KH 02/20 D4* was written in blue dry-erase marker just above the lowest line, *uf 02/20 D6*. Kendrick Haymes, and unidentified female.

The attendant led us around the flat metal examination tables to the wall of drawers, and then stopped and turned to Willard.

"Go ahead," Willard said.

The attendant pulled hard on Drawer 6 and it opened slowly, releasing a thicker waft of cold air along with the rotting vegetation smell. A thick blue plastic sheet covered the body inside. The body's weight made the long drawer sag a fraction of an inch, as if threatening to tip.

She pulled back the plastic sheet very carefully.

The face underneath was horrific. There was no other word for it. The bullets had gone through Elana's nose and forehead and shattered every bit of bone and cartilage in their path, until the little nubs of metal and their shock waves had burst out of her skull altogether. Her splintered facial bones had collapsed inward. Even her hair was dull and grayish, as if trying to match her pallor. It was almost impossible to tell that she'd been young. Or even female.

Willard stared at her, suddenly red-faced and breathing through his mouth.

"There's also this," the attendant said, and drew back the lower corner of the sheet to reveal a tattoo in faded red and black on the body's calf. Roses, in a loose bouquet, one tumbling out and down in a graceful curve.

I reacted an instant before the deputy did, both of us grabbing Willard as he slumped. Damn, he was heavy. We kept him roughly vertical as the attendant grabbed a chair and got it under him.

"Sir?" Deputy Banks said over and over.

" 'M all right," Willard said, even as he threatened to topple to the floor. The attendant rushed to cover Elana and close the drawer.

"I'm terribly sorry," she said.

"Mr. Willard, can you identify that woman as Elana Coll?" the deputy said.

"I can," said Willard. He shuddered and put his face in his hands. The deputy looked embarrassed, and the attendant edged away.

"Give us a minute," I said. The deputy nodded, not ungrateful, and they left the room.

I sat on one of the examination tables. Willard took a dozen deep breaths, each getting longer and a little less ragged. When he took his hands away, his eyes were bloodshot but mostly dry.

He fished out a pack of Camels and a lighter from his red raincoat. He offered me one and I waved it off, after an instant's hesitation.

He lit one. The smoke didn't smell good, but it was better than the other lingering odors in the room.

"Talk to me," Willard said. I told him what I'd seen at the cabin. He listened. The busy fans caught the smoke as it trailed upward, yanked it from the air to vanish like a small, startled ghost.

"So maybe the little shit killed her," Willard said when I'd finished.

"Yeah. Maybe."

45

"You don't think so?"

"I think the cops will start with the obvious and see if the evidence backs it up. Was Kend nuts? Did they fight a lot?"

"I don't know. She didn't share her love life with me, for Christ's sake."

"Would she have left him if he was getting rough?"

He glowered. "You knew her."

The Elana I remembered wouldn't have taken a guy who slapped her around. She'd have left, or stabbed him with a carving fork, or something. But I hadn't seen her since we were teenagers.

Willard tapped his ash and watched it fall. "She was still the same girl."

"Okay. So let's say that violence was out of character for Kend. You said they went to the cabin at the last minute?"

"I said that was the feeling I got."

"Kend had packed for a stay," I said. "Elana hadn't. She just brought her shoulder bag."

"So what?"

"I don't know. It just strikes me as weird, if they drove up together. Who doesn't bring underwear and a toothbrush, at least? There were other tire tracks around the cabin. People had been there, and left. Maybe they saw something, or heard an argument."

"You said the gate was locked. Weren't they alone?" he said.

"Unless somebody decided to lock it behind them when they left. Maybe Kend asked them to."

Willard rumbled. "Possible."

"Call some of Elana's people," I said. "She must have shared secrets with somebody."

"I didn't know her friends. She liked running with Kend and his crowd. I guess she thought they were exotic. Or rich, anyway."

"A new start? Was she running from something?"

"We didn't talk. She took the job with me because she needed it. But"—he dropped the cigarette to crush it under his size eighteen wingtip—"she didn't share much."

That seemed to run in their family. "Maybe her parents know."

"Her parents are in Australia, last I knew, or cared. I haven't seen my sister and that fried egg she married in three years. I'm not sure Elana has, either."

"But you and she don't talk."

"Van. Let it alone."

I looked at him. "What's going on, Willard?"

He shook his head. There was something missing, I realized. The threat of violence, which was almost always present with Willard, which had been boiling right at the rim when he'd walked into the hospital, was gone.

"Do you know something?" I said. "Did one of your scores lead to this?"

"I don't know shit," he said. He took a slow breath. "I'll check. I'll make sure it's not on me. But I already

47

know the answer. My life has been quiet and level for a long time. How I like it."

"Okay," I said. "There still might be a motive on Kend's side."

"You think that'll explain anything?"

"How hard will the cops dig with the Haymes family?"

He shrugged. Not knowing. Or not caring. But my question was almost rhetorical. If rich kid Kendrick had killed his girlfriend and then himself, the Haymeses would bury this faster than all his daddy's excavation machines could manage.

Willard looked at Drawer 6. "I've lost a lot of people, Van. You too, I suppose. Knowing why never gave me a damn scrap of comfort."

The masking smell of smoke had been scrubbed completely from the air by the cold artificial breeze. We were back to the lower notes of decay.

"I'm sorry she's dead," I said.

Long after I thought he wouldn't answer, Willard turned away from the drawer.

"You were right the first time," he said. "There's no fixing it."

Chapter Six

By late afternoon I was back in my house on the east side of Capitol Hill in Seattle, trying to cook pancakes. Pancakes because a box of Bisquick was one of the few things I had in the pantry, and late because I'd skipped lunch after seeing Elana's body. The trying part was courtesy of my elderly neighbor, Addy Proctor.

"You need to use the spatula," Addy said from where she perched like a stout cockatoo on the tall leather bar stool. She wore a wool sweater the color of cream with a Scandinavian pattern woven in blue around the shoulders. The sweater came down almost to her knees. Because the furnace was still struggling to warm the house, Addy kept her loose-knit scarf wrapped around her neck. "Separate the batter from the pan a little."

"I like them a little crispy."

"Did you oil the pan? That helps."

"I'll make you your own, if you want."

She grimaced in horror at the idea. Her dog, Stanley, looked up from where he lay, ever vigilant where food was involved. Stanley took up most of the floor of the cramped kitchen, so that I had to step over him. I had no clue as to what breeds had combined to make Stanley.

49

Pit bull crossed with white rhinoceros, maybe.

Addy Proctor lived in a yellow house down the hill. Her home was small and quaint. Mine was big and dark blue and looked like a dented helmet on the top of our street. She had seen me return from the Peninsula in the truck, and within half an hour she was knocking on the door, inviting herself over to talk. She'd done that most every day in the weeks I'd been home. I didn't mind. And even if I did, I owed the old woman a favor, or ten. She'd helped look after Dono while he was in the hospital. And she'd kept his house from falling apart, or being taken over by squatters, while I completed my final year in the Army. I'd spent one more short rotation in Afghanistan before impatiently waiting out my last few weeks at Fort Benning in Georgia. They'd assigned me to RASP— Ranger Assessment and Selection—where I was up hours before dawn every day, pushing the candidates to their limits, and usually beyond. I was discharged from the Army in better shape than I'd been in years.

Just Donovan Shaw now, my grandfather's namesake. No longer Sergeant First Class.

The dining area of the house was right next to the kitchen, so that the two rooms made one large space. An ancient scarred oak table and three rickety chairs were the only furniture. The table had one of the better spots in the old house, with bay windows that looked out at the backyard with its overgrown lawn and tangles of wild rosebushes. I sat down at the table with my crunchy short stack and a bottle of syrup from the Pike Place Market.

"Your friend, Willard," said Addy, "he and his niece were close?"

I wasn't exactly a friend of Willard's. Dono had been.

"Willard isn't even sure where Elana was living," I said between bites.

"But he's upset. Of course he is, stupid of me to even ask. That poor girl."

"Mostly, he's angry."

"That's how men get upset. My Magnus once broke a plate that had been his mother's—the only thing he had of hers, from his childhood in Sweden—and he shouted the rafters down about any little thing for a full week. I understood, even though I was perfectly happy not to have a reminder of that old witch around anymore." She waved a hand, too late to stop me tossing a golf-ball lump of pancake to Stanley. He snagged the treat before it hit the floor. "Don't encourage him."

"I'm just staying on his good side," I said.

"And I'm late giving him his dinner." She lowered herself down from the bar stool. Stanley leapt to his feet, tail wagging. "I hope you'll serve Luce more than burnt flapjacks."

I had told Addy that Luce would be coming over. It was the one night per week Luce allowed herself off from running things at the Morgen.

"We're going out," I said, although I wasn't really sure what our plans would be. I hadn't wanted to tell Luce about Elana's death over the phone during my long drive back from the Peninsula. However long the two friends had been out of touch, it wasn't going to be easy for her to hear.

"Good. Put on something nicer than a tank top, take her out on the town, and show her off."

"Addy."

"I'm simply saying young ladies like her don't come around every day."

"Are you sure you don't want to take her out yourself? You could hitch up Stanley to a hansom cab."

We both turned at the sound of a knock and the front door opening. "Clearly it's too late for you," said Addy.

"Hello," Luce called.

"In the kitchen," I said. She came down the hall to where we were.

I was always a little bit stunned at the sight of Luce Boylan. She was taller and more alive than my memory could hold, somehow. She wore a knee-length black wool coat, silver scarf, and black boots. Her blond hair was free and fell down between her shoulder blades, much longer than when we'd first reconnected last year.

Luce leaned down to kiss Addy on the cheek. "Afternoon, Addy."

"Good evening, I believe. Which means I have my own date with Alex Trebek. You two have a lovely night." She cocked an eyebrow at me. "Remember what I said."

She and Stanley left. Luce looked at me. "What was that about?"

"Addy needs a hobby. Come here."

She put down her overstuffed shoulder bag and we kissed. I might have given it less than my usual enthusiasm.

"What's wrong?" Luce said.

"Let's sit down."

"Van." She didn't like suspense.

"It's bad news, Luce. Elana is dead."

The fact took an extra few seconds to sink in. It usually did. I'd had to tell a lot of people about unexpected death in the past few years. Mostly guys in my platoon. Soldier or civilian, the first reaction was usually stunned quiet.

"Oh. Oh, Van. What . . . ?"

"Take your coat off. Here."

We sat on the rickety chairs of the dining room, and I told her about the sad end of her friend, and of Kendrick Haymes. She cried. When I came to the part about it looking like Kend had killed them both, she stared at me like I was insane.

"Why, for God's sake?"

"I don't have the first clue. I guess you don't, either."

Luce took another tissue but didn't wipe her eyes, just twisted it in her fingers. "Last time I saw Elana was just after high school. I guess she would have been nineteen or twenty. That was before she followed some guy to Chicago, I heard."

"She do that a lot? Latch on to guys?"

"I don't know. I don't really know who she was, as an

adult. You know what her life was like, as a teenager."

I did. Better than most.

"She was a really good friend, when we were kids," Luce continued. "Helped me a lot, when I needed an extra hand taking care of Albie."

Luce and Elana had a lot in common, when it came to defective parentage. Elana's folks were space cases. Luce's mother had left the family when she was a baby, and her dad had wandered in and out of her life while Luce lived with relatives. She'd finally settled with her uncle Albert when she was ten. Through a combination of the bottle and his own misadventures, Albie wasn't the most dependable, either, for as much as he loved her. Luce had grown up fast.

"I'm sorry," I said.

She nodded and leaned forward for a long hug.

"We'll stay in tonight," I said.

"No. No, I want to be out. That's okay?"

"That's okay."

I found a clean pair of jeans and a shirt in the single bedroom upstairs. It was still odd to think of it as my room. Dono's books filled most of the shelves, and the flat-screen on the wall was preset to his news and sports stations, with an emphasis on European football matches.

We took my truck up the hill to the row of restaurants and bars on 15th Ave, and found a table with no waiting at Smith. One side of the restaurant had rough portraits of unknown people from the first half of the past century, and a long, very tall bar. The opposite wall was sparsely decorated with stuffed animal heads and the occasional pheasant trapped forever in flight. Our table was on the wall of taxidermy, under the head of something vaguely like an antelope. We ordered drinks—a cocktail with rum for Luce, bourbon neat for me—and held hands across the table. Her phone buzzed in her pocket. The second time since we'd left the house.

"You're not answering?" I said.

"It's either Marcie in a panic because she's low on a brand of vodka or something, in which case she should learn to deal with it herself. Or it's Fye, letting me know she's really okay after her latest breakup, really. Either way, not tonight."

Or it was someone else. I'd been back in Seattle barely a month. Luce and I hadn't talked about being exclusive. I knew other guys had called her.

"Not tonight," I agreed, and took a sip after we'd clinked glasses.

Luce hesitated before drinking. Maybe the toast felt too cheerful, half an hour after crying for Elana.

"Speaking of work," I said. "I have a lead on something. It might even match our weird nocturnal hours."

"I didn't know you'd been thinking about that," she said. "Matching our schedules."

"I have. I'd be teaching night classes."

"In military work?"

"Training, for police. Or at least survivalist types. A

major from our battalion started his own firm. Eberley Tactical Instruction. He says there could be openings, if he lands a couple of contracts. It would be short-term, to start. He'll let me know."

"Well. All right." She grinned then, and I would have leaned across to kiss her but the waiter arrived to take our orders.

"It might mean some travel," I said when we were alone. "It wouldn't be as close as working together at the bar."

"No."

"There are too many memories there. With Dono, and after."

"I understand," she said. "I wouldn't even set foot in the place, if I were you."

We fell silent again. Luce looked up at the antelope head on the wall. I drank a little of the bourbon. I'd learned enough about the lovely Miss Boylan in the past weeks to know that when she was distracted in the middle of a conversation, she was hauling on the reins on something inside herself.

"Do you think the police will learn why Kend killed her?" she said.

"They'll try. But mostly, they'll try to confirm Who and How."

"Two out of three."

"They take what they can get." I held her hand, which was cool from holding the iced drink.

"It's still a crap deal," Luce said. "Willard must be terrible. And terrifying."

"I think he's in shock. Elana was his last family member he gave a damn about."

The waiter brought our food. We concentrated on our plates for a few minutes. I tried to show some restraint while eating my venison pie. Luce picked at her salad. After a few bites she gave up.

"I took some numbers off Kend's contacts," I said, tapping the phone in my chest pocket. "If you know any of them, maybe they should hear about Elana from you."

"Let me see," she said. She took my phone to scan the short list of names, and shook her head. "I don't know them."

"I'll call them anyway. Willard said she hung out with that bunch, mostly."

"Because they might know if things were bad between Kend and Elana?"

"Or they may have seen it happen," I said. "There were other tire tracks at the cabin."

Luce leaned back.

"You're wondering if Kend didn't do it," she said.

"I don't know one way or the other," I said. Luce raised her eyebrow. "And yeah, I want to. I saw how they were left, Luce. Like bags of trash."

She considered it. "If there's really a chance."

I knew what her hesitancy was about. My way of looking into things tended toward the extralegal. After growing up around thieves and robbers, Luce preferred her life less complicated. She'd met enough bail bondsmen.

"If I find anything useful, I'll hand it to the cops," I said. "Any evidence that points to Kend Haymes being murdered will make them very motivated. They don't want to fumble this one."

"All right. Elana deserves that." She tapped her rum drink. "And afterward, I want to go someplace very warm, with a lot of these for hydration."

"A vacation? You?"

"Us. Before you start whatever job you find. After that it'll be tough to get time off for a while. What's that face?"

"I had a horrible vision of a pension fund chasing me."

Luce stole a bite of my pie crust. "I think you can take him."

*

I dreamed of dark wings. They formed patch by patch in midair, each new sweep of feathers announced by long orange flashes of rifle fire off to my right, as if the gun were painting in precise strokes. I kept thinking that I would turn to see who was shooting, but the wings held me rapt. The next burst would be straight at my face. As I was tensing for the coming bullets, I woke.

I knew where I was. Lying in my bed, Luce beside me,

turned away and curled half into a ball like she did when sleep was at its deepest. Her hair was a pale splash in the black room.

Safe.

Safe. Say the word a hundred times. It loses its meaning but gains something in power.

Sweat beaded on my forehead and chest. The natural cool of the old house in winter felt like the hospital morgue had. I got out of bed and pulled up the covers so the cold wouldn't touch Luce, and went downstairs.

Moonlight cast everything in the front room into shades of indigo and navy. I sat in Dono's old leather chair. And breathed.

Dark wings, and automatic weapon fire. A new dream, mixed with an old one.

I had believed that the nightmare that started with the three flashes was gone. Or at least subdued. I'd beaten it down over time with treatment and medication and a lot of sleepless nights.

But it rattled its tail from time to time, just to remind me it was still there. A subconscious stress response, the therapists had called it. The sight of Elana's blood splashed wide and sweeping across the cabin wall had given the dream strength, and determination.

I didn't believe in ghosts. There were too many dead people in my past to buy the notion that any of them cared enough to tap me on the shoulder, symbolically or otherwise.

Still. The wings, Elana's wings, had my full attention, if that was what they were asking for. I could be pretty damned determined myself.

Age Seventeen

The first question on the employment agency's application form, after the boxes for name and address and all of the usual identification details, was:

WHAT SPECIAL SKILLS DO YOU HAVE? SEE LIST OF EXAMPLES ON PAGE 3

I could think of a few talents. None that I should put in writing.

Sitting around me in the agency's waiting room were a dozen other kids about my age and a handful of older people. Some scribbled on their own copies of the same application, while the rest waited to see if they would be called for what the agency called a pre-interview. I guessed that the other teenagers had either just finished high school, or had dropped out.

I pretended to fill out sections on the form for a couple more minutes, until the receptionist stepped away from her desk. Then I folded the papers in half and left the office. I followed signs to the stairs. Instead of going down to the lobby, I went up two flights to the top floor.

The stairwell door was locked. I used the pick gun in my pocket to open it.

The hall on the other side of the door was empty. The employment agency was open until seven o'clock, to allow potential candidates to come in after work or after school, but most of the other offices in the building were empty at this hour. I listened for a moment, just to be sure. Then I walked softly down the hallway to the firm of Gallison Engineering, to see what I needed to see.

Five minutes later, I was leaving through the building's lobby, employment forms still in my hand. I passed Dono. He was chatting amiably with the security guard. His voice had no hint of an Irish accent, as it often did when he was at home. He wore a polo shirt with a Verizon Services logo, and a matching baseball cap. His face was angled away from the lobby camera.

Outside, I crossed the street to the brown Sentra that Dono used when we needed to be inconspicuous. While I sat and waited, I looked at the back of the building.

At one of the fourth floor windows, to be exact.

Behind that window was the secure storage room of Gallison Engineering & Equipment. Where I would be in thirty more hours, sharing space with about five hundred thousand bucks' worth of top-quality optical lenses. We'd clear ten percent, with another twenty grand going to the guy who'd sold us the information. Dono had already made the arrangements for the sale with Hiram Long.

Dono came out. He checked his surroundings and

when he was sure no one was watching him, he ambled across the road and climbed into the driver's seat.

"Well?" he said.

I drummed my fingers on the dashboard. "It's really soft. There are no cameras in the stairwells or anywhere on the fourth-floor hallways, except by the elevators."

"What about the office door? What kind of lock?"

"Key card. A Jackson Command model."

He frowned. He'd been hoping Gallison would have a punch code, or even a plain old deadbolt. "So we'll use the frequency scanner. But I don't like you standing out in the hallway that long."

"Or I could use this." I held up a GE&E employee badge.

"Where'd you acquire that?"

"Lifted it from a guy leaving for the night as I came in. With luck he won't even know it's gone until Monday morning."

"Without luck, he's already reported his badge missing. In which case it won't work when you need it. And maybe the system will alert the guards at the front desk."

"What's worse? We take a chance on the card, or I just cross my fingers that the scanner works before a guard wanders by?"

Dono looked at me. He didn't like my tone. But he also couldn't deny it was a better choice.

Still, I was a little more polite when I spoke again. "How'd it go with the guard?" I said.

"Let's find out." He took a handheld receiver out of the center console and switched it on, and tuned it to the right frequency. A male voice came through like he was in the back seat of the Sentra.

—tol' her that if she wanted to have them over for damn dinner she shoulda tol' me sooner and I coulda stopped—

Dono smiled and switched it off. "I pasted the bug right under the desk. A little advance notice if someone hears you and calls it in."

"Nobody's going to hear me." I grinned.

"Not if you go slow. You've practiced enough with the cutter?"

He knew I had. But my grandfather would check everything ten times for himself, and make me take another lap through the plan just for good measure. Even if he was letting me run the plays from the field, he couldn't let it go.

"We're ready," I said.

"Not without transport we're not. You recall where Willard lives? Near Green Lake?"

"The little house." It always struck me funny that such a huge guy lived in a house that had less square footage than our home's first floor.

"He'll have a suitable truck for us. You go up there tomorrow morning and fetch it."

"Is Willard going to be there?" The notion made me a little nervous, even though all I had to do was ask Willard for a set of keys. I'd met him a dozen times, but it was hard not to be uneasy around a guy whose face never told you what he was thinking. Plus, he could probably pop my skull like a grape with just one hand.

"Don't bring the truck to the house. Park it three blocks down from us here." Dono pointed out the direction. "Take a bus home."

I gaped at him. "Come on. We're forty miles from Seattle."

Sultan County was north and east of home. One of the latest hubs of business real estate, as the population swelled and pushed farther and farther inland. The office complex where Gallison was located was new and shiny and stupidly generic, one of a dozen just like it in a square mile. "I don't even know if they *have* buses out here."

"There's a park-and-ride two miles west."

"Geez."

*

Saturday morning came up hot and quickly got hotter. Short sleeves in October, and made even weirder when the overcast skies refused to clear up with the heat. Even the Halloween pumpkins on the lawns were sweating beads of water.

Willard's house was walking distance from Green Lake, on a short cross-street packed close with other homes, most of them larger than Willard's. His was a little older, too, just a bungalow with a porch and maybe a loft. It was painted about the same dark brown as the suits Willard always wore.

From behind the house, I heard a faint clink of metal on metal. The driveway ran along the side of the house, and I walked up it toward the back. Most of the fenced yard was paved. A big silver Lincoln and a white Toyota pickup truck with a covered bed took up all of the cement. On the remaining strip of grass was a chaise lawn chair, and on the chair was Elana Coll. She wore big gold sunglasses and jeans shorts, and a red T-shirt with the WSU Cougars logo. The shirt was tight enough to show the complete outline of her bra. She held a plate piled high with eggs and sausage and diced potatoes.

"You made me breakfast," I said.

"Ha ha," Elana said. "This is all mine, and I need it. My sure cure."

"That explains the shades. Where was the party?"

"Shit. I forgot my coffee. It's in the kitchen. Would you? I'm settled in." She stretched her legs out to their full length on the chaise.

"Where's Willard?"

"Out of town." Elana flipped her brunette ponytail behind her shoulder, picked up the fork, and took a big bite of eggs.

"Do you have the keys to that truck?"

"D'you have my coffee?"

To hell with it. I could jump the ignition. I started toward the truck. Elana waved her fork like a little home-team flag.

"I'm kidding, I'm kidding. God, you're so serious. Willard left me the keys for you. Lemme eat something and I'll get them." She took another bite. "There's 'nuff coffee for both've us."

"You could have opened with that," I said.

Willard's kitchen was just inside the screen door. It was so narrow that he could cook and wash dishes and put them away, all by just turning his body. I wondered how he lived here without going nuts. Maybe he had to spend all his money on custom clothes. I found Elana's coffee mug on the counter—still messy from her cooking—and poured another cup for myself.

"Are you living here now?" I asked Elana after I'd taken a seat on the back stoop.

Mouth full, she shook her head. Her plate was already half clean.

"Mom'n Dad are somewhere in South America. Chile, I think."

"What are they doing there?"

"Shit, what do they always do? Commune with the vibrations, get naked with the other hippies."

I grinned. "Not your thing."

"*Hell*, no. Even if I wasn't in school."

"What's sharing a house with Willard like?"

"Like living with your vice principal. He's always

66

checking on me. I've got a curfew, if you can believe it."

Yeah, I could. Dono had been like that when I was fifteen, too. I had to be home by ten o'clock on the dot, except when he and I were working on a job.

"Doesn't matter. End of this semester, and I am *gone*," Elana said.

"Gone? Dropping out?"

She chair-danced in triumph. "Meltoun Academy. I got the letter last week."

"What's Meltoun Academy?"

"Boarding school, in Oregon. *Very* exclusive, thank you very much."

I smelled bullshit. "They needed a ringer for the high jump?"

"Hey, my grades are kick-ass." She saw my expression. "No shit. Straight As. And Dad went there on account of his folks being rich once. Even if he screwed that up for us, I'm a legacy. It counts."

"Willard's going to throw a hell of a party when he gets his house back."

"He's too cheap," Elana said. Her fork stopped in mid-air. "Well, no. Uncle Will doesn't have a lot of money. He's real careful, you know?"

"Cautious. About what work he takes."

"Yeah."

"Dono is, too. I guess he wasn't always. He used to be kind of crazy, when he was young."

"What happened?"

67

I shrugged. "Prison. The last time was when I was about ten."

"No shit? What'd you do? Stay with relatives?"

We had no relatives. I'd gone into foster homes for a year and a half.

"You have the keys?" I said.

Elana looked at me for a moment, then set the empty plate on the grass and stood up. "Hang on." She walked lightly on the balls of her bare feet to the truck, and leaned deep into the driver's window to snag the keys off the seat. I tried not to stare.

She spun like a ballet dancer and tossed me the keys. "I'll follow you there."

"Forget it."

"You're going to walk all the way back?"

I started to reply that I was hopping a bus, but that sounded even more lame than walking. Elana had a point. We'd be leaving the truck three blocks away from the Gallison building. It wasn't like I was going to point and show her which office Dono and I would be breaking into later tonight.

"Try not to get busted on the way," I said.

She lowered the sunglasses to blink her green eyes at me. "Please." Then she frowned. "Wait. You really think I don't have fake ID?"

I really had.

But as Elana was fond of implying, I was an idiot.

Chapter Seven

The condominium building where Kendrick Haymes had lived was off of Galer, on Queen Anne Hill. Twenty-eight or thirty large units arranged in a wide H-shape to maximize sun and privacy. And profits.

It was seven in the morning. A lousy time of day to break into a place, with all the neighbors likely to be home and getting ready for work. But if I waited, I might lose my chance to be the first inside.

I turned onto the cross street and parked a few doors down. The morning was damp. A black vinyl carrying case that had belonged to my grandfather made a warm rectangle under my jacket. I'd found the case the week before, where it had been hidden behind the ventilation mesh in one of the house's eaves. Dono had kept it out of the reach of a standard police search.

As I walked back to the building, I heard a mechanical clacking and the gate to the parking level began to rise. A late model Acura flew up the short ramp from the garage and zoomed down the street without pausing. I ducked under the gate before it closed again. A good omen.

Kend's driver's license had listed his unit as #D8. I found the garage stairwell and went up. The fourth-floor hallway was dead quiet, and carpeted in a deep wine color that matched the accents on the wallpaper. Nicer than any room in my house.

Number D8 was at the end of the hall. It had a cream-painted door, like all the other apartments. And like the others, a Baldwin brand single-cylinder, jimmy-proof deadbolt. I rang the bell. No answer. I could barely hear the chimes from out in the hallway. Another point on my side. High quality condo equals good soundproofing.

I opened Dono's vinyl case. Inside, held in place by elastic loops, were a dozen key rings. Each ring had multiple keys. All of the keys had their jagged cuts filed down to stubby points.

Bump keys, arranged by brand name—Schlage, Kwikset, Master, and more—and by type of lock. I took out the Baldwin ring, and picked the key that matched the 8200 series. It went into the lock like it was coated in goose fat.

The hallway was still quiet. I took a screwdriver from the case, put a little tension on the bump key, and tapped it with the screwdriver's rubber handle. A couple more taps, and the pins inside the lock lined up neatly on the shear line, and the key turned.

Now came the fun part. I stepped inside and closed the door.

Ten seconds. The air inside the condo was stale and odorless. Twenty seconds. No blaring siren. I locked the door behind me.

The entryway was wide enough to allow for a bench, and a wrought iron coatrack hung with half a dozen coats. A man's coats, mostly, leather and microfiber jerseys and Gore-Tex from a higher price range than most outdoor enthusiasts could afford. There was one woman's jacket, a sleek waterproof raincoat in dark green. Assuming it was Elana's, she might have chosen it to match her eyes.

There was a narrow chance that the condo had a silent alarm. I searched around the entryway for a telltale keypad, and found only a closet stuffed to the ceiling with more clothes and shoe boxes.

His home was spacious. I guessed it at two bedrooms and maybe thirteen hundred square feet. But despite the size, the apartment felt stifled, like a cocoon. The soundproofing blocked any exterior sound, creating a private little world.

The first piece of furniture after the bench was a thin table with a stack of junk mail on it. The envelopes were addressed to Kendrick B. Haymes, or K. B. Haymes, or to just to Resident.

The flat anonymity of *Resident* summed Haymes up for me, too. Beyond his famous name, he was a blank. Had Kend been a violent whack job who'd killed his girlfriend in a rage and then taken the express train to Hell himself? Was he just some sorry bastard tormented by depression or fear? That was another kind of victim, I supposed. But any pity I might have felt was swept away by the memory of Elana's wings.

Kend must have had friends, other than his girl. His phone had given me a few names and numbers. Maybe I could learn more here, find the people closest to him. Or I could paste the pieces of his life together myself. Figure out what he was thinking behind that crooked smile in his license picture.

You think that will explain anything? Willard had asked.

I started in the bathroom, checking the medicine chest. Kend had a Mantelukast prescription for seasonal allergies. Elana had a mild antidepressant. I'd taken shit a lot heavier when I'd been in therapy. There was nothing in the cabinets to imply Kend was bipolar or fighting anything more serious than clogged sinuses. Nothing that might signal that the poor bastard was a risk for suicide. Unless of course he'd decided to flush his meds.

In the living room, a brocade sectional couch took up a majority percentage of the living space. Broad sliding glass doors revealed a narrow balcony. Real hardwood floors and eight-foot ceilings, with the walls painted the color of eggplant. The furniture was sleek and low to the ground. It was a toss-up which had cost more: all of the furniture, or the eighty-inch flat-screen that looked like a glass tabletop bolted to the wall.

Everything was so immaculate there had to be a regular cleaning service. Even the appliances shone. I wondered what days the service came, and what time. Hopefully not first thing in the morning.

The living room also had a black walnut desk with a Macintosh laptop in a docking station. I tapped the space bar and saw the password prompt. No checking Kend's e-mail, unless I wanted to steal the machine and find a way to hack into it. Better to leave the forensics for the cops.

There were photographs in wooden frames on the shelves, and taped to the fridge. One on the wall showed Kend as a young boy, red curls flying as a woman who I guessed was his mother swung him around. I didn't see any pictures of Kend's famous father, Maurice. Elana appeared in half a dozen pictures, in groups at parties or candid shots. She looked good in the candids, striking when she turned her gaze on the camera. A few faces repeated in the party pictures. I took snapshots of each with my phone.

I found one other picture, facedown in the desk drawer. The photo showed two white women in their midtwenties, both in glossy black dresses. The woman on the left was short and gamine, with bobbed hair the shade of thick honey. The other was taller and darker. A beauty mark accented the corner of her mouth. The girls were winking broadly and brandishing champagne flutes at the photographer. Both of them were good-looking. That seemed to be the kind of circle Kendrick Haymes ran in. All the men were rich, all the women beautiful. At the bottom of the picture was a line written in neat feminine cursive—*Barr and Tru at Bob's wedding.*

The rest of the slim drawer was full of Post-its and bits of notepaper. The one on top read *You're So Much Marvelous, Mister* written that same cursive, inside a felt-pen heart. Love notes that Elana had written to her man, and a few that Kend had scrawled back. The notes ranged in tone from cute to NC-17 for sexual content. None of them seemed to have been written as apology, or in anger. Maybe the lovers only kept the nice ones. Sweet, even if they were all stuffed in a drawer.

My phone buzzed. It was Bill Eberley. Major Eberley, of Eberley Tactical. Calling to give me news about the possible job, most likely. It buzzed once more while I decided. The walls here were probably thick enough.

"Yeah," I said, my voice low.

"Van?"

" 'M in a library, but didn't want to miss your call."

"Okay. I'll do the talking. It's not good news. We couldn't make the deal with the Oregon state troopers. They want us, but February's just too late to get onto their budget for the year. I'm still talking to Olympia, but those conversations are looking bleak. Short answer, I don't think we're going to have capacity for extra resources soon. I'm sorry."

"Thanks for letting me know fast."

"Like I said, these things wax and wane. Oregon might have funds free up later for extra SWAT training. But I expect you'll be settled into another job well before that."

In other words, don't stare at the phone expecting it to ring. I said thanks again and we hung up.

Shit. Double shit. I had been counting on that job, maybe more than I'd let myself realize. But I couldn't dwell on my employment situation right now. I might not have much time left in Kend's apartment. Kend's really upper-fucking-class apartment.

I went to the master bedroom. It had the same dimensions as the living room, with the same identical set of glass doors to the balcony. Framed large-print photographs decorated the blue walls, artfully time-lapsed prints of a Japanese street, a casino floor, an empty restaurant. In the nightstand drawer by the California King bed I found sticky buds of pot in an unlabeled aspirin bottle, along with rolling papers and an ashtray with a few layers of smudged resin. I examined the nightstand surface and the inside of the drawer closely. Addicts nearly always kept their works close to the bed, the better to collapse. There were no pinprick holes or scratches, like clumsy handling of a syringe might leave. No scorch marks in the soft wood from a hot pipe set down quickly.

Elana's things were neatly tucked away in the dresser and the closet. She had lived simply. Almost minimalist. I got that. When you relocated every couple of years, you found you could cast off a lot.

There was something else I hadn't found, I realized. No box of 9mm Parabellums, or a carrying case or gun cleaning kit. Had Kend lifted the Glock from somewhere? Or had he kept it hidden?

A small dog barked in the hallway. Then more barks, loud and frantic, right outside the door.

Crap.

I liked dogs. K9 units had saved our company's collective ass in the Army more times than I could count. None of that kept me from wanting to punt this particular canine through uprights from twenty yards out.

The owner called to it from farther down the hall. The little terror kept up with its yapping. Finally I heard footsteps and the dog protesting as it was being carried away.

I couldn't stay much longer. Maybe I'd been heard on the phone. Or the neighbor down the hall would start thinking about his dog's sudden interest in the Haymes apartment.

I'd searched Kend's place for drugs, or signs of psychological distress. There were other ways a person might be pushed to the limit. Even a rich man. Romantic woes. Family suffering. I knew a little something about that.

An antique rolltop desk and matching file cabinet took up the bedroom corner. I rummaged through stacks of bills on the desk. Most were standard. I found a bank statement and a car registration. Maybe Kend had been buying himself new wheels. He could've done all the window-shopping he wanted at Willard's card game.

The registration wasn't for a purchase, I realized with a second look. It was the seller's record for a Porsche Panamera, two years old. Kend had signed over the car to someone named Torrance X. Broch about three weeks ago. There was no entry in the space labeled *Sales Price*.

I glanced through the recent bank statement. Kend's checking account had less than two hundred in it at the time the statement was printed. His savings were non-existent. Maybe he had another account, or kept all his money elsewhere.

A rich guy with a practically zero balance. Thirty seconds earlier I would have said I had nothing in common with Kendrick Haymes. But based on the quickest of glances, he looked just as broke as I was.

The file cabinet was a mess. I had just figured out which drawer held the scattered piles of bank and credit card statements when I heard voices from the hall.

" . . . a court order if we have to, but given the state of the family . . ." said a man's low voice.

"Of course. Let me just . . ." Keys jingled.

Terrific. I was missing the mutt already.

I grabbed the stacks of papers and stuffed them into a canvas messenger bag that was next to the desk, and slung the bag over my back. The key turned in the front lock just as I eased open the sliding door to the balcony.

Fourth floor. I'd have to hope Kend's downstairs neighbors weren't at home. I climbed over the railing to clamber down and hang. My feet touched the railing on the third-floor balcony below. I jumped down and without pausing did it again, down to the second floor, and then I dropped the last ten feet to the alley.

My landing slammed my knees all the way up to my

chest and gave me an instant headache. But no busted ankles. I eased back to a standing position and walked away, picking up speed and a little more oxygen as I went.

Chapter Eight

Back in the truck, I tossed the messenger bag on the passenger seat and started the engine. I wanted a look at the guy asking the manager to unlock Kend's apartment. A family member, maybe, or a cop. It might be useful to know if it was Peninsula deputies working remote, or if they'd passed the case off to SPD. I drove around the block to park where I could see the building entrance. It had started to rain, graduating rapidly from a drizzle to an insistent pelting shower.

The large stack of Kend's bank and credit statements took some reshuffling to put in order. I read through them as the precipitation streamed down the windows.

They told a story. Kend's finances were a holy mess. Every month he received one deposit into his bank account in the whopping sum of twenty grand, from something called GLV. The deposits stretched back as far as the statements went. I assumed it was Kend's trust fund. That was the only bright note for him.

Then the money went right back out again. In cash. During each of the past few months Kend had made withdrawals in large round numbers, until he'd completely wiped out his monthly allowance. The trust fund money was usually gone within four or five days after it arrived.

The credit statements proved he was living on borrowed time, charging everything from groceries to the cable bill. At least it looked like the condo was paid for.

He hadn't bought another car, though. No gas receipts, either. The Panamera he'd sold seemed to have been Kend's only ride. I checked the bank statements again. No deposit of extra cash from a few weeks before, when Kend had signed off on his hundred-K Porsche.

What was burning through Kend's money like this? Drugs? No sign of that in the apartment, and he'd have overdosed long ago at this rate. Was he dealing? That was possible. If he were buying in quantity and laundering the money somewhere else. But why max out his credit cards?

The door to the building opened. A stout, middle-aged guy in a blue business suit and tie came out, walking so fast he verged on jogging. He held Kend's Mac laptop under his arm, hunching to shield it from the rain.

He had the look of a cop, from the stone scowl to the bristly mustache. But a cop wouldn't grab just one piece of evidence and remove it with his bare hands. Ex-cop, I decided.

I got a closer view through the river running down my windshield, as he crossed the street to a gray four-door Taurus two cars in front of me. His face was as chubby as his body, made rounder by a comb-over that swooped light brown hair over his tanned pate. Fat but strong looking, like a junior college lineman gone to seed. He hustled his gut behind the steering wheel and the Taurus zoomed away.

I began putting Kend's financial statements back into his monogrammed messenger bag. The bag had looked empty, which was why I had grabbed it. There was an interior pocket, half unzipped. Inside the pocket was a large piece of paper, folded in quarters. The paper was thick and a little waxy, like a blueprint. I unfolded it.

It was a schematic. For an alarm system.

With pencil notes around the sides, pointing out how and where to beat it.

Kendrick Haymes, scion of old money, had suddenly become much more interesting.

Of course, just because the schematic had been tucked away in Kend's monogrammed bag didn't mean it was his. Elana was more the type to be familiar with burglar alarms. Was it hers? Both of theirs?

The alarm was complex. In a quick scan of the diagram I spotted redundant power sources, and both hardwired and wireless zones. Not the toughest system to beat, but not DIY crap from Radio Shack, either.

Where was it installed? The design was intended for a commercial building, or a series of connected smaller buildings, I guessed. There was no company name or identification number. A blank white strip showed at the bottom, maybe where those details had been masked before printing it on this strange waxen paper.

And had Kend or Elana or both already followed the penciled instructions, and broken into the place? If so, I had to assume there would be a police record of the burglary. But matching that to this diagram would be tough, without access to the same reports.

I knew how I could get those police reports. Or who could get them for me.

While the truck's vents were laboring to defog the windows, I checked the faces in Kend's and Elana's snapshots against what I could find on their social media accounts. I got a handful of matches. Barrett Yorke was the elfin girl with honeyed hair, Trudy Dobbs her taller friend with the beauty mark. Barrett had a brother, Parson, who had been a looming presence in the background at a couple of the parties.

No doubt they had heard of their friends' deaths. Kend's had been reported, with very careful wording, on last night's news. The reporter had named father Maurice as one of the dozen wealthiest people in Seattle, according to *Forbes*. And a quick check on my phone showed me the socialverse was on fire with rumors. One gossip claimed Kend and Elana had been only two of dozens secretly killed in the forest that night.

I sent a group text message to Barrett, Trudy, and Parson.

My name is Van Shaw. I was a friend of Elana's. I was the one who found them at the cabin.

And then a following message:

Someone else was there, too.

If that didn't pique their interest, I'd have to get drastic. Maybe I'd start my own horrible rumor circulating. I had a doozy about a bear.

Chapter Nine

The morning traffic jam was making like an inchworm by the time I reached Belltown. I could have low-crawled the last four blocks in full battle rattle—body armor, weapons, and all—and still beat the pace I set in the Dodge.

I stashed the truck in its usual spot at a garage three blocks from the bar. The morning's rain hadn't let up. I pulled my jacket tighter and strode down Western Ave, through people hurrying to work and Pike Place visitors seeking the shelter of the vendor stalls.

Only the panhandlers stood in place, one staking a claim on every corner. I gave my last single to a woman with ratty scarves wrapped around her head, framing a face with more deep wrinkles than teeth. She held a cardboard sign saying 4KIDS. I didn't know if that meant she had four kids or intended to use the money for her kids, or if the sign was bullshit and my charity would just fund the woman's next bottle. A dollar wouldn't go far in any case. A drop of malt liquor on a bonfire.

The door to the Morgen was halfway down an alley off Lenora. It was bright green. Nothing on or around the door told you the bar's name. When the bar opened at noon, Luce or one of her people would put out a sandwich board that directed customers to the right place.

I knocked on the door. No answer. Luce was probably hustling around somewhere in the back, in that efficient frenzy she always had while working. I tugged on the brass handle, and was surprised when it opened.

Most of the Morgen was a single room, long and wide, with thick ceiling beams and banged-up wooden tables and chairs. The overhead lights were turned off, making the interior murky. The walls were painted black, and so were the planks of the pine floor. Dust motes floated in the soft light coming through the high windows.

A man was seated at the table farthest from the door, half in shadow. I could make out a wispy black beard, but the rest of his face was hidden by a fraying cotton hood. He wore a dark blue wool coat over the hoodie. On the table in front of him was a plate of what looked like half-eaten chicken wings from the bar's kitchen. Luce wasn't in the room.

"Hey," I said.

The man didn't answer. His hands were out of sight under the table. His face could have been Asian, but it was hard to tell from just his chin and mouth. On the floor next to his bench was a large backpack. It was stuffed near to bursting and stained and faded from hard use.

A couple of street people made a habit of coming by the Morgen before opening, looking for food or spare change or whatever Luce could offer. If they weren't drunk or high, Luce usually found something to wrap up for them.

I'd never known her to invite one of them into the bar. Where was she?

"Anybody home?" I called. No answer from the back rooms.

I walked toward the bar counter, a lengthy stretch of pale birch. On the wall behind the bar hung a tapestry. A medieval image of a nude woman riding a horse into the sea, which gave the Morgen its name. I watched the man in the hood as I walked, and he watched me in continued silence.

"You got a name?" I said.

He nodded. Hands still under the table.

"That's a start," I said, moving behind the bar. Luce kept a collapsible police baton taped under the lip of the counter. Albie had kept a Louisville Slugger in the same spot for decades. The steel baton was both a nod to his legacy, and an improvement. The eight-inch handle would telescope out to triple its length with a flick of the wrist, a lot quicker and just as effective as a baseball bat. I reached underneath for it.

The baton was gone. The loose ends of masking tape where it had been stuck to my fingertips.

The beard moved in a smile. His left hand came out and picked up a chicken wing, and dipped it in the plastic cup of blue cheese dressing.

"Lemme finish these," he said around a mouthful, " 'fore you shoot me."

I knew that voice. And saw his combat boots, scuffed from their original tan to a patchy gray.

"Pak?" I asked.

"Hey, Sergeant."

Leonard Pak had been a specialist in the Seventy-Fifth Ranger Regiment, serving in Afghanistan. On his second deployment, he'd been assigned to the platoon I had led. Leo got into the rhythm of working with his new fire team faster than most. He was smart and quickly proved his rep as a hell of a shot with a sniper rifle. As happy as I was whenever any of my guys went home safe, I'd been sorry to lose Leo from the unit.

"Goddamn," I said, and walked down the bar. He wiped his hand on his pants before shaking mine.

"Sorry to yank your chain," he said, "but the look on your face when you walked in and saw me . . ."

Leo tugged the hood all the way off. His ink-black hair had grown long enough to touch his shoulders. He had the same broad, square face as I remembered, with a few extra creases framing his eyes. Handsome enough that at least two girls on post at Benning had labored through killer crushes on him. The way his facial bones pressed at his skin, I didn't think Leo had been eating a lot of home-cooked meals.

I sat down on the bench across from him. Up close, spots on his wool coat shone bright with wear. "Luce let you in?"

"The hot blonde? I told her how I knew you. She made me prove it. I dug my Ranger tabs out of my pack." He grinned. "And I told her about when our team extracted that HVT in Kabul, and you had to cold-cock one of his wives when she jumped you."

Jesus. "I apologized to her."

"That's what I told the blonde girl. The woman was unconscious, but you said 'Sorry' to her just the same while we hauled ass out of there." He shrugged. "Saved us from having to shoot the crazy bitch."

Of all the stories, Leo had picked that one.

"Nice beard, Pak."

"Huh. Still better than you can do."

He wasn't wrong. Ever since the left side of my face was stitched back together, any attempt I made to grow facial hair looked ridiculous.

"How'd you find me here?" I said.

"You told me and Johnny Hargreaves one night about a bar near Pike Place that your dad owned. I thought, what the hell, I'd knock on a few doors, see if you were around."

"Granddad," I corrected automatically. "You could have just asked the battalion office to pass along a message. They've got my e-mail."

The lines around Leo's eyes crunched together. "I'm done with all that, Sarge," he said. Before I could ask what he meant, he pushed away his empty plate. "Man, those were good. Are you working here now?"

I shook my head. "It's not in the family anymore. I just help out sometimes."

"Uh-huh." He nodded pointedly toward the back. "You and her?"

"Yeah." I said. "Me and her."

"Good deal. You haven't been out very long, right? Your hair still looks reg."

"Middle of January. How long for you now?"

"Over a year." He said it like the amount of time surprised him.

"Did you go back home?" I remembered Leo was from Utah. His mother had emigrated from South Korea, and his dad was serving a full thirty-five in the Army, which was why Leo had signed up.

"I was there for a while, after I got out." Leo nudged the loaded backpack with his foot. "Then I went for a hike."

"From Salt Lake to Seattle?"

"Not directly. Medford, first."

"They have these things called buses now," I said.

"I took 'em. When I had to." The half-hidden smile appeared again.

"You didn't come to Seattle just to find me," I said.

"Nah. Figured I'd look you up while I was north, something to do before the next leg. It's nice, you know? Peaceful out there." His eyes went to the closed front door of the bar, then over to the doorway leading to the storage rooms. Then back again.

"I can open that, if you want," I said.

"How's that?"

I spread my hands. "You picked a table where you can see the whole place. Watch the points of entry. Which you haven't stopped doing since I came in. You squared away, Leo?"

He met my gaze. The muscles under his eyebrows tightened.

"Good days and bad," he said finally.

"I hear you on that."

There was a thump from the back rooms. Leo twitched. I knew it as the sound of the small loading hatch off the alley closing.

"Need any help?" I called to Luce. She yelled back that she had it handled. Leo's right hand was out of sight again.

I looked at him. "You packing?"

He smiled, a little sheepishly. "Security blanket," he said, pulling up his hand to show me a foot-long iron rod, like a bigger, heavier Kubotan self-defense stick. "Can't carry a gun or a knife. Not when cops take any excuse to pat you down."

Luce entered the room. I stood up, and Leo followed along. He was only about five-eight, boots and all, but his thick wool jacket added to his naturally muscled build.

"Hi," said Luce. She wore her work togs of black jeans and white button-down oxford. It was a man's shirt, but no one would ever guess that when she was wearing it. "I'm sorry that took so long. I figured you two would be on your second round by now, nine in the morning or not."

"Crap," I said, turning to Leo. "A whole damn bar and I didn't offer you a beer."

"Forget it," said Leo. He quickly picked up his back-pack and slid the iron rod into a sleeve in its base. A good place for it. It would look like a reinforcing brace on the pack if he were searched, and still be within quick reach.

"Thanks again for the wings," Leo said, wrestling his pack on.

Luce nodded. "You get enough? I'm running late, but Van can throw something on the grill for you both."

"I'm cool," said Leo, looking at the closed green door.

I wanted to talk to Leo in private. Despite what he'd claimed, I had the feeling that I was the reason he'd come to Seattle. But he was acting squirrelly enough that I thought he might bolt for the exit before he could spit out the reason.

"Hang out a minute," I said to him.

I steered Luce toward the back. We went to her cozy, surprisingly feminine office. Running the bar allowed her very little time to sit and enjoy it, but she had still papered the walls with a lilac pattern and decorated with photographs of friends and happenings at the Morgen. Now they reminded me of the pictures Kend and Elana had left behind, and I pushed that dark idea away.

Luce had framed a snapshot of me on the shelf above her computer. I'd dredged it up and mailed it to her from overseas when she'd asked. I didn't have a lot of pictures of myself. This one had been taken at Camp Eggers in Kabul, not too long before the raid that Leo had told her about. I was dressed in ACUs and plates but no helmet, sitting on the hood of a Humvee and grinning stupidly at the camera, with the scarred side of my face angled away.

"Leo said you checked his story," I said.

"Yeah."

"Still."

"I was careful, Mr. Ounce of Prevention." She took the collapsible police baton out of her back pocket.

First Leo, now Luce. Everyone was walking around armed like ninjas today.

"Good," I said, and stepped forward to kiss her.

When we parted Luce's face was flushed. I spoke before I changed my mind.

"Leo's going to go out and find a place to crash. On the street," I said.

She nodded. "I thought our plans today might change. Are you going to put him up at the house?"

"If he wants. I have to ask."

"Yeah. Okay." She sighed, exaggeratedly. "Guess I'll show you what I bought at Bellefleur another time."

"Jesus."

Luce laughed, but had one eyebrow raised. "He is a friend, right? I mean, you trust him? He's kind of edgy."

I trusted every Ranger I'd served with. It was part of what made us the best at what we did.

"He's a good guy," I said. "And maybe he needs some-body who can hear what he's saying. Thanks for giving him a meal."

"Another night, then."

I made myself let go of her. "You have no idea."

Her smile, full of promise, stayed with me all the way back to the main hall.

I had spent more minutes with Luce than I'd planned. Leo might have taken off, his restlessness forcing him out of the confines of the bar. But he was still there, studying the stained glass of the windows intently.

"Hang with me," I said to him. "I have a friend to see. Then we'll set you up at the house. You can crash there." I had meant to say it casually, but it came out with the undertone of platoon sergeant. I wasn't sure if Leo heard it, too.

"You don't mind?" he said.

"Mind, hell. It'll do me good to talk to somebody who doesn't think a magazine is what you read at the hair salon."

He grunted a short laugh. "All right, hell with it. Let's go."

On the way out I lifted a case of Saw's Porter from the storage room, and left a note for Luce saying: *I owe you for the beer and a lot more. Looking forward to paying the tab.*

Chapter Ten

Hollis Brant kept his powerboat the *Francesca* moored in one of the bigger marinas of Shilshole Bay, one pleasure craft among hundreds. Raindrops pinged off aluminum masts and brasswork. Tiny puddles had formed wherever the dock's planks were warped. Our steps made slapping sounds on the sodden wood as we walked. Leo stayed a step or two behind me, scanning each boat as we passed. So alert that I could feel his gaze when it swept across my back.

I knew the slip number, but I hadn't seen the boat before. All of Hollis's boats had been named *Francesca*, without any trailing roman numerals to let you know how many vessels had come before. Hollis once said that slapping a number on the name would be like asking a lady her age.

The latest incarnation of the *Francesca* was a fifty-foot Carver. I guessed it at about a dozen years old. A hell of a lot sleeker than his previous Nixon-era Chris Craft. But maybe a little less personality, too.

I rapped on the hull, and heard the cabin door thump open at the stern.

"Come aboard, for savior's sake!" Hollis called. "It's raining, or haven't you noticed?"

Leo and I each made one high step up, and climbed over the rail to shuffle sideways back to the enclosed aft deck. Leo had to take his backpack off to squeeze through.

Hollis clasped my right hand as I shook the water off my cap with the other. With his round face and long, muscular arms, Hollis would have looked simian even without the orangey curls that reminded me of an orangutan. He was dressed in madras shorts and a blue-and-white-striped Ballymena United jersey that had been new around the same time I'd started preschool.

"Hollis Brant, Leo Pak," I said.

"You've finally come to visit," said Hollis. He gestured expansively to invite us into the cabin. I entered. Leo stayed in the open doorway. The main salon was a show-piece of teak cabinetry and tan leather settees. Because the boat was newer, the surfaces were shiny and without stains. Because it was Hollis's home, it was untidy.

Hollis lived aboard, and sometimes worked aboard as well. He was a smuggler, and a scrounger. While most of his work wasn't as directly larcenous as Dono's, or as prone to violence as Willard's, he was still a long throw from being a straight citizen.

"It's got class," I said.

"Doesn't she?" said Hollis. "You should feel her take the swells. I'll give you the tour."

"I'll hang here," Leo said, angling his head at the aft deck.

Hollis looked uncertainly at me. I nodded. Leo staying outside would allow Hollis and me to talk business without couching any words. I fished the folded alarm schematic out of the messenger bag and set the bag outside by Leo's backpack. Leo tugged a chair over to where he could see the dock through the glass.

Hollis led me below and I made approving noises over the staterooms and the engines. I was curious what compartments he had built in for smuggling, but I didn't ask. Bad form.

"Your man, there," Hollis said softly before we went back up to the main cabin. "Am I right in guessing he's a soldier, too? Or was?"

"He turned up at the Morgen today," I said. "I haven't seen him in three or four years."

"And home safe, like yourself. That's a blessing."

"Better than the alternative."

"Coffee's on, if you'll have some. Or something stronger?" I stuck with coffee, and brought a mug out to Leo. He nodded and went back to watching the rain.

Hollis swept some half-folded laundry off one of the chairs and sat down.

"Got your message," he said. "What's this about Willard?"

I filled him in on the sad fate of Elana. Hollis had been my grandfather's closest friend, and he knew Willard well enough. He seemed to know someone everywhere.

"Poor bastard," Hollis said, "and those poor fucking kids."

"That about sums it up."

"You and Miss Elana, you knew each other. Or am I misremembering?"

"You're not."

"Ah. And you want me to do what, now?"

"Two things. First I want the police records for Elana and for Kend. They may come up blank, but it's better to check. We know part of Elana's history. I don't know about Kend." Maybe whatever burglary Kend was planning with his alarm schematic wasn't his debut.

Hollis pushed against the floor with his bare calloused feet, letting the round chair swivel from side to side. "This, ah, isn't something I should tell our large friend about, I'm guessing."

"No." Willard was torn up enough about Elana's death without telling him I was looking into her life. "Elana Coll, and Kendrick Haymes." I spelled them out for Hollis.

"What's the second thing?"

I unfolded the schematic and spread it out on the table for him to see.

Hollis whistled. "I don't know such things as well as you and your granddad. Wasn't he a wizard? But this looks like serious business to me."

"Industrial," I said, "and expensive."

"What was it for?"

"That's the question," I said. "The pencil notes tell me somebody planned to grease the system. But I don't know if it was ever used, or if they were successful. The design looks American—see the way the zeroes are made, and the wireless frequencies noted here—but I couldn't swear the score was even in this country."

"And if I may ask, *who* was it for?"

"I found it in Kend Haymes's apartment."

"Did you now?" He looked up at me. "I'm feeling better about our decision to keep this from Willard."

"Yeah."

Heavy rain always sounded different inside a boat. The hollow shell of fiberglass and teak trim making a drum that bobbed gently with the beat of each gust.

Hollis felt the corner of the schematic with his fingertips. "Is this a blueprint?"

"It's blueprint paper, I think. Maybe that has something to do with it, too."

"So you want to know if there were any break-ins, or attempted monkeyshines, at larger businesses that involved cutting an alarm. Maybe in the U.S. and maybe not. That's pretty damn wide."

"I figured it was a stretch."

"I said wide, not unworkable. We can start asking locally and see if anything matches. If we find a lot, maybe that's good, maybe that's bad. Would you like SPD, King County, or State?"

"Show-off."

"Times are tight, lad. There's always a friend willing to make a few extra dollars, so long as it doesn't hurt anybody."

"How many dollars makes a few?"

"Their sheets shouldn't run more than a bill apiece, with some bargaining. I'm not sure about the other. The schematic."

I had taken my roll of fifties from its hiding place in the truck, where I kept it for emergency gas money, or whatever. Bribery counted as whatever.

I tossed the roll to Hollis. "Here's five hundred. If you need more, let me know."

My cell phone buzzed as he was happily pouring himself a second round from the coffee pot.

"Would this be Mr. Shaw?" Female. The barest touch of an accent, maybe British.

"It would."

"This is Carissa Lee, calling from the office of Maurice Haymes, sir. Mr. Haymes would like to meet with you at your earliest convenience."

Maurice Haymes. The late Kend's father. The twelfth-richest man in Seattle, if Channel 3 news had it right.

"Would nine o'clock tomorrow morning be acceptable?" she continued, managing to imply that turning down such an offer would be unthinkable.

"I think I can rearrange," I said.

"Wonderful," she said. "Our offices are in Columbia Tower. Do you know where it is?"

Everybody in Seattle knew where it was. Columbia was the tallest building north of Los Angeles. It took up most of a full block of downtown.

"We're on the thirty-fourth floor," said the assistant. "The reception desk downstairs will have your name."

I stifled a wiseass urge to ask her if the event was white tie, and said I'd be there. She thanked me again and the line clicked off instantly. Efficient.

"Who was that?" said Hollis.

"I've been granted an audience." I told Hollis about Kend's family. He hummed softly.

"Elana didn't aim low, did she?" Then he grimaced. "Sorry. I'm speaking ill of the dead. If there's a service for the girl, you let me know."

I hadn't even thought about whether Willard would be holding a funeral for Elana. Even Hollis Brant was ahead of me when it came to social niceties.

He slapped a hand to his forehead. "Christ, I'd nearly forgotten again. My mind these days. Here." He handed me a small key attached to a plastic disk. "Locker twenty-four, up at the office."

"What is it?"

He grinned. "Presents. Some items of your granddad's. He asked me to hold them, years ago, and it wasn't until I was cleaning through all my things to move aboard the new *Francesca* that I even remembered I had them tucked away in storage. I brought 'em here for you."

He wouldn't say more.

When I opened the door to the aft deck, Leo was looking at Kend Haymes's bank statements, lost in thought.

"Hey," I said.

"Sorry," he said, not glancing up. "I was looking for something to read. Got distracted. These aren't yours, right?"

"Right," I said.

"Good," said Leo. " 'Cause this guy is shit at managing his life. And that's coming from me."

That was the first joke Leo had made today. I was a little pissed at him going through the messenger bag, but counted any humor as a good sign.

Hollis peeked around my shoulder, curious. "Those are young Kend's?"

"Dude needs to stop partying and pay his bills," Leo said, shuffling the papers back into a stack.

"Partying?"

"Yeah." Leo picked up the first credit statement and handed it to me. "He's taking rides everywhere he goes. See?"

He pointed to an entry from a company called Faregame. The entries repeated, sometimes three or four times a day. The amounts were small, less than twenty bucks each. In Kend's overcrowded credit statement, I hadn't noticed.

"He doesn't have a car," I said. "Faregame must be a taxi service, or some kind of ride-sharing deal."

"I figured he was drunk off his ass all day, with that many rides," Leo said.

Maybe he was. And I'd seen Faregame before. I pulled out my phone to look over the list of names and numbers I'd copied from Kend's.

There it was. Selbey Faregame. Likely it was Selbey *at* Faregame, instead of firstname-lastname. Selbey could be Kend's favorite driver.

"Leo," I said, "you're hired."

"Hired? For what?"

"I don't know yet, but you're already earning your keep. Come on."

Leo and I bade farewell to Hollis and walked up to the marina office to use the key Hollis had given me. Locker 24 was large, big enough for sail bags or fishing rods. Inside it was a rolled-up Persian rug.

"Your friends are strange," Leo said.

The rug was a lot heavier and lumpier than it should have been. We carried it out to the truck, and I opened the tailgate and canopy to lay the rug on the truck bed.

Nobody was nearby. I unrolled the rug to reveal two long guns in soft carrying cases, three pistols wrapped in oiled cloths, and a cotton drawstring sack. The handguns turned out to be two Smith & Wesson Sigmas and a larger Glock, all with the serial numbers etched away. The long guns were a Mossberg 12-gauge pump shotgun and a very nice Merkel .30-06 rifle, with a burled wood stock and a Nikon scope. The drawstring sack was full of plastic baggies, sorted ammunition for all the guns, including a few non-lethal rubber shells for the Mossberg.

Leo looked at me, expressionless. "What kind of work did you say your grandfather did?"

Chapter Eleven

The ride-sharing company Faregame had an online app. The app allowed you to request specific drivers. It showed Selbey, Kendrick Haymes's regular guy, coming on shift in half an hour.

I didn't want to give Faregame my own name, so while Leo was still outside, scouting the outside of the house, I opened Dono's hidden compartment in the pantry. He had kept his false IDs and credit cards secreted there, among other useful items. I picked one Washington State driver's license under the name Varrick, and used it to book Selbey for a pick-up on 24th, going down to the Market. Hopefully no one would notice the thirty-year age difference between me and what the license claimed.

Leo came in through the open front door.

"Big place," he said, looking around the rooms of the house he could see from the foyer. "You guys build it?"

"Restored it. Dono was a general contractor, part of the time." In between his less legitimate and more profitable jobs. Contracting work and owning a bar had mostly been convenient ways for Dono to launder his money.

"I'm still getting used to being back," I said.

"Uh-huh." Leo didn't show any signs of removing his

pack. He'd slung it over both shoulders the moment we got out of the truck. "But you like being home?"

The heavy cloud cover outside wasn't allowing much daylight through the windows. I set the case of beer down and flipped all of the switches on the wall. The first floor flared to sudden color.

"I like coming and going whenever I want," I said. "I haven't had time to figure out much else yet."

He nodded. "I looked at the calendar a hundred times a day the first week, like I was counting down to the next deployment. Gearing up, you know?"

I knew. Some rotations, the op tempo was so high we'd break a hundred missions in ninety days. You learned to hit the ground running.

"I keep waking up startled, thinking I've missed my report date," I said, trying for a joke.

Leo just nodded. He took his pack off, almost reluctantly, and leaned it against the wall.

I was hungry. Hunting around the kitchen, I found a full box of pasta left in the cupboard, and an unopened jar of red sauce. I put on a pot of water to boil and the sauce on simmer, and opened the refrigerator to see if there was anything like a vegetable.

"I used to take Prazo," Leo said, looking out the window. "And Ambien. And some other shit I forget."

I looked up. "But you don't now."

"No." He turned away from his reconnaissance of the trees. "You ever?"

"Clone." I said. Clonazepam. Antianxiety. "And sleep aids."

"Man, they had me on all kinds of crap at the V.A."

"It wasn't Army for me. I picked a city doctor off base, when I was on rotation back at Benning." I had decided to keep my troubles to myself. Seeing Army shrinks couldn't do my career any good, no matter what they decided to put on their reports. What the brass didn't know wouldn't hurt me.

"What'd it do for you?" Leo said

"Cognitive therapy. It gave me some coping tools, when my heart rate would go crazy or when I had nightmares. Some of them worked."

"Nightmares." It wasn't a question. But it needed answering.

I used the pot lid to keep the noodles from sliding into the sink while I poured out the boiling water. Steam snaked along the upturned lid, the hairs on the back of my arm catching scalding droplets from the air.

"I was a brand-new sergeant and fireteam leader," I said. "We were just part of two platoons sent to raid a Taliban village. The locals had left, and the insurgents had hunkered down in the houses during bad weather."

"Wintertime?" Leo said. There was something in the way he said it, something hesitant.

I nodded. "First storm of the year. No visibility, and too much wind. Enough that our air support was cut way back. Our squad was covering one side of the village, in case any bad guys ran to hide and attack from the hills nearby."

Leo waited. I put the pot down. I hadn't even told Luce this story.

"Somebody in our group spotted a cave," I said, "way up above the village. There was movement around the entrance. We got the signal to climb the hill and secure it, in case they had heavy weapons they could use to make it rain down on the village."

"I hate caves."

"This one wouldn't have changed your opinion. We called inside for surrender, and threw in grenades when there was no reply. Still no sign of the enemy. The cave turned out to be a long son of a bitch. It went back into the hill and broke up into side tunnels and dead ends. The Taliban had turned it into some kind of depot for old AK-47s and other junk. So we had to go through it one yard at a time with our night optics on, checking every twist and turn in pitch-black."

Leo's eyes flickered. As a sniper, he might not have dealt with as many holes in the ground as other Rangers. But we all knew that clearing a cave of hostiles was like chasing a cobra down its den. "Was there another exit? Did they rabbit?"

"We thought maybe. Our team just kept going deeper into the mountain, tossing a grenade around every blind corner and clearing more ground. Then we came around one bend and everything went to hell on a rocket."

"How many were there?" His voice sounded tight.

"Five. One of them fired a burst in the dark."

Three shots. The same three flashes that I saw every time I had the dream.

"Then the rest of them just panicked. They were shooting anywhere, and the whole place lit up like it was noon. Bullets and rock pieces off the walls and I was sure the whole damn cave was coming down around us. We took them all out in thirty seconds, but—"

I stopped.

"You thought you were done," Leo said.

I'd had close calls before that day, wounded and knocked unconscious, shocked when I woke up alive. This firefight hadn't been like that. It had its own surprises, especially when our team checked ourselves for casualties after, and were astounded to find only a few deep cuts and one guy with rock fragments in his leg.

During the fight, I had felt aware of everything. The way the dirt crunched underfoot. The blurred ghost of my rifle's reticule dot in the green night vision, as I moved it across targets. The thud of a ricochet hit on the armor plating of the guy next to me.

I hadn't believed I was dead in those moments, like Leo assumed. I had felt more alive than I ever had before.

It was what came after that night which had seemed so unreal.

My phone buzzed with a message. It was an automated text from Faregame, telling me that Selbey would be at the top of the block to pick me up in five minutes.

"Look," I said, "my offer still stands. Hang with me for a while."

"I don't need watching."

"Okay."

"I just like it better outside."

"So camp in the backyard if you want. I gotta go. There's a lady down the street named Addy. Tougher than stale jerky. I'll write down her number. If you need to find something and I'm not around, you call her. Understood?"

It was my command voice, back again. Leo grinned for the first time I'd seen since Kandahar.

"Roger that," he said.

I jogged up the street to the corner, wishing Selbey had been a little slower to reply to my ride request. Leo had been ready to talk. Maybe not about everything that was weighing him down, but it was a start.

Then again, I hadn't been completely truthful with the former Specialist Pak myself.

It wasn't really the gunfight in the cave that still lurked in the back of my brain, after so many years. It was how I had felt in the days after the fight.

Separate. Insensate. Going through all the motions of walking and talking and even thinking as an outside observer.

The feeling of distance had faded eventually, buried under the constant pressure of new missions, new dangers. Then one night in a dream, months later and back stateside, I saw the three muzzle flashes at the right edge of my peripheral vision, and somehow all the fear I hadn't felt on that day came in like a howling banshee. I woke in a panic. And for the rest of the next day, I felt that same disconnection again, shrouded from reality.

Like I wasn't meant to be on the Earth anymore.

Chapter Twelve

I walked up the hill to catch my ride. The rain had finally abated after a long final drizzle, but the tree leaves and gutters were still dripping.

A metallic blue Forester wagon pulled up to the curb, so new that the chrome trim gleamed even under the gray sky. The driver rolled down his window halfway. He was a college-age white guy, with a long face and even longer neck with a pointed Adam's apple. Tufts of dirty-blond hair poked out from under his bright red wool cap.

"Selbey?" I said.

"And you're Mr. Varrick. Cool," he nodded. "Pike Place, yeah?"

I climbed into the backseat. The Forester had that leather-cleaner smell of showroom cars, along with just a hint of sativa smoke.

"If you need a ride back from the Market, I can hang," Selbey said. He banged the gas and the Forester lurched into a gap in the traffic. Selbey didn't match his pristine suburbanite ride. He wore a dull gray wool sweater over a T-shirt I could tell was paper-thin just by the collar. His jeans were frayed at the knees and a two-inch split showed at the thigh seam.

"Nice car, man," I said.

"Bought it for this gig. Gotta spend to make, you know?" His head nodded along with unheard music.

"I know," I said. "Kend told me you were his go-to wheels right now."

"Hey, you know Kend?" Selbey's face fell. "I heard on the news. He was a cool guy."

"He said you were solid, too. That's why I called." I found myself imitating Selbey's parrot-like head bob.

"Yeah? That's all right. I liked him."

"I'm trying to let people know. Like maybe have a gathering or something. For his tribe."

Selbey gave me a big grin in the rearview mirror. The Forester drifted a little out of its lane. "That's very cool of you, man."

"Problem is, some of his friends, I just know their first names or nicknames from Kend. No phone numbers. It would help me out if you could tell me where he'd been going. So I can get in touch with them."

"Uh. Hey, I'm just allowed to drive people where they send me, you know. I can't just go anywhere."

"It's cool." I laid two bills, a twenty and a hundred, across the shoulder of the passenger seat. Held them there with my hand. "So you take me to the Market, and Faregame gets the twenty bucks and we're done with them. Then you can do whatever you want. Free country, man."

Selbey's eyes were working triple-time, between me in

the rearview and the money and the traffic down Olive. "I suppose it's okay to drive you someplace myself."

"Car payments are steep. You show me the list of the places he went. I pick one, and we'll go there."

He couldn't hand me his phone fast enough. "Under the spreadsheet app. That logs all my rides."

It was easy enough to sort by Kend's name. He had taken forty or fifty rides during the past month with Selbey. I scrolled through and used my phone to photograph the whole list. A lot of the destinations were obvious—his apartment, downtown at the Columbia Center and the HDC offices, his neighborhood in Lower Queen Anne.

One location stood out, in the southwest part of the city, almost to Burien. Kend had made at least ten visits to it. Two during the daytime, the rest in early evening.

"What's this one?" I said, showing it to Selbey. He was busy running the yellow light through Pine Street and waited until traffic had stopped us to look.

"Yeah, that's the long trip. Twenty-five bucks from his house. It's just a building, man. I figured he worked at the place part-time. Here we are." He stopped the car in the middle of the brick road at the Market, and took back the phone to press a couple of buttons. I signed off on the ride. A car pulled up behind us and honked.

"Take me there," I said.

"You sure you know Kend, man?" Frowning wasn't a natural expression for Selbey, but he gave it a shot. The car behind us backed him up by laying on the horn.

"You ever meet Elana? How hot was she?" I said.

"*So* hot," Selbey said, unable to keep from laughing.

"Help us out," I said.

Selbey popped the Forester into gear and we zoomed off as the car behind us stalled, still honking.

*

The address from Kend's phone turned out to be a brown brick-and-cinder office building. It had seen better decades. The front wall showed as many FOR LEASE signs as iron-barred windows. Selbey dropped me at what he said was the same spot where Kend had gotten out of the car on every visit. We exchanged fist bumps and the two bills and he zoomed away, probably happy to be out of the neighborhood.

I was the only person visible on the street. The eroded brickwork showed a lot of very old graffiti. The four-story building wasn't even interesting enough to be tagged anymore. Besides a couple of homeless guys sitting across the road from the back half, the block was just as lonesome all the way around. What the hell was Kend Haymes doing here?

Then the dreary anonymity of the office building struck a familiar note. I'd never been there before. But I had visited another location a whole lot like it, and recently.

On my way back to the front entrance I spotted the satellite dishes. Two of them, up near the roof on the

113

south corner. Brand-spanking-new, with cables leading down into a rough hole in one of the top floor windows.

I kept my distance from the front doorway. There was a steel intercom with a keypad. Dial the right number and reach the right extension, back when the building had phone service. I thought about the kind of security I might install for myself, and then edged just close enough to see the camera. It was inside the lobby, pointed through the glass door where it could get a clear view of anyone standing by the intercom. The camera wasn't the ancient closed-circuit type that would have matched the building. It was a new wireless model, and crudely bolted high on the wall.

It would be good to see inside the building, and confirm my suspicions. It would not be good to have my face on camera doing it.

The building had fire exits, steel doors one inch thick on ball-bearing hinges. Old doors like that could be opened from the outside with a large special key, more like a wrench than a house key. With proper tools, a crowbar and a sledge, I could force the steel door or beat the lock. I didn't have tools. I didn't need them.

Twenty feet from the fire exit, embedded flush with the building's brickwork, was a black metal box that looked like a very small safe. A Knox-Box. Used by fire departments to gain access to the building without the trouble and expense of chopping big holes in the doors and windows. At the center of the Knox-Box was a little hinged cover, and under the cover was a keyhole, slightly rusted from disuse. The SFD would have a master key that fit every Knox in the area, and I had the equivalent. No one was nearby. I used Dono's lockpicks and had the box open in moments. Inside was a set of keys and one larger hollow hexagonal tube that looked sure to fit the fire exit lock.

Abracadabra.

The downside, of course, is that fire exits are also hooked up to extremely loud alarms, with flashing lights and automatic alerts to the nearest fire and police stations. Most burglars give them a wide berth.

Unless the burglar is pretty damn sure that someone has disabled the alarm already. I inserted the hexagonal tube and turned. The fire door opened to blessed silence.

Whoever had greased the fire alarm hadn't cared enough to hide their work. The metal doorframe near the latch been pried open and peeled back. I could see where someone had crudely bypassed the circuit, leaving the disconnected wires exposed. The young professional criminal that I used to be grimaced at the hack job.

I ran up the stairwell to the next floor. It was completely empty. No walls, no furniture, just a dusty void waiting for renovation. I took a moment to mark where the other stairwells were located. One in each corner.

On the fourth floor was a dank hallway with glued-on linoleum and blank eggshell-colored walls that had more scuff marks than paint. There was a freight elevator, and a single windowless door with cheap wooden veneer leading to the interior.

I listened. Under the normal hums and clicks of office heat ventilation, there was something else. Voices and music, in a very staccato beat.

Inside the windowless door was a longer hallway, which led to an open space beyond. The voices and music were coming from televisions. Many televisions, with the sounds of bumper jingles and cheers and rapid-fire announcers competing for dominance.

. . . *Villanova, with half the game to go, needs to* . . .

. . . *Hess, for three! That makes him five for seven* . . .

. . . *superb engineering that turns your carpool into a carnival* . . .

Then all of the broadcasts were drowned out by a very enthusiastic roar of live male voices. Somebody's team was doing well.

There was a rubber wedge on the floor of the hall, for propping the door open. Just as useful for keeping the door closed behind me. I shoved it underneath, as another burst of appreciative shouting and claps came from around the corner. Before the celebrating had died down, I risked a glance.

Someone had transplanted a sports bar into the middle of the barren office space. Ten flat-screens, arranged on tables in a semicircle, with cushioned chairs and sofas at the circle's center. Eight or ten men lounged in the chairs, watching the games. Their backs were to me, and I took advantage to extend my look.

From behind, it was hard to assign a type to the men

seated on the sofas and chairs. They ranged between twenty-five and fifty. Expensive haircuts on most. A couple of business suits. Today was a Tuesday. The executive types might be blowing off afternoon at the office to be here.

One young guy in jeans and a puffy winter coat was seated on a swivel chair off to the side. He wasn't watching the games. Instead he typed away on a laptop with frenzied concentration, occasionally tapping the wireless headset in his ear.

There was one last man, over six feet tall and brawny, with sparse black hair and a thick beard. He stood by a table stocked with booze and an ice-filled cooler underneath. As I watched, one of the spectators raised a piece of paper and the bouncer walked quickly forward to grab the proffered slip and take it over to the laptop jockey.

That was why the building's derelict exterior, with its shiny satellite dishes, had been so familiar. Willard's mobile card game operated on the same principle. A dull layer of paint disguising a gold brick.

I'd heard of operations like this, but never seen one in person. A ghost book.

Washington State was hard-nosed about online gaming, and sports betting in particular. A Class C felony, last I knew. If a state resident wanted to play anything heavier than their company's March Madness pool, they needed a go-between. The ghost book was the middle man. Live viewing, and up-to-the minute gambling. The book would be set up in an unobtrusive location, and relocated whenever necessary. A few trusted high rollers would be clued in to the new spot. And if those gamblers wanted to stay part of the inner circle, they would bet like they meant it.

This was a bigger cash cow than Willard's little rolling casino, however. The geek at the laptop would be working the phones and instant messaging as well as the whales in the room. He'd have stolen or false identities to lay down bets with international sports books via satellite. The gamblers would pay the ghost book a hefty percentage, win or lose, on top of whatever the bookies themselves charged. It might be the only heavy game in town. It was definitely for suckers.

Like Kend. It was clear where all of the trust-fund kid's allowance, as well as his Porsche, had evaporated.

The door behind me thumped. Someone was trying to open it and running up against the rubber wedge.

Time to leave. I checked my mental map of where the nearest corner stairs were, as the door banged again, and someone shouted *Hey!* from the lobby. I stepped into the room and sprinted past the screens for the stairwell door.

The bouncer reacted pretty fast, but there was half a showroom's worth of furniture between us. The men hollered in confusion as he crashed through their midst. I had a thirty-foot lead when I hit the door. I took the stairs three at a time, sideways, like running downhill with a full ruck.

At the bottom, there was another fire exit. The alarm on the fire door had been disabled just like the first one I'd seen, with the disconnected wires exposed to the air. I yanked the makeshift circuit apart and touched the exposed wire back to its other half.

The bouncer, still two flights up, wheezily tried to shout again. It sounded like someone had stepped on a rat. That was the last thing I heard, before the alarm kicked in. A shrieking pulse filled the air, so loud that it went beyond deafening and into blinding. Halogen lights began to flash in a disjointed rhythm.

I ran out the door. Behind me, I could imagine the gamblers, their bets and the game forgotten in the sudden panic, scattering like roaches.

Chapter Thirteen

It had started raining again during the few minutes I'd been inside. I was drenched by the time I made it to the nearest bus stop, and still dripping when I caught the next one headed uptown.

The ghost book had been blown. Whoever was running the game would have to move locations, and leave the televisions and satellite dishes behind for the fire department to find. I had considered waiting around to watch the show. But there was no point. I'd seen what I could see, and I had no car to follow them, whoever they were.

It had been a bad week for that book. Besides my visit spooking the regulars, they had also lost Kend. Judging by his parched bank account, he might have dropped enough cash there to be considered a gold-star mark.

Something didn't fit, and I let my mind relax, watching the drops stream down the window. By the time the bus connected with the arterial, I had it.

Kend was visiting the ghost book at least once every few days, based on his rides with Selbey. But his available funds were down to zip every month within a week after his allowance.

So what money was he gambling with? Was he selling

things? I thought about his Porsche Panamera. Two years old, signed away, and no money deposited in his bank account for it. If Kend had sold it, he might have taken cash under the table.

Or maybe he didn't sell it. Maybe it was given as payment, to cover what he already owed somebody. I searched my memory and came up with the name on the sales record: Torrance X. Broch.

Kend gambles. Kend needs money. Kend goes to the kind of guy who lends money to people who gamble it away, and when he gets in over his head, he gives the shark six figures' worth of automobile. That could be it.

So then the question became: who was Torrance Broch? I didn't know the name. Then again, I didn't know many loan sharks. They swam in different seas than the ones Dono and Willard navigated.

I did know a few bookies, though. One in particular had probably thrown customers to every shark in town. He could tell me about Broch, if he was still shambling around. And if I could find whatever rock he was under.

My cell phone was in my inside jacket pocket, the only completely dry spot on me. I pulled up one of the handful of numbers in my contact list.

"Ganz and Quinlan," answered a female voice.

"Van Shaw. Calling for Ephraim." From across the center aisle, a gaunt woman in a tan pantsuit and pink parka frowned at me. She had a face that looked as though she frowned more than she blinked.

"One moment please, Mr. Shaw," the voice said.

I waited. The woman across from me made a little grunt of annoyance. I gave her a smile that was two teeth too wide to look sane. She turned away, rolling her eyes.

"Van, hello," said Ephraim Ganz quickly. Ganz did everything quickly. He probably took the stairs when he lunched with clients at the Space Needle because he found the elevators too slow.

"Hello, Ephraim," I said. "That's a new receptionist."

"I married the other one, and she won't answer the phones anymore."

"Congrats."

"You've been back in Seattle, what?" he said. "A few weeks, I hear."

"You're annoyed that I haven't called?"

"I'm astounded that you're calling at all. In trouble already?" The last time I'd been in Seattle, Ganz's legal maneuvers had kept me from spending a lot of years sitting on a built-in bed, staring at steel bars.

"No trouble," I said. "At least not your kind."

"I wish I could say that sounded encouraging."

"Is Fred Fogh still a client of yours?"

"No. Not for some years now." Ganz's voice was dry enough to mop up the rainwater puddle I had left on the floor of the bus.

"Was he too cheap to keep paying your retainer?" I said.

"You remember Freddy well."

"Then you and I don't have to dance around attorney-client privilege."

"Not unless you're inquiring about anything that happened during the two excruciating decades within which I deftly handled Mr. Fogh's concerns."

"Nope. He's still in business, I take it."

"Freddy is what Freddy is."

"You know where?"

Ganz laughed. "He switched attorneys. It would take much more than saving a few pennies to get him to switch taverns. The Laughing Friar. You know where that is?"

"On Meeker. Thanks."

"My pleasure. Say, if Freddy looks to be in need of representation, you remind him that I don't hold grudges. My door's always open."

"You said he was excruciating."

"So I'm pragmatic. It's a flaw." He hung up.

Ganz hadn't asked me why I was looking for a pocket-change bookie like Fred Fogh. He was probably in the habit of not asking questions. The kinds of answers his clients gave might make him an accessory before the fact.

*

Most of the light inside the Laughing Friar came from neon signs. The main room was long and narrow and smelled of dry rot. There were three booths at the end. All

123

of them were empty. A few old men who had the look of permanent fixtures propped up the bar.

The bartender was no younger than the customers, but he was a little more vertical. He watched me from the moment I entered the door, eyes as narrow as the sides of dimes.

"Freddy here?" I asked.

"Don't know him," said the bartender. His downy white hair made a tangled ring around his bald head, with the same thick pale tufts for eyebrows and covering his forearms.

"Sure," I said. "He's only been coming here since the Civil War. I'll wait."

"Not without a drink, you won't."

I wanted to ask him about the house wine, but decided that wouldn't further my interests. Each of the regulars was nursing a bottle of Budweiser, or Coors, or Miller. The microbrew revolution would never storm the gates of the Friar. I bought a Bud.

I sat in the back booth where I could see the door, and thought about Kend, and Elana. Mostly Elana. Why was she with a guy like Kend Haymes? Sure, Kend must have seemed like a catch. Megabucks family. His own place. Even close to good-looking. Everything a girl might want, on paper.

Unless the paper you were talking about was Kend's bank statement. Zero was zero, whether it started from mutual fund dividends or working a double shift at Arby's.

Had she known about his gambling? Had she loved him anyway? Or at all? I thought about the love notes I'd found in their apartment. Sticky notes not stuck to anything. Stuffed haphazardly in a drawer. But not thrown away or burned in a fury, either.

My beer was empty. I bought another.

Elana was smart. And the picture of Kendrick Haymes I was piecing together looked like a guy who couldn't successfully hide his gambling addiction from the woman who shared his life. So she must have known. And chosen to stick by him. I didn't know if I admired that or not.

My phone buzzed with a text. It was a reply to the message I'd sent Kend Haymes's friends early that morning. The answer came from Barrett Yorke, the elfin girl holding the champagne in the wedding picture.

Meet us A. Borealis on 5th at nine tonight.

Couldn't fault her for wasting words.

At three fifteen Fred Fogh walked through the door of the Laughing Friar, moving slow enough that I had all the time in the world to recognize him. He was probably pushing seventy now, thinner than he'd been fifteen years ago, and buried under multiple layers. I counted two worn dress shirts and a moth-eaten green cardigan and a brown raincoat and a fishing hat and a scarf. The ruddy skin of his face sagged like wax off a pillar candle.

The bartender nodded to Freddy and jabbed a thumb in my direction. Freddy saw me and stopped. There was a flash of panic on his face. When I raised a finger off the bottle in greeting his expression shifted to puzzlement. He risked coming a few steps closer.

"I know you," he said. "Right?"

"Yeah."

He gave himself another dozen seconds to think about it, then shook his head. "Frigging brain," he said, "Half the things now, I remember that I remember them, but that's about it. Tell me."

"I'm Dono Shaw's grandson."

He stared at me, mouth drooping to match his jowls. "Jesus. Jee-Zuss! You really are." He plopped down opposite me in the booth, bringing a waft of nickel cigarillo. "Christ, how could I forget those black peepers of your grandpa's. What's your name? Wait, don't say it. It's the same as his name, of course, stupid bastard I am. Donovan."

"Van. Good to see you, Freddy."

"You too. Jesus. Dono Shaw." Fogh gave another shake of the head, or maybe it was a shudder. He dropped his wet hat on the bench next to him. His hair was still brown, but the color was buoyed by liver spots on his scalp.

"Sorry about your grandpa. I woulda known who you were right off, if not for—" He waved a fingertip at his face, miming lines at the same places where the scars marked mine. "Been a long time. It must have been at the Morgen, last you saw me."

"Taking bets from Albie." Luce's uncle had liked to play the horses at Emerald Downs without having to drive the half hour south.

126

If the ghost book I'd found this morning was action for high rollers like Kend Haymes, then Freddy Fogh was the bookie for the guys who trimmed Kend's lawn. Freddy would probably get altitude sickness if he ever covered more than a couple of grand.

"Right, right, Albie." Freddy's face lost a little of its excitement. Maybe his memory caught up enough to remind him that Dono and Albie were in the ground now. "So, uh, you here to put something down yourself? I got a good line on tonight's Thunderbird game."

"I need some information."

"Ah." Noncommittal. Freddy angled his head where he might see out of the corner of his eye, in case any of the bar's regulars had somehow managed to lurch within earshot.

"I want to know about a guy named Torrance Broch," I said.

"Know what?"

"Know anything. Where he is. What he does. Start with that."

"Sure. And what's your own line of work nowadays?"

"I'm not a cop."

"Who ever said that?" His eye twitched again toward the bar. " 'Course you're not a cop. You don't have that look, like you own the whole frigging place. In fact, at first I thought maybe you were some kinda muscle, sent here to push on me a little."

"You underwater?"

Freddy made a noise like coughing out a cotton ball. "Not seriously or nothing. I just need a little extra cash until the Saturday games."

"Sure." There it was. The dry palm wanting for grease. I was throwing money around like confetti lately.

"I got about eighty bucks in my pocket," I said, "not counting bus fare. You give me everything you have on Broch, we'll decide what that's worth."

"You're joking me."

"That's the offer. You want a drink, too, it'll come out of your cut." My beer bottle was empty and I clinked it. "Or do I leave now?"

"Hang on, hang on. I can tell you who T. X. Broch is. He's a bear trap. He sets up big-money games and tries to get suckers to overextend, so he can squeeze them long-term. He's into legit businesses, too, used cars and auto lube joints, I think. But most of his money comes from squeezing vig out of guys."

"Do people really still say that? I thought 'vig' went out with phone books."

"Hey, screw you, too."

"You said he's the house for big games. Does he run sports?"

Freddy traced one of the innumerable scratches in the tabletop with a nicotine-stained fingertip. "You wanna stay clear of him, Van."

"Big Bad Broch."

"I'm not shitting you. He may not be the Gambino

128

family but he's still plenty. One of my regulars? He had a sure thing and he wanted to lay it down big. More than I could cover. I heard he borrowed twenty thousand off of Broch."

"And the sure thing wasn't."

"*And* the next thing I know, the poor son of a bitch is in the ICU at Overlake. Broch's guys took their time on him, with the number of things they broke."

"Busting bones is kind of the daily grind, for a loan shark."

"You don't understand me. I mean Broch did this the same frigging day. He knew my guy couldn't pay it back, not anytime in the foreseeable. Broch coulda milked him forever, but how much would he get? A hundred a week? He let my guy make his bet, and by the time it went in the shitter Broch had already decided the poor prick was worth a lot more as an object lesson. The twenty large didn't mean squat."

"Decisive."

"Fucking nuts."

"Has Broch made any permanent lessons?"

Freddy stared at me. "Eating through a tube isn't enough for you?"

"I mean it. Is Broch a killer?"

"Hell, I don't know. Maybe? It's not anybody's first choice, not even for an animal like T. X. Broch."

He was right. Loan sharks dealt in pain, not death. You can't squeeze a dead guy. Murder didn't even make a great example to others, because if enough people heard about the killing, the cops would, too. Better to populate a whole ward at Overlake than to knock one deadbeat off.

Broch lent money. Kend needed money, if he wanted to keep gambling. Broch probably ran the ghost book, too. But why might Broch kill Kend? Haymes still had his trust-fund thousands coming in every month. Plenty more juice to be had there. Was Kend in so deep that he had threatened to go to the cops?

Freddy was watching me, not wanting to interrupt my reverie.

I put my four twenties down on the table. "Okay. I'll give you what I've got. But you keep your nose up. Tell me if you hear anything more about Broch in the next week."

"I'll ask around, yes indeed," said Fogh, taking the bills and folding them three times before slipping them into his cardigan.

"Good luck with Saturday."

Fogh nodded and waved a happy hand at the bartender, who continued to give me the stink-eye as I left. He was warming to me, I could tell.

Chapter Fourteen

In keeping with its name, A. Borealis had an arctic motif. The glass ceiling of the rooftop bar was held up by sandstone pillars, each carved with Inuit-inspired designs. Eagles and humpback whales and caribou. The cocktails on the menu started at fourteen bucks. I ordered a rye, neat. If I enjoyed it, I could mortgage my house and have a second round.

From where I sat at the center bar, the mirror allowed me to watch most of the tables. Borealis was a big place, designed for large wedding parties and small convention crowds on the weekends. The midweek rush of business people from the Mansfield Georgian hotel downstairs still left plenty of elbow room.

Most of the business types were still wearing their suits, though the men had loosened their ties and the women had slipped off their high heels under the tables. The few who weren't completely engrossed by their phones or laptops engaged in animated chatter with one another. In my jeans and flannel shirt, I was the gamekeeper crashing the country estate's cocktail hour.

Barrett and Parson Yorke came off the elevator lobby into the bar. I knew they were siblings from their social media posts, but in life I never would have guessed. One or both may have been adopted. Barrett was recognizably the petite fashion plate I'd seen in the snapshots. The honey-eyed bob had been restyled in a wedge cut that fell over one eye. Parson was a very big boy. Not a square slab like Willard, but round, with a midsection that made his head look undersized by comparison. The shearling coat he was wearing must have set him back two grand at the Big 'n' Tall. He towered behind his sister, carrying her coat. The princess and the palace guard. Or the whole palace.

They scanned the crowd and I raised a hand. Barrett glided across the room, a sharpened shadow in a black sleeveless blouse and black pants. She extended a hand to shake, frowning.

"How d'you do," she said.

"I'm Van," I said. Parson was inexpressive, and his handshake was soft and damp. Still, I had the feeling he could have squeezed until my fingers gushed out between his like toothpaste.

I motioned for them to sit at the bar, but Barrett chose a table and sat at it without a word. Parson followed. I took my drink from the bar—still a few dollars of liquor left in the glass—and sat with them. A server came over immediately and took their drink orders. Vodka for Barrett and a Newcastle for her brother.

"You knew Elana," Barrett said to me.

"Back when we were kids. Our families are friendly."

"Then you don't really know her now," Parson said.

He was younger than I'd first guessed, perhaps only twenty or twenty-one, and his mud-brown goatee was more attempt than reality.

"Well enough to say hello. That's why I was at the cabin."

"Can you prove that?" said Barrett. "You could be anyone. We've already had calls from the press, wanting quotes about Kend."

"I can prove I know Elana's uncle Willard," I said. "He's the one who told me she was on the Peninsula."

"That's not quite what I want."

One well-tailored young businessman two tables over found Barrett much more interesting than his cell phone. It was understandable. She was very poised, as cool as the single large sapphire stud pierced through her upper ear. The gem was real. I wasn't sure about the ice princess act. Her black-coffee eyes gave off a challenge.

"Okay. How's this?" I said. "Kend and Elana drove her blue Volvo hatchback up to the cabin. Sometime after that, Elana was shot twice in the face at close range, and then Kend probably put the gun to his own head. Both of them died immediately. I've seen enough gunshot wounds to be sure. The cabin door was left open, so animals and decomp had a couple of days to whittle away at both of your friends before I happened along. The last thing I did there was drag Kend's body, which was mostly in one piece, back inside to protect what was left."

It was cruel. Maybe crueler than I'd intended. But it

had the right effect. They were both openmouthed and pale. In Barrett's case, paler than usual.

"I'm sorry," Barrett said. "That—that must have been awful."

"Worse for them. Tell me about their relationship."

"Their relationship?"

"Were they happy? Did they fight? Was one of them in trouble? I'm trying to understand what happened at the cabin."

"I-I don't think they were fighting. They argued some, but not like angry arguments."

"What did they argue about?"

"Oh. Who said what when, and who was right about so-and-so." Barrett shook her head minutely. "Inconsequentials."

I turned to Parson. "How about you? When was the last time you saw them?"

"I saw Kend last week," he said.

"At the cabin?"

"What's that supposed to mean?"

"There were lots of new tire tracks around. Somebody visited them."

Parson frowned. He suspected trickery, but maybe that was normal for his attitude. He seemed easy to trick.

"It wasn't me," he said.

"So you believe the rumors are true?" said Barrett, regaining some of her earlier self-possession. "That Kend killed Elana?"

"No," said Parson flatly.

"I don't know if he did or not," I said. "Just what the scene looked like."

"He didn't."

Barrett reached over and squeezed her brother's prize ham forearm. "Parson was a great friend to Kend," she said, smiling sadly at him. "And Kend looked out for Parson."

"He was my best friend," said Parson.

"Then I'm sorry, Parson," I said. "I know what it's like to lose guys who'll have your back, no matter what."

He nodded, looking at the table.

"Barrett, it's probably time for your own special friend to join us," I said, pointing to the businessman in the navy suit. He saw me pointing and scowled.

She flushed. "That's just Charlie."

"No point in Charlie sitting alone."

She waved him over and he came, reluctantly. By the time we shook hands he'd apparently decided to pretend the whole secret-agent thing didn't happen.

"Charlie Shearman," he said. He was a GQ-cover match for Barrett, with curly dirty-blond hair and sideburns. His navy suit had been fitted down to the quarter inch, until it was practically scuba gear.

"We were telling Van that we don't know why Kend might have done what he did," Barrett said. "What the police *suspect* he did," she amended, off Parson's hurt look.

"Hmmm. And is that all you're wondering about?" Shearman said. He sat down and placed a protective hand over Barrett's.

"I was curious whether you use a laser level to get those sideburns just so," I said. Shearman's jaw clenched.

"Van described the cabin to us, Charlie," said Barrett. "It sounded horrible."

"I'll bet," he said. "Enough to file a mental distress suit against the Haymes family, if the official ruling goes his way."

"Charlie!"

"You're a lawyer for them?" I said.

"I'm a financial consultant," Shearman said, like I'd impugned his honor.

"A junior partner with Lyman and Goode," said Barrett.

"Good for you," I said.

He scowled. "Go to hell."

"All right," I said. "We got off on the wrong foot. Was the idea to hang around until I left Barrett and Parson, and then follow me and make sure I was who I claimed?"

"You can hardly blame us," Barrett said.

"You're protecting your friends. I get that. But the idea of spending years wrangling a settlement out of Kend's family makes me want to jump off this roof."

Civilians had a range of reactions to my facial scars. Some people pretended to ignore them, like Barrett, who had glanced once and then studiously kept her eyes on mine. Charlie Shearman couldn't help examining the

136

white grooves every time I looked at someone else. I wasn't sure Parson had even noticed my scars at all.

Shearman's eyes flicked back to me. "So this isn't some angle?"

"I've had enough stress in the past ten years. I don't need to pretend to having more."

He didn't reply, but as the server took his drink order, he asked me if I wanted another round. I took it as a peace offering.

"No matter what happened up at the cabin," I said, "nobody wins. But the cops are likely to ask Kend's friends all kinds of rough questions, looking for motive. Like whether he was ever violent with her, or anybody else. Or if he got into fights."

Head shakes all around. Parson was getting agitated again.

"Was he taking anything?"

"He wasn't some *drug* addict, if that's what you mean," Shearman said.

"What about antidepressants? Mood elevators?"

"God, isn't everyone?" said Barrett. "But Kend was a very positive guy. It was part of why everyone liked him so much."

Shearman's eyes flickered to his girlfriend, then down. I remembered the picture of Barrett and Trudy Dobbs in Kend's apartment. Facedown in a desk drawer, instead of up on the wall with the rest.

"What about money?" I said.

"What about it?" said Shearman.

"Did he have any? I know his family does. But that's different."

"We wouldn't be so rude as to ask."

"Even as a junior partner at Lyman and Goode?"

Barrett stiffened. "It's not a requirement for our friendship. No matter what you might think."

"I don't care about your entrance criteria," I said. "I want to know if Kend was broke."

"We were friends with Elana, too. Unless you believe she was some token."

Damn it. I was digging myself a hole, and fast.

Worse, the whole private-school bunch of them seemed to be genuinely out of the loop. None of them was giving any sign that they might know of the ghost book, or T. X. Broch, or even that they knew Kend had liked to gamble.

"Your other friend didn't show tonight," I said. "Trudy Dobbs."

"She's away on vacation," said Barrett.

"Away where?"

Barrett downed the last half of her second vodka rocks in an impressive shot, and exhaled slowly through her nose. "Trudy's my best friend. And Elana's. If you have any questions for her, I'll ask her myself."

Shearman took out his wallet and handed an Amex card to the server as he passed. The Black Card, of course.

"Sorry we couldn't help you more," he said to me.

"We're all very upset, and we just want to make sure Kend gets every consideration."

Over any considerations for Elana, was what I took from that. Closing ranks.

Shearman sipped the last of his scotch. Parson's beer was mostly untouched. We all stood up. Shearman took Barrett's thin leather coat from Parson and draped it over her shoulders. He led Barrett back toward the bar.

Parson lingered behind.

"If you make trouble for us," he said softly, "I'm gonna break your spine."

They left.

No-limit credit cards. Sapphire earrings. And threats of bodily harm. I was coming up in the world.

Five minutes later, I was standing around the corner of the hotel, watching each of them drive out of the parking garage. Shearman chauffeured Barrett in a Mercedes sedan. Parson scraped the bottom of the curb with his red Chrysler 300C.

No sports car with fishhook treads. No dually.

I shrugged to myself. It had been worth a shot.

Age Seventeen

The office park where Gallison Engineering & Equipment made its home was beyond quiet, as Saturday night ticked over into Sunday morning. Just me, and Dono, and the occasional squirrel, startled by our truck cruising slowly behind the building without its headlights on.

Willard had chosen the truck well. The little white pickup could be a landscaper's, or a utility truck, or a personal vehicle. As a bonus, the hard plastic cover over the truck bed had hinges and stiff pneumatics to open and stay open, like a box top. Or a coffin.

Dono came to a stop at a precise spot, right under the fourth-floor window I'd been examining the day before.

He handed me a burner phone. "Don't forget this." Like I would have left it behind. I plugged my headset into it.

"You remember the right frequencies?" I said, pointing to the police scanner. He had already programmed the SPD dispatch channels in, I knew. I was just giving my grandfather shit for treating me like I was in kindergarten.

I shouldered the backpack, which contained most of the gear I'd need during the next hour or so, and walked quickly around the corner of the building. I wore a black baseball cap and dark, long-sleeved Henley and black sweatpants with running shoes. Except for the surgical gloves, I could have been out for a jog.

A small delivery door near the loading ramp had a Schlage-brand deadbolt, a six-pin model from a few years ago. With the lockpick gun, I had it open in one minute. From there, it was thirty paces across the dark mailroom to the hall, and another twenty-four to the same stairwell I'd used before.

At every corner I paused and listened, for patrolling guards, or cleaners, or anything at all. I was in no rush. Not yet.

Opening the door of Gallison was the part that made me nervous. Not that it was tough. I had the keycard; how much easier could it get? But the doors and walls were windowless. No way to tell if some GE&E employee might be behind one, still at his work computer at midnight, frantic to make a deadline. I took an earbud out for a moment to listen hard at the door. Nothing.

I took a deep breath and swiped the card. The scanner gave an answering chirp, and the thunk of the lock opening sounded as loud as a hammer whacking an anvil in the empty hall. I opened the door a few inches and stuck my head in for a look. The place was dim and deserted, every third ceiling light glowing with minimal wattage. I exhaled.

North wall. Third room from the end. The secure storage room with the small fortune in optical lenses had a keypad code for its lock. I could beat the lock, and without even burning a lot of time. But the guy who'd sold Dono's fence, Hiram, all of the information about the lenses had also known the code. Some underpaid or laid-off desk jockey, probably. The human element could screw up even the best security, and Gallison wasn't exactly a bank vault. A quick punch of 4-1-4-3 and I was in.

Once the door was closed behind me, the room seemed pitch-black. My eyes gradually picked up a faint blue glow from the night sky through the floor-to-ceiling windows. I tapped the microphone button. One beep to Dono. One beep in reply. It was safe to talk.

"I'm all the way in. Anything from the guards?"

His voice was clear but sanded smooth of emotion through the phone. *"All quiet. There are two on duty tonight. One is walking the halls now. He's been gone six minutes."*

We had timed the guard's rounds at fifteen minutes. With five floors, three minutes per. That was during the workday. It might be a little faster at night. So he'd be on this floor within two or three minutes, and gone in six or seven.

I used a pencil flash to scan the shelves of the storage room. Loads of equipment whose functions I could only guess at, maybe bit and pieces of laser generators, and some kinds of thermal imaging cameras that looked like tiny televisions on sticks. Gallison specialized in optical engineering, which was why they had the top-quality lenses I was looking for.

I found their cases bungee-corded in place on two of the lower shelves. Twenty-six cases in all, in varying sizes. Each was made of hard black plastic with a built-in handle, like a toy suitcase. The smallest case could hold a baseball glove, and the largest could hold all three bases stacked together. I undid the bungee cords around one of the small cases and clicked the plastic latches open. Inside, wrapped in clear oiled plastic and tucked into gray protective foam, was a thick circle of glass that cost about five thousand dollars, retail price. The biggest cases would be worth ten times that. The value increased exponentially along with the size. I grinned as I stacked the cases neatly by the window. You could light one hell of a campfire with one of these magnifiers.

The contents of the backpack came next. Fuel tanks. Hollow alloy rod and attached torch. Plexiglas safety mask. Gloves. Tongs. And two hundred coiled feet of slim cotton rope, with rubber-coated carabiners attached to it on little loops every four feet.

My watch said seven minutes had passed since Dono and I had talked. The guard would be off my floor by now. I attached the fuel tanks to the torch, put on my gloves and mask, and beeped Dono three times. That was the signal that I was ready to start. Four minutes later, I heard his answering beeps. The guards were back in the lobby.

I lit the torch. It whuffed to thick orange life, bright as a birthday cake in the black room. I quickly dialed it back to a narrow flame that ran along the inside of the hollow alloy rod. The rod tapered to a point. It was a very special piece of metal, as expensive as some of the lenses for its ability to retain heat. Over twelve hundred degrees Celsius, once it really got rolling. The tip glowed red, then white, then almost clear. I could feel it even through the silicone-coated Kevlar gloves.

I picked a spot on the window, about one foot above the floor. And started melting through the glass.

It was slow going. The window was two panes of tempered safety glass with a thin layer of argon in between for insulation. The panes would crumble if I created too much stress. So I let the heat do the work, just like a hot blade cutting frozen butter. The glass popped and sizzled in tiny beads, almost launching itself away from the superheated rod. I wondered if one of the hot beads might somehow fall four stories to land on the truck. We'd have to check, later. It could be evidence.

I needed to make a hole about one foot by two feet, for the largest cases. After five minutes, I'd melted a three-inch line. If I kept the same pace, I'd have my hole in two hours. The liquefied glass smelled like candle smoke and paint thinner.

This was the first big score—not just a house job or piecemeal stuff—that Dono and I had done together in months. He'd had other work, with other crews. Dono didn't like involving me in scores that required a team. He said the fewer people who knew about me, the better. I was at the age where the law might prosecute me as an adult. It made some sense.

But I wondered if his secrecy was also to keep me from branching out. I knew I could get work with some of his partners. Maybe even set up my own scores, with Hiram as the buyer. Hell, I'd have to chew through the leash, someday.

The earbud beeped once. I kept cutting. I was nearly to the end of the first side. It beeped again, a longer blast.

I spoke as it was starting again. "Yeah?"

"*You're supposed to signal back before talking,*" Dono said.

Jesus. "I'm here now."

"*They're making rounds. Two min—no, three minutes in now.*"

The torch was quiet enough. The guard didn't come into the Gallison offices from the hallway. "All right."

The guards finished that patrol, and made one more an hour later, while I was closing in on the last inch of uncut glass. The piece I'd carved out of the window was warped into tiny crocodile bumps at the edges. A cool bit of sculpture. If it wasn't a dead giveaway, I might want to keep the thing. I gripped the big rectangle with the tongs in my left hand, lifting its weight off the rod. Drops of sweat had been rolling off my forehead and the tip of my nose for the last hour, drizzling the inside of the face mask.

Then the rectangle of glass was free, and I had to drop the tongs to catch the sudden burden. I set the glass aside and rolled out my shoulders. The night breeze came in through the open hole and chilled the perspiration on my chest. I shivered, and it felt great.

I took off the face mask and heavy gloves, and beeped Dono. He responded instantly.

"Fresh air," I said.

"*Go.*"

I grabbed the end of the hundred-foot rope, and fed the end out the open hole. When I came to the first rubberized carabiner on its short loop, I grabbed the nearest carrying case—one of the little ones, no need to risk fifty grand on the first try—and clicked the carabiner onto the handle. The case went out the window, and down a few feet before I got to the next loop. I heard the case tap softly against the side of the building. I repeated the process with the next case and carabiner, and the pricey pieces of custom glass steadily inched their way down the side of the building.

I worked quickly now. The cases could be spotted as we lowered them, from the inside or by someone who happened to walk by the building, not that pedestrians were likely in an office park at two in the morning. But there were other buildings, other guards who might step outside for a smoke. And I didn't like the way the cases tapped randomly against the building. Faster was better.

At the bottom, Dono was receiving the first of the cases, unhooking them, laying them in the open truck bed. I couldn't hear him over the wind, but I felt the tug on the rope as the weight of each case came off.

Onto the last of the cases now, the big ones. They fit through the hole I'd made with an inch to spare. Hot damn. I let the cord play out, giving Dono just enough slack.

Then there was a sound from outside the storage room. The heavy clunk of a door closing.

I stuck my head out the window. The last case was still two stories above Dono.

My earbud beeped. He must have seen me looking.

I beeped back.

"*Everything all right?*" he said.

It could be a janitor, in the outer offices. Or just a regular spot check by the patrolling guard. No reason to panic.

"Keep going," I said.

"*That's not an answer.*"

Someone turned on the lights in the outer office. The yellow glow came under the storage room door with an almost audible rush.

"*Talk to me,*" Dono said.

From the outer office, a radio receiver squawked with an indecipherable voice. And footsteps. I definitely heard footsteps now.

Coming right toward the storage room door.

Chapter Fifteen

At eight the next morning I was carefully shaving around the scar that followed my jawline. The slim furrow had a bad habit of catching the razor. I'd long since learned that going very slowly was the only way to keep from adding another mark to my face.

Leo had still been awake when I'd gotten in the night before from A. Borealis. He'd nodded hello and then gone back to reading a year-old *Sport* magazine. Dono had subscribed to the UK weekly to follow the Ulster coverage. Addy Proctor had collected Dono's mail while I'd been overseas, and a tall stack of issues had grown in the front room.

I'd heard Leo go out around midnight. This morning he was still gone, and his pack was leaning against the hearth.

As I scraped the stubble from my face I thought about Kend Haymes's strange flock of friends. Suspicious Charlie Shearman. Controlled Barrett Yorke. And her loyal and potentially spine-cracking brother, Parson. Were they just circling the wagons around one of their own, out of class courtesy? Maybe they did care for Elana, but more so for Kend. Or perhaps there were secrets between friends that the new guy with the suspect pedigree should never know.

And Trudy Dobbs. I'd see if I could get a line on her. Had she been gone on vacation before any of this went down? Or had she left in a hurry?

I had an hour before my appointment, or whatever it was, with Maurice Haymes. Charlie Shearman had done me a small favor, without meaning to. I hadn't considered whether the Haymes family might be worried I was going to sue them. That might be the reason for Maurice's sudden urge to meet me. Hell, maybe they were thinking about suing *me*, just for hiking over their private land.

Over breakfast I found Trudy's profile online. Her latest post showed a stock picture of a tropical beach at sunset, with the caption *Off for a week in Paradise!!! See you later!!* It was followed by a couple of dozen replies, including one from Barrett, marveling at her trip and asking where she was going. There was no response from Trudy.

The time stamp on the post was near nine thirty in the morning on Saturday. Elana and Kend had been shot sometime Friday night.

It could be coincidence. Trudy leaves at the end of the workweek, for a vacation off the grid. Her bestie Elana and Kend go to the cabin, also away from civilization. Taken separately, neither event sounded unusual. But put them together, and I was very interested in talking to Trudy Dobbs.

On my way out to the truck I heard Stanley woof excitedly, from down the block.

Leo was standing in the street outside Addy Proctor's house, holding a stunted length of heavy rope. He tossed it high in the air and Stanley leapt to catch it. As I came closer I spotted Addy sitting in her usual wicker chair on the porch, wearing a white snowsuit trimmed with fake fur. Stanley's leash lay on the table next to her.

"Drop," Addy said. Stanley chewed on the chunk of rope, and danced side to side, his eyes on Leo. Leo didn't move. His attention was as focused on the dog as Stanley's was on him. Addy repeated the command. Stanley set the rope down and ran in a big circle, off the street and into the lawn, tearing up wads of earth and grass, and back to Leo again. I walked over the mud-splattered flagstones to Addy. She tutted.

"Ready for Westminster," I said.

"Ready for a nap," she said, "just too excited to know it."

Leo picked up the rope and tossed it again. Stanley's pale flanks were covered with his own slobber and splashes of dirt.

"Everything okay?" I said.

"With me and Stanley, sure," said Addy, speaking under her breath. "I don't know about your friend."

"Leo's safe."

"Well of course he's safe. I've never seen Stanley take to someone so quickly. But he's been throwing that toy for an hour, with hardly a word beyond saying hello. I never even had to start our morning walk."

"How'd you know he was with me?"

"From what I choose to see as an advantage of being old. I hardly sleep more than two hours at a time. Mister Pak was sitting out on your stone steps half the night, without the decency to smoke like I do, and then I suppose he went for a long walk. Stanley and I met him when we came out. I had to take the first step to make introductions."

No kidding. "Leo's the quiet type."

Addy frowned at me. "Give me more credit. I've worked in hospitals. I saw plenty of young men there, after Vietnam."

"Okay. So you know. Leo takes life piece by piece, I think."

"As do we all."

"I'll ask him to join me this morning."

"Nonsense. Leave them be. If Stanley sleeps through lunch I'll save hundreds on dog food."

I nodded to Leo as I passed, and he nodded back. Happy. Maybe.

*

The Columbia Tower elevator opened on the thirty-fourth floor to reveal three large letters in brushed steel on the opposite wall. HDC. The glass door separating the offices from the elevator bank elaborated that the letters stood for Haymes Development/Construction.

The receptionist managed to leap to attention while remaining seated when I told her whom I was there to see. She picked up her phone to announce my arrival, and then whisked me to the far end of the building, past a couple of hundred office people doing office things. I didn't see anyone who looked like an actual construction worker.

We reached a set of large wooden double doors. Maurice Haymes's name was on the right-hand door in the same aluminum letters as in the lobby, but smaller. Downright humble.

The receptionist didn't pause, but opened the door and nodded me inside.

Haymes's office was about the same square footage as the ground floor of my house. There was a full-sized conference table made of dark walnut, and another sitting area with a coffee table and club chairs.

The man standing behind the giant wraparound desk looked enough like Kend for me to know I was looking at Maurice Haymes. His short red curls were liberally sprinkled with gray. He wore a dress shirt and tie, but his jacket was draped over his chair. He looked fit and energized.

"Mr. Shaw, please come in," Haymes said, in a voice that an anchorman would have envied.

Another man was sitting in a chair in front of the desk. He angled himself to look at me, but didn't stand. Even sitting, he was very tall, and very thin. About the same age as Maurice Haymes, sixtyish, and immaculately dressed in a gray three-piece suit and tie with a Windsor knot.

"Thank you, Bonnie," said the thin man in the chair. The receptionist nodded and left, closing the door.

Haymes came around to shake my hand firmly. "I'm pleased you could come and see us, Mr. Shaw. I'm Maurice Haymes. This is Arthur Ostrander."

Ostrander nodded. His gray hair was combed straight back from a widow's peak.

"Please," said Ostrander, gesturing to the chair the chair across from him. I sat down. He leaned back in his chair, seemingly satisfied to have us both at the same altitude.

Haymes sat on the edge of the desk. "First of all, Mr. Shaw, I want to say thank you for what you did for my son."

"I'm sorry for your loss."

"Kend was—everything a father could want. I truly do not understand what may have happened."

Haymes's sorrow sounded authentic. Maybe it was. But his polished manner gave everything that he said the impression that he was working from a script.

Ostrander jumped in. "We understand from the county sheriff's office that you frightened away the animal. That took some courage."

"Perhaps not for a soldier," said Haymes.

Ostrander nodded. "Indeed. But we wanted to talk to you about something else. Could we offer you a coffee first?"

I was starting to get dizzy from the glad-handing. "I'm fine, thank you. You're an attorney, Mr. Ostrander?"

He raised an eyebrow. "That's a concern?"

"Just trying to understand why we're all here."

"Of course, of course." Ostrander tried on a sympathetic smile. His gaunt face and widow's peak made him look like a cartoon mortician. "It's a difficult time for the family. I'm sure you can appreciate that."

"For Elana's family, too."

"Yes. You knew Miss Coll?"

"When we were kids."

"And her uncle? William Willard?"

They were well informed. I shouldn't be surprised. The Haymes name probably swung enough weight to have cops and hospital workers lining up to share details about the case.

"Was Kend in trouble?" I said.

"Excuse me?"

"In trouble. Under stress. Did you know of any reason he might have hurt Elana, and himself? Stop me if you want to take these one by one."

Ostrander stiffened. "That's hardly your—"

"I want to ask you for your help, Mr. Shaw," said Haymes. "We're as upset by Miss Coll's death as you are. She was a victim. But I believe Kend was, too, of his own emotions. Perhaps one day we'll understand. For now, all we can do is deal with the pieces."

"What sort of help?"

"Kend worked for HDC. Not full-time, you understand, but he was a trusted employee. He had taken some

HDC property with him to the cabin, we believe. Boxes of documents which he was sorting through for me. Did you notice those, while you were—with Kend and Elana?"

Documents. I looked at Ostrander, who was poker-faced, and back to Haymes. "Not that I saw."

"You wouldn't have missed them, the boxes would be large. The material isn't top secret—not like the information you've had clearance to see, I'm sure." Haymes gave me a manly smirk. "But it is proprietary. The documents might be of interest to competitors, and we would like them back."

"I imagine. But they weren't there."

"You're certain?"

"Like you said, I wouldn't have missed them."

Haymes looked at me. He didn't say anything. Despite his strong energy, there were bags of fatigue under his eyes that even the year-round tan couldn't fully conceal.

"Perhaps Kend was working with the files elsewhere," said Ostrander. "Miss Coll may have had another apartment."

"Would you keep an eye out for those, Mr. Shaw?" prompted Haymes. "I'd consider it a personal favor."

Ostrander gave a slow nod. "Should you happen across any HDC property, we would of course reimburse you for your efforts."

"Handsomely," Haymes said. "You have served your country with valor. In Iraq and Afghanistan, and else-where." He paused, maybe to let me be impressed by the extent of their reach. "It can't be easy to reintegrate after so long away. This could lead to bigger things. Much bigger."

He stood up off the desk. The interview was over. Ostrander made a business card appear and handed it to me without getting up.

"Good luck, Mr. Shaw. I do hope we'll speak again," Haymes said, giving me another handshake of precisely the same firmness as the first one.

*

The Columbia elevator was fast, but going down thirty-three floors still gave me time to think.

Boxes. Of papers. I could believe the first part, because of what I had seen, or hadn't, in the back of Elana's Volvo hatchback. That empty space could have held plenty of large, heavy cartons. But if Haymes and Ostrander really thought I was buying the part about proprietary documents, I should be insulted.

Still, they had painted the carrot a nice bright orange. *Get whatever Kend had at the cabin back for us, and we'll make it worth your time.*

It was an easy bet that the alarm schematic I'd found in Kend's apartment was linked to the boxes Haymes and Ostrander were so eager to reacquire. Taken from HDC or one of its many sister companies by Kend himself, most likely.

So why ask me, and not pressure the cops, or hire some P.I. to track down their precious boxes?

Ostrander had asked me about Willard. It wasn't a

long jump to assume they knew about the big man's criminal history. They had also pulled a few strings to learn my military record. In which case, they might have dug deep enough to learn about Dono.

I could follow their reasoning. Willard's a crook. Dono was a crook. So maybe Elana and I are as well. And I happened to be at the scene, with two dead bodies and however many missing mystery boxes.

I modified my previous thought about the carrot: *Give us our stuff back, and we'll pay you your ransom.*

Back in the Columbia's underground garage, I turned the corner to walk down the long ramp. The garage was brightly lit, maybe to reduce the tomb-like feeling of being a hundred feet below ground underneath a skyscraper. The workday morning ensured that every parking space was filled. A flash of light caught my eye.

Near my pickup truck.

I ducked and moved silently down the row of parked cars. Someone was near the truck, only an outline from behind. The light shone again. A small flashlight. And the door of the truck was open.

The figure turned slightly and I crouched behind a Prius's fender. It was a man, broadly built, and dressed in a suit and tie.

The stocky man who had unlocked Kend's apartment, and taken his computer.

He quietly closed the door on the cab of the truck. Then he shone the light through the canopy's smoked glass, taking a scan of the pickup's bed. I was very grateful that I had removed the Persian rug with Dono's rifles and pistols at the house.

The stout guy walked around to the far side of the truck. I slipped past the few cars between us. The last car was a black Acura RLX Sport. List price about sixty K. Factory alarm standard.

I stomped on the Acura's bumper. The horn blared and the flashing lights threw the man's startled face into view through the canopy windows. He rushed to the rear again. As he rounded the corner of the truck we collided. In the tangle of limbs I lifted his wallet from his breast pocket.

He swiped at it. "Give that—"

I sidestepped, already looking at the driver's license.

"Rudolph Rusk," I read, almost shouting over the klaxon shriek of the Acura. I matadored him as he lunged again. With the echo in the garage, it was like being inside an air-raid siren. Rusk stopped trying to catch me. He wasn't built for chasing.

"You're on camera. Hand it over and I won't bust you." He even sounded like a cop.

I fished one of his business cards out of the wallet. "Haymes Development. Director of Corporate Security." I guessed Rusk to be in his fifties. Probably joined the private sector after qualifying for his department pension. I pocketed the card.

He took out his cell phone. "Last chance, shitbird." The Acura's alarm clicked off. My ears were ringing.

"No reception way down here, Rudy. What were you looking for?" I asked. Boxes, no doubt. Or whatever had been in them.

His face was nearing the same shade of maroon as his necktie. "We check the payload of all large vehicles at Columbia Tower. Standard procedure."

I laughed. "You personally? Come on."

"You're dirt. I don't have to explain a fucking thing to you."

"And you're not calling the cops. Not with that slim jim under your coat." I'd felt the flat metal strip next to Rusk's kidney when I'd lifted his wallet. "Popping the lock is a little retro. But it's an old truck," I admitted.

I snapped his picture with my phone and the flash made him blink. "That's a good one. Why the search and seizure, Rusk?"

"Fuck you."

"Bank of Seattle, platinum plus. Haymes pays that well?" I flipped the debit card like a small, rectangular Frisbee. It sailed far off into the dim of the parked cars and I heard it clack off a windshield.

"Cocksu—"

I threw another card in the opposite direction, over the divider to the next level. This one we didn't hear. "Everywhere you want to be. Better tell me something before I get to your Jenny Craig membership."

Rusk fumed at me. Probably wishing he had pepper spray in the pocket of his Brooks Brothers. Then he turned and walked quickly up the ramp toward the elevators.

Had the invitation to meet with Haymes and Ostrander been a misdirect the whole time? Just to let their pet bulldog nose around the truck?

I dropped Rusk's wallet into a trash can on the way out of the garage. Half of his two hundred forty in cash went into the donations box at Union Gospel Mission on my way to grab second breakfast.

I may be dirt, but I was hometown dirt.

Chapter Sixteen

My phone rang as I was waiting for the crosswalk light on Stewart.

"Van. Can you talk, lad?" Hollis.

"What have you got?" I had to speak up. The sidewalks were momentarily crowded with a rush of people braving the cold streets on their lunch hours.

"Less than you might like, I'm afraid. Your Kendrick Haymes has no police record to speak of. Two moving violations in the past six years, and neither of them would make for a good story."

"Any firearms under his name?" I said. I was still wondering where the Glock at the cabin had come from.

"Nothing listed here. You wanted Willard's niece as well."

"I do."

"The poor child. She was a bit more like us. There's a note here that says there's a juvenile record, but it was sealed."

I already knew about Elena's teenage history. "Give me the other stuff."

"Nothing serious, mind. But Elana had been brought in for questioning, twice. Once when some money went missing from a club she was working at in Coeur d'Alene. No charges, but she left for Washington State not long after. Then again two years ago. That time—and this is the part I enjoyed thinking about"—Hollis paused, enjoying the suspense—"jewelry was taken from a dozen high-rent apartments during a fire alarm. Later on they found the superintendent's keys were also missing. The Spokane police estimated that particular night earned some lucky soul about forty thousand."

"Sounds serious enough to me."

The crosswalk light had changed while I'd been listening. I hurried to catch it.

From the corner of my eye, I saw a tall guy in a long gray raincoat on the opposite side of the intersection turn quickly to match my direction. He jaywalked through the cars stopped at the light. As I walked down Stewart, he stayed parallel to me on the other side.

"Well, at any rate, Elana had no convictions," Hollis said. "And she's dead now, so all is forgiven."

"What about the company that matches the alarm schematic?"

"Not a thing. No reports anywhere in Washington of a break-in at any larger than a home or mom-and-pop store. Do you want me to look farther afield?"

I slowed to catch a look at the guy in the gray raincoat in the reflections on the windows. He had thin hair and a thick black beard. The bouncer from the ghost book. He stopped to urgently check something on his phone. Cell phones had apparently replaced newspapers as the go-to disguise for clumsily shadowing people. Just another blow for print journalism.

"Forget it," I said. "It was a long shot. Thanks, Hollis."

It couldn't be random chance, the bouncer finding me here. Had someone made me at the ghost book? Or maybe there had been another camera I hadn't seen.

I didn't want to lead him to the bar. Instead of going right on 1st Ave I kept going, down into the Market. A few of the outdoor vendors were open, but their business was more hopeful than actual. Not a lot of tourists in February to buy artisan jams or ladles handcrafted from black walnut. I crossed the cobblestones of Pike Place. My gray-coated buddy hurried to follow me through the absurdly colorful row of flower vendors.

I knew the Market well. It was one of my favorite places to kill a Saturday afternoon as a kid, once I was old enough to catch the Metro on my own from Capitol Hill. I would buy comic books and read them on the long flight of steps between the shops and the waterfront. Later on, the Market became where I practiced picking pockets. Not a time of my life that I was proud of anymore, but it had taught me every possible exit from the rabbit warren of stalls and stores on its enclosed lower levels.

My shadow was thirty feet behind me when I took the stairs down to the first level. Once I was out of sight I could race to the far side and wait in one of the alcoves, while Gray Coat ran around trying to figure out if I'd gone farther down or into one of the shops. When he gave up and left, I'd give him a little lesson in how to properly tail someone.

The hall on the first level was nearly empty, with half the stores closed for the slow month. There were only a half-dozen shoppers in the hallway. I started my sprint.

And stopped almost immediately.

Another large guy was coming fast toward me down the hall, walking with the rolling gait of the overly muscled. The fabric of his red-hooded sweatshirt was pulled taut over his armor-plate chest and shoulders. He had a cell phone pressed to his ear. It wasn't hard to guess who he was talking to.

God damn it. It wasn't a tail. It was a trap, and I'd been suckered.

Gray Coat would be coming down the stairs behind me. I moved right, near one of the few shops still open, an emporium selling magic tricks and large illustrated posters of illusionists and circuses from centuries past. I didn't see the shopkeeper inside.

A skinny boy was in front of the shop, feeding quarters into a penny arcade fortune-teller, a glass case with the top half of a mannequin in grandma curls who would robotically cast its plastic hand over tarot cards before the machine spat out your future. I grabbed a buck and thrust into his hand.

"It's broken, come back later," I said. He looked at my face and ran off at full steam.

164

The machine started to make whirring noises. Bulbs flickered. I put my back to it so neither guy could get behind me. I didn't need tarot cards to know that would be a bad thing.

They converged on me together, stopping a little out of reach. Gray Coat was on my left, and the bodybuilder in the red sweatshirt was on my right. The bodybuilder had black sweatpants on as well, probably the only choice that could encompass his thighs. His face was pockmarked and his hair slicked back straight from his forehead. He was a little shorter than I was, but at least two inches wider on every side.

Gray Coat was taller than both of us, at least six foot three, and while he wasn't a walking distended vein like his buddy, he was no stranger to barbells, either.

"This him?" asked the bodybuilder to Gray Coat.

Gray Coat nodded. "Saw him on the street. When I was coming to meet you. Saw the scars." He was out of breath from hurrying after me through the Market. He'd been wheezing when he'd chased me at the ghost book, too.

"Cardio," I said, "in between sets on the bench press. Give it a try."

Gray Coat frowned. The bodybuilder smiled. He wasn't in any hurry.

"That's funny," he said. "You like messing with people, yeah?"

"You pissed off a friend of ours," said Gray Coat.

I shrugged. "You'll have to be more specific. I piss off lots of people."

"At the book," said Gray Coat, confused. "Yesterday."

"He knows where you mean," said the bodybuilder mildly. "He's just being a comedian."

I smiled back. "A comedian and two jokes. How'd you morons find me?"

Keys jingled behind us as the magic shop owner started locking his display cases. Leaving for lunch. The four of us were the only people in the hall now. Soon it would be only three, with no witnesses.

The bodybuilder's chest muscles bunched under his sweatshirt in anticipation. I could feel my breath slowing. The tension in my shoulders eased. A relaxed muscle is a fast muscle. I'd have to be very fast.

"Maybe," said the bodybuilder, his voice high and excited, "you're a slow learner."

"You mean like this guy?" I pointed to Gray Coat. "He's the one who plays in traffic."

I glanced over the bodybuilder's shoulder and grinned, like I was pleased as punch to see someone. He turned to look—his whole body, his neck didn't move very far—and I jabbed my pointing finger as hard as I could into Gray Coat's right eye. Gray Coat yelped and staggered back, hands flailing.

I spun, swinging a looping hook at the bodybuilder's face. Power over style. But the gym rat was already moving, and the hook caught him on the side of his neck. It felt like punching a tire. He grunted and slammed forward into me, trying to tackle me to the ground. Instead we crashed into the fortune-teller machine. The glass case made a sharp and agonized crack. The shop owner shouted behind us.

The bodybuilder kept pressing, head lowered like a bull and swinging haymaker punches at my ribs. I took two bruising shots on my elbows and cupped my hands behind his head to drive my knee up into his face. He snorted again and grabbed at my forearms. It was a mistake. My second knee strike broke his nose and blood gushed over the hardwood floor and my jeans. His legs wavered and I tore my arms free and, with my fists still clasped together, swung them like a lumberjack swinging an axe into the bodybuilder's temple. He spun halfway around and fell onto his face.

Someone yelled again. Gray Coat ran at me blindly, arms extended and hands grasping. I ducked low and got a shoulder into his gut and lifted him like a sack of flour, his momentum carrying him up and over and down onto his forehead. The boom echoed, as loud as a dropped shotput.

The yelling hadn't stopped. The magic store owner was screaming for the cops, which I only half-heard over the rasp of my own lungs. Maybe I needed more cardio, too.

I went to the bodybuilder, who was still on the floor and lost somewhere in the mental mist between out cold and trying to wake up. His hand pawed at me. I slapped it aside. He had a wallet in the pocket of his red hoodie and in the wallet was about eight hundred dollars. Maybe his advance on putting me in intensive care. I took the bills and slipped them through the crack in the glass of the fortune-teller machine. They fluttered down over the tarot cards. The store owner stopped shouting.

The machine had spit out a thin lavender card, which had fallen to the ground. I picked up the card and read it.

A BRIGHTER TOMORROW WILL BE YOURS

"You and me both," I said to the mannequin. Its blue ceramic eyes stayed inscrutable behind the fractured glass.

Chapter Seventeen

Luce kept a Costco-sized first aid kit in the kitchen of the Morgen, equipped to handle everything from grease fire burns to deep lacerations. She hauled the blue bag from under the cabinet while I ran cold water over my hands. My knuckles were swollen from the fight.

"You should ice," she said.

"Did you buy that bag?" I asked. "Or has it always been that size in case a saloon brawl breaks out?"

"Funny."

"Yet you're not smiling. It wasn't my plan to get jumped, Luce."

"And it wasn't those two assholes' plan to have you be tougher than they were. This whole kit wouldn't have been enough to patch you up, if they had their way." She swabbed my neck with antibiotic gel where I had a cut, probably from when the bodybuilder and I had cracked the glass on the fortune-telling machine.

"Okay. You're right," I said. "Those two were more sinew than skill."

The next guys Broch sent might be better, or at least more numerous. But I decided to keep that thought to myself.

"So will you go to the cops?" asked Luce. "You trust that detective you met last year."

"John Guerin," I said. "Yeah. But I don't know what I can tell him that's usable. Kend was probably in deep with Broch. There's no way to prove it. Loan sharks don't give out receipts." I looked at her. She peeled the paper wrappers off two Band-Aids and stuck them on the back of my neck. Her touch was warm and I felt her breath on the little hairs at my nape.

"I'm not worried for myself," I said.

There was a knock at the rear door of the bar. "It's Leo," he called.

I went to let him in. The Morgen's rear exit was one of half a dozen unlabeled doors on that side of the building. I hadn't shown Leo where it was.

"Did you recon the block when you were here before?" I said.

"And again just now," said Leo. "Nobody's watching the place, unless they bought a condo across the street."

Luce looked at Leo, then me. "You called for backup," she said.

"Occasionally I use my brain," I said.

I caught Leo up on events, while Luce put some ice in a Ziploc bag for my hands. Leo stood at the kitchen door where he could see the front entrance of the bar.

"The two guys weren't tailing you?" he said when I'd finished.

"No. I think they were coming to look for me here,

170

before I practically ran into one of them on the street. So Broch must have learned who I am. And my connection with the Morgen."

"Or with Dono, which amounts to the same thing," Luce said.

I nodded. "Freddy Fogh sold me out. I paid him to tell me about Broch, and he probably ran straight to Broch to double-dip."

"Little worm," said Luce.

"Ganz warned me: Freddy is what Freddy is."

Leo spoke without taking his eyes off the front. "Maybe we should talk to Freddy."

"We?"

"Unless you got other volunteers, Sarge," he said.

"Freddy's not the problem," I said.

"You think this Broch dickwad will try again?" said Leo.

"Jesus," said Luce.

I flexed my hands. The ice had turned them stark white around the edges and pink in the middle, and seeing them move was a separate thing from how they felt.

"I don't know if Broch will take another run at me. He wanted to warn me off, I think. Even if they didn't put me in a body cast like they planned, his apes still delivered the message."

"Maybe he'll back down," Leo said.

I shrugged. "There's no percentage in wishing and hoping."

Leo nodded. "So I'll watch your six for a while."

"No," I said. I turned to Luce. "They know about the Morgen. I don't like you being here without me, or without Leo, if that works for him."

"I could eat more wings," said Leo.

"Fantastic," Luce said. "Who'll be looking after you?"

"I'll have my guard up," I said. "They can't tail me. If I have to go anywhere they might be waiting, Leo backs me up."

"While I hide," she said.

I turned to Leo. "Give us a minute."

He looked a little startled, but he nodded and wandered out to the front of the bar. I closed the swinging door with the Plexiglas porthole behind him.

"I'd ask what's wrong, but that's a dumb question after the past couple of days," I said to Luce.

"It's multiple choice," she said, lowering her voice. "There are hired thugs coming to my bar. Leo's going be your bodyguard, and he's so twitchy I wonder if that will be more or less dangerous for you. And every rock you've turned over makes Kend and Elana look even worse. The lousiest thing is that you're happier than I've seen you in weeks."

"I'm happy with you."

"Yes. And I am with you," she said. "But there's always part of you that's somewhere else. You know that's true, even if we haven't talked about it."

My hands were throbbing. I made my fingers move the

right way to open the bag and pour the mash of ice and water out into the big dishwashing sink.

Luce touched my arm. "This trouble with Elana—you're focused on it. Completely."

"It's just how I'm used to thinking," I said. "Tactically. I've spent years going from mission to mission. That doesn't mean it's more important than you."

"I'm not jealous," she said. "I just don't want you to have blinders on. Your kind of tactics might get you into a mess that even you can't get out of. Already you've broken into two places and been involved in an assault. If it escalates—"

"I won't let it. I'll tell Guerin what I know, or suspect. Maybe I've missed something that he can piece together for the D.A."

"Thank you."

"In the meantime Leo and I will keep our guard up. He's good, Luce. He's struggling when it comes to normal life. But I trust him to stay cool."

Luce looked at the closed swinging door. After a moment she stepped forward and put her arms around me, and we stood there holding each other for a long moment.

"We talked about going away," she said. "Could that be soon?"

"It could."

"It's a slow time of the year right now. And you aren't waiting for Eberley any more."

I leaned back to see her eyes. They were the steely color of the Sound waters only a thousand or so feet to the west of us. And somehow warmer than the Caribbean.

"How you'd know I didn't get the job?" I said.

"You haven't mentioned it in two days. It wasn't hard to guess. Sorry."

"I'm that easy, huh?"

Luce just smiled and angled her head for a kiss. When we parted I took a long breath to clear my head.

"Let's leave on Sunday," I said. "You pick which direction we go."

"I'll spin a bottle."

She went back to her office, and I found Leo behind the bar, examining Luce's police baton. He snapped his wrist and it clacked out to its full length.

"Not bad," he said. "Beats an iron pipe."

"If we're going to keep Broch from steamrolling me, I'd better have something with a longer reach." The Glock and the two Smith & Wessons from Dono's oriental rug were back at the house. Carrying around a concealed, unlicensed, untraceable firearm. Luce would definitely count that as escalation.

I knew I could handle being arrested, or even serving time. That wasn't true of everybody.

"I got other people who can stay with Luce," I said to Leo.

He looked at me. "Meaning what? You think I'm off the rails?"

"Meaning I don't want to make things worse."

"You aren't making shit. It's my choice. Unless your *other people* got our kind of training, you know I'm your best option." He banged the tip of the baton on the tile floor, collapsing it back into its handle. "And fuck you. You're not exactly one hundred percent, either."

I tried bending and unbending my arm. The elbow ached where the bodybuilder had punched it.

"Guess I can't throw stones at that glass house today," I said.

"Hell," said Leo, "if I'd known Seattle was going to be this interesting, I'd have come north a long time ago."

Chapter Eighteen

I had sent two messages and left a voice mail for Barrett, trying to get more information on Trudy Dobbs. At around nine o'clock I got a reply.

Meet me at Haunt. I'm here for the night

I looked up Haunt online. It was a nightclub south of the stadiums, in an area that I used to associate with body shops and recycling centers.

It didn't take me long to decide. I wanted to talk to Barrett about Trudy, in person. The more time that passed, the more uneasy I felt about Trudy's sudden vacation. I'd checked her profile online again. There were still no posts from her since the first one announcing her arrival in some unnamed place with palm trees.

I texted Barrett that I was on my way and threw on a black button-down while walking to the truck.

An answer came twenty minutes later, just as I was handing the truck keys to the valet.

3rd floor stage Hurry!

There was a line outside, swaying with the electronic music that reverberated through the walls, as a bouncer checked IDs. He was big and black and dressed better than anyone waiting to get in, in a dark blue two-piece and white necktie. He did a double take as I passed, headed for the end of the line.

"What's your name?" he said.

"Shaw."

He nodded and motioned me in, past the grumbling couples at the front. Barrett must have told him to look for me. To look for the scars. Of course she had an in with the guy at the velvet rope.

Inside, the blend of music was so close and loud as to be almost white noise, felt more than heard. The entryway broadened into one wide blue room, every wall a mosaic of cobalt tile and shards of mirror. It wasn't packed, but crowded in clumps that shifted like seaweed floating between heavy piers on each side. Drifting more than dancing. Through the flashing silver lights I could see more rooms in back, and stairs leading to other floors.

Third-floor stage, she'd said. I shouldered through the crowd to the stairs. Most of the men wore tees. Most of the women were sheathed in spandex microdresses. A defined range of ethnicities, each in their circles. Asian, Southeast Asian, Anglo. No Latinos, and no black faces now that I was past the guy guarding the door.

The stairs ended on the third-floor landing, at closed double doors with THEATRE painted on them, large and ornate in glittered silver.

The room inside was blue as well, but darker and made up to look like a library, with navy-colored columns and the outlines of shelves and book shapes stenciled in copper. Everyone inside was grouped at the far end, by the stage. The music was still electronic, but lower and softer, almost dreamy.

Up on the stage was a girl in a pink pageboy wig and candy-cane lingerie. She sat on a stool in front of a vanity table and its oval mirror. Very slowly, she took a rolled-up stocking off the table, extended one lean leg in a ballet point, and rolled the white stocking up to her thigh, careful to smooth out any wrinkles with long strokes.

A reverse striptease. Apparently I'd missed the grand commencement, if she had started out naked. I should've driven faster.

The slow-motion girl had garters in place by the time I got near the stage. I hadn't spotted Barrett yet. Her petite frame was lost somewhere in the throng. I spared a glance—not my first—at the dancer, and was surprised when she winked one leisurely red eyelash at me.

It was Barrett.

She held my eye as she stood up languorously from the vanity table. She'd either had dance training or a lot of natural ability. Her figure, which had looked so angular in the black clothes from the night before, was delicately but very distinctly rounded, in all of the desirable places. She started shimmying robotically into a dress that looked like cotton candy, and held the crowd's attention all through her exit, coiling herself in a feathered boa. They whooped approval as she vanished, and the tide immediately surged toward the bar.

Damn. The cold, polished sapphire that was Barrett Yorke had a few hidden facets.

One person didn't move with the crowd. Parson. He walked toward me, parting the waves of people without effort as he went. With the performance over, the music synced with the lower floors and swelled in volume and intensity.

"What are you doing here?" he shouted over it, a little louder than required.

I'd already had one scuffle today. A second round wasn't appealing.

"Barrett invited me."

He glowered at the stage, then back at me. I hadn't figured out if Parson was actually slow of mind, or if he was just socially awkward.

"She's got a boyfriend," he said.

"Nobody here saying otherwise, Parson. You want a beer?"

"No. I told you to stay away."

I'd known a bouncer in Georgia built like Parson. If someone gave him a problem, he'd just lean on the guy. Being mashed against a wall by four hundred pounds took the fight out of anybody real damn quick.

"We want the same thing, Parson," I said over the pounding beat. "To protect our friends."

"You told us you hadn't seen Elana since you were kids. You didn't even know Kend."

"I know he liked to gamble."

Parson stared. He started to say something, and then closed his mouth with a snap I could almost hear over the music.

"You probably knew that, too, right? You guys were tight. How much trouble was he in?"

Parson looked away.

"Enough to get him hurt?" I said.

"You made it," Barrett said. She was at the point of a clump of girls. One of them handed her a red plastic cup with a mixed drink. The sapphire stud in her upper ear had been replaced with a tiny, bright ruby. Parson gave me one last sullen stare and walked away. He wasn't going to tell me anything, not right now. But I was convinced that the huge lump had something on his slow mind.

"Can we go somewhere?" I said to Barrett.

"Oooo, he's ready," the girl closest to Barrett laughed, "after that show."

"Wait here," Barrett said, and downed the last of whatever was in her plastic cup, and left it on the edge of the stage. She squeezed past me, angled toward the tech platform where the light board and sound equipment was run by club staff. She had changed into a dark purple dress, cut low in front and lower in the back.

"How do you know B?" one of the girls shouted. I read her lips more than I heard her.

"I'm her choreographer," I said. The girls nodded but cast doubtful glances at my faded black jeans and hiking boots.

Barrett came back and tugged at my arm. "Come on." We wove our way off the floor. Her purple dress wasn't form-fitting like most of the outfits on display, but shaped to her waist on top, and the skirt swirled around her thighs as she moved lithely through the crowd. If there was a way for underwear to be involved, I couldn't see it.

I followed her down what looked like an exit hallway. She stopped at a side door and opened it with a key. "The sound guy lets me use this."

The room inside was small, about fifteen square. A spare dressing room for performers, with recycled school lockers and faux velvet couches and mirrors on the wall.

"I'm worried about Trudy," I said.

"I am, too. She doesn't answer her phone, which is more than strange for her. And look. This is from Trudy's boss."

She showed me her phone. Barrett had exchanged messages with someone named Zelle. Trudy had sent Zelle a text saying she had to take emergency leave and would be back in a week. Zelle said that Trudy hadn't replied to urgent follow-up questions. That was on Saturday, the same day Trudy had posted about her tropical vacation.

"So she lied to her boss about taking a last-minute holiday?" I said. "Trudy loves her job," said Barrett. "She's a graphic designer, and she's really good. She wouldn't leave them in the crunch like this. Unless something was wrong."

"Where does Trudy live?" I said. I could go check it out tonight.

She thought about it. "I'll come with you."

"Better if I check it on my own."

"Don't be stupid. I know where it is and I have the codes to get in."

I couldn't very well explain to Barrett that her friend's security system wouldn't slow me down for very long.

"We'll take my car," she said.

*

Trudy Dobbs's house was almost directly across the city, on the shore of Lake Washington. Barrett parked on the opposite side of the street, against the flow of traffic. I suppose she could afford a ticket. Her Lexus was new enough that it hadn't hit its first oil change.

We sat and looked up at Trudy's home. It was very vertical. Three stories, not counting the garage. Each squareish chunk of the house was offset from the others like carelessly stacked child's blocks. It would have a hell of a view of the lake, in the daytime.

"Maybe she's here," Barrett said. "There's lights on upstairs."

"She lives alone?" I asked. The house had to be three thousand square feet.

"Since her dad died two years ago." She leaned to peer around the side of the house. This close, I could smell her shampoo over the car leather.

I opened my door and got out. "Let's see if anyone's at home."

We walked up a long flight of concrete stairs to reach the first deck and what seemed to be the front door. The stairs were painted white, the house in a sedate neutral that reminded me of modeling clay.

I knocked, with the echo from inside the only answer. The place felt empty. I cupped a hand to peer into the darkness through the door. I could see part of a kitchen counter, and a table. No coffee cups or dishes on the counter. All the chairs pushed in flush against the table.

"Nobody home," said Barrett. "Maybe Trudy *is* on vacation."

"Does she have a cleaning lady?" My eyes had made out a small neat stack of mail in the kitchen.

"I guess. Why wouldn't she?" Barrett dug for a key in her purse. "I've still got it from feeding her old cat last year. Hang on."

She unlocked the door and immediately a soft chirp sounded from the kitchen. Barrett walked over to punch in the alarm code.

I took a deep inhale. No stink of death in the air. That was something, at least.

The front half of the house was an open floor plan, with the kitchen and dining room and living areas all visible from one another. Every room had large paintings hung on the walls, and most of the paintings looked to be by the same artist. Trudy's own work, I guessed. The images were abstract, but evocative. There were similar canvases propped up here and there.

"All ours," Barrett said. "What are we looking for?"

"Purse. Phone. Anything that's here that she would have normally taken on vacation with her. Or if she did leave, anything that tells us where she went."

"Gotcha. I'll take the upstairs." Barrett ran up, dress swinging. She was a hell of a lot livelier tonight than yesterday. Enjoying the mystery, with the dead friends momentarily just an abstract concept.

I couldn't blame her. There had been times, after I'd lost men, lost friends, that the missions were almost fun. Jubilant, in a dark way. The action helping to keep grief at bay, and give me purpose. It never lasted.

Trudy had posted online, and texted her boss. Then she had dropped off entirely. Was it intentional? Did she not want to be traced?

In the neat stack of mail was an Amex statement. I opened it. It had been printed too many days ago to tell me if her purchases had included any last-minute plane tickets to Jamaica. But it gave me an idea.

I found a large office room off the kitchen, with an angled drafting table and light boxes and about a thousand books on art. More of Trudy's big paintings on the walls. She was industrious. There were stumpy file cabinets on one wall, and I searched until I found the file with her credit statements. On a Post-it at the back of the file were four digits. Her PIN code.

It amazes me, how easy it is to find the random codes that banks assign. The randomness is the problem.

Everyone writes them down. Everyone puts them by the computer, or in the files. It would be embarrassingly easy to be an identity thief.

I picked up the wall phone and called the service number on the statement. I entered Trudy's card number and PIN and had the system read me a list of the last ten purchases.

The first eight charges were small random debits at Starbucks and bookstores and a deli.

The last two entries were different. Both on the same day. Saturday. The day Trudy had supposedly left on vacation, or had her family emergency, or whatever it was. Two hundred thirty bucks in groceries at a Safeway in Ballard. And a cash advance of four hundred dollars.

If I still gave any credence to the tropical vacation story, the groceries erased it. Who buys half a carload of food before getting on a plane? And four hundred dollars felt like a maximum daily amount for a cash advance.

So Trudy had grabbed food. As much money as she could get. And there had been no more purchases on the card after that.

She'd gone on the run, or she'd holed up somewhere. If she was on the run, I had no way of knowing where or how. If she had holed up, then it was probably a place she already knew. Somewhere she could go, and stay, at a minute's notice. She'd already been there four days.

I walked upstairs, checking out the rooms as I went. A second bedroom, and a third, both large and lonely. Two bathrooms and a sitting room. The top floor was taken up by the master suite, where I found Barrett nodding with satisfaction.

"Okay," she said, pointing to each area. "No purse. No phone or charger. There are clothes laid out on the bed. Her laptop is gone and so is one of her pieces of luggage." She folded her arms triumphantly. "On vacation, clearly."

"Clearly," I said. "What's that?"

A shoe box was open on the dresser. It was the cloth lying next to it that had caught my eye when I walked through the door. Yellow silicone. A gun cleaning cloth. In the box were a squeeze can of oil and an empty box of .25-caliber Hornady brand ammunition.

"That's Trudy's dad's gun," Barrett said, inaccurately, since the pistol wasn't here. "Why would she want that?"

Good question.

The master bedroom was large enough that Trudy had wall space for yet another half-dozen paintings. And I realized what I hadn't seen, among all the square footage of her house. No easels, or tubes of acrylic, or blank canvases. Maybe she stuffed all of that gear in a closet every time she worked, but what person living alone in a house made for five or six people would bother doing that?

"Where does Trudy do her painting?" I said.

"Oh, she rents a studio. In Ballard. She says the light is better on that side of the city, more western exposure."

The Safeway where she'd bought groceries last Saturday had been in Ballard, too. I didn't have an address on the cash advance, but I was willing to bet it was in the same neighborhood.

I went downstairs to look at the Amex statement again. Barrett followed. There it was, near the start of the month. Studio Oceania, six hundred dollars. I had taken it to be some outlandishly elite hair salon.

"What is it?" Barrett said.

I'd had Miss Yorke as a sidekick long enough. "Just hoping to find plane tickets here. But no luck. Let me check one last thing."

I walked down the stairs to the garage, saw what I expected to see, and came back up.

"Her car's here," I said. "She probably took a cab to the airport."

"Sure, who wants to park down there for a week?" Barrett glided up to me. "I feel a whole lot better. Thanks for helping me. Us."

"No problem."

" 'My pleasure' is I think what you mean." She pressed herself gently against my side, backing me an inch into the counter, and reached up high with her lips to brush them against the skin under my ear. "We have the whole house."

"What about Charlie?" I said.

"Charlie's not the only man in my life. We have an understanding." She arched her back and made a sinuous movement that I'd seen her do on stage. Definitely no lingerie under the dress.

"Ah." I placed my hands on her upper arms.

"You don't want to?" She smiled against my throat. It was clear from the evidence that part of me did. I pushed her gently away, her body still moving.

"I'm with someone." My voice was a little raspy.

She paused in midwrithe. "Only her?"

"Right. Sorry."

She withdrew. "My poor choice, then." Her posture changed into the formal deportment she'd shown me at Borealis. "I suppose you think I'm ghoulish."

"Grief is about the best reason I can think of. I'm just not your guy."

"We should go."

As she angrily tapped in the code to leave, my mind went to what I'd seen in the garage.

I hadn't lied to Barrett about Trudy's car. It was down in the garage. A Jaguar convertible. Its sleek looks marred only by the reddish, claylike mud, caked dry and flaking on its sides and tires. Tires with treads like fishhooks.

Chapter Nineteen

First thing in the morning, I went to meet John Guerin outside the East Precinct on Capitol Hill. There was a group of bike cops at the curb preparing to set out on neighborhood patrol, in black helmets and black rain jackets and pants. I was dressed similarly, in midnight black running gear and my worn-in Asics. Give me a pair of big-ass mirrored sunglasses, and I'd blend right in.

Guerin came out of the tall lobby. The detective was in his late forties with wire-rimmed glasses and prematurely white hair. He'd grown a mustache since I'd last seen him, and it was white, too. He wore a camel's-hair overcoat and a sharp blue suit. Guerin looked more like a successful stockbroker than a cop.

"Coffee?" I said.

"Always," said Guerin. We turned and walked down 12th. "How's civilian life treating you?"

"More downtime. Fewer options."

"What kind of work are you looking for?"

"Until recently, I thought I would teach cops."

Guerin made a whisper of a chuckle. "Interesting."

"Not exactly the family business."

Guerin nodded. His posture was so vertical that he

hardly seemed to lean at all as we walked. I knew he'd been in the Marines once, but my guess was that he was born like that.

"What would you teach? Combatives?" he said.

"Urban tactics, probably." We rounded the corner onto Pike toward Caffe Vita. "But it's moot. No openings. Maybe I can learn bicycle maintenance."

"How's that?"

"Private joke."

We went in and ordered and waited for the coffee. The machine took a long time, and a lot of coaxing and prodding from the barista. We took the cups and sat in a two-top on the upper floor, by the window.

"I want to tell you some things about Kendrick Haymes," I said.

"Maurice Haymes's dead son," said Guerin.

"I have some facts and some guesses. They might help. They might not. Either way, I can't tell you how I came by the knowledge."

"Can't, or won't?"

"Won't, then."

"Haymes was found with William Willard's niece," Guerin said. "Found by you, I heard."

"Word travels."

"The Jefferson County sheriff called me three days ago, checking on your bona fides. Have you been looking into Haymes?"

I sipped my coffee. It had been worth the barista's trouble.

"Never mind," Guerin said. "It's obvious. If what you know gives a motive for Haymes killing himself, then going on the record is better. It might give their families closure."

"If he killed himself."

"You think it was homicide?"

I shrugged.

"Okay," said Guerin, "off the record."

"Haymes was a gambler. Sports junkie, mostly. There was a ghost book in Burien where he lost a whole lot of money."

"Was."

"It—ah—might have had some trouble lately. Packed up and moved."

"Which does me no good whatsoever."

"Haymes was also broke, or as broke as it's possible for a guy with guaranteed dividends to get."

"Did his friends tell you this?"

"No. You heard of a guy named T. X. Broch?"

Guerin had been leaning forward to take a drink. He looked up at me over his glasses. "Broch."

"Kend Haymes signed his Panamera over to Broch. A Porsche. That's worth at least—"

"I know what it is. Is this a guess, or are you sure?"

"I'm sure Kend forked over the car. I'm guessing he was in up to his eyeballs, or worse, with Broch and maybe others."

"T. X. Broch," said Guerin.

"A guy I talked to described him as an animal."

"Any animal you could name would be better. Broch beat a felony rap a while ago, I recall. Assault with intent, on a woman. I don't know if it was personal or business."

"Personal to her."

Guerin grunted. "Nothing has stuck to him yet. He's not flashy, but his lawyers are."

"Kend was a loan shark's dream," I said. "Broch must have had a very compelling reason, if he killed him."

Guerin seemed to think about it. I looked out the window. These few blocks of Pike Street were the part of the Hill that always came to mind when I was far from home. I wasn't sure why. Broadway was busier, and 15th Ave was closer to the house where I'd grown up.

Maybe it was because Pike was a little off the main thoroughfares, and yet always active, pedestrians outnumbering the cars most any time of day or night. All of the schools and parks and hospitals were just around one corner or another, but not in sight. Pike was the narrow stream flowing between the boulders.

"All right," said Guerin. "Kend's death gives us some justification to look into his accounts, if I can get backing."

"Backing?"

"This is a Jefferson County case, not SPD. And officially it's still murder-suicide, last I knew."

"Do they really believe that? Or is it just the theory of the moment until they dig up something better?"

Guerin moved one side of his mouth, making about five percent of what might be called a smile. "The sheriff's no rube. My guess is that he's cross-checking every piece of evidence, hoping to find something that will move the needle toward it being a homicide. He might formally request that SPD assist, if I ask him to do so. But I heard that the residue test came up positive on Kend's hand."

"Just in casual conversation, huh?"

"I took an interest in the case after your name came up. One of the deputies in Jefferson was with our precinct years back, when he started out."

"Spies everywhere."

"Friends. Not spies."

"The residue test doesn't mean much, you know. If it was murder, someone could put the Glock in Kend's hand, fire one off into the high trees, take the brass and replace the round to make the count right."

"Simpler is better. The murder-suicide tag will remain for now. No point in getting the press and the family all riled up without cause."

I drank my coffee. It didn't taste as good now.

"Which brings up another point," Guerin said. "SPD will need the family's permission to look into Kend's finances. A court order is out of the question. This isn't a homicide case."

Even if it was, I doubted the SPD could get a judge to sign off on poking into Haymes family business. Hollis's contacts had found no police records of a break-in at HDC, which could mean it was never reported. Or that the report was quashed. Haymes probably had that kind of political muscle.

And there had been no photograph of Haymes senior anywhere in his beloved son's apartment, among all the dozens of snapshots. Somehow I knew there weren't any pictures of Kend in Maurice's home, either.

"You won't get permission," I said.

"Then that road is closed," said Guerin. "I can question Broch, but we know he won't melt under a little heat. Broch deals in used cars. He could just claim that the Porsche was intended as a trade-in that Haymes hadn't claimed yet."

"Shit."

Guerin tapped the edge of his empty cup with the wooden stirrer. "This is what off the record earns you. A bunch of knowledge without a lot of results."

"Thanks a lot."

"This wouldn't be the first time a killer skated for lack of evidence. You know that. Better than most, I'd say."

We looked at each other.

"I'm just hunting down clues, Detective. Junior Crimestopper," I said.

"Spare me. You're not a cop. I don't think you're a crook, although some of my fellow officers have different opinions. I'm not sure what you are. And not knowing worries me."

"I'm not going to kill Broch for Kendrick Haymes," I said.

"Would you kill him for Elana Coll?"

"No."

"Would you feed him to that monster Willard?"

I didn't answer.

"You see where this goes," Guerin said. "I won't have you or Willard making this city into a hunting preserve. You've given me a lead. Thanks." He stood up. "Now call it a day before I jail you on suspicion of whatever-the-hell-I-choose, just to keep you safe from Broch."

He walked down the stairs and out of the cafe. Leaving his coffee cup for me to clear. Subtle.

Chapter Twenty

Trudy Dobbs was a pretty girl. All the pictures I had seen of her online verified that. Even in the lousy snapshots, she was clearly better-looking than average. She was tall and attractive and brown-haired, and the more photos I looked at, the more I disliked her face.

Because I couldn't get a solid handle on it. Some people had a face that immediately stuck in your mind, because they were beautiful or ugly or just damned unusual. My face fell solidly in the last category, if not the second. But Trudy's was elusive. She had a beauty mark in a couple of the party pictures, but it seemed to be gone in others. Her nose was strong without being hooked. Her hair was always brown, but sometimes dyed either lighter or darker. She even went soft on the makeup.

If I were going to ID Trudy Dobbs on sight, I would have to get a very close look, in person.

Studio Oceania was deep into Ballard, half a block from 65th on one of the few streets that the tsunami of gentrification hadn't touched. It occupied the upper part of a squat structure, brick on the street level and poured concrete above. An austere Brothers of Scandinavia lodge claimed the bricks. Through its window I saw a meeting in progress, a herd of old walruses in wool sweaters and chambray shirts, sitting in rigidly spaced rows as they scrutinized the speaker.

The upper two stories looked like an apartment house, except for a forest of wind chimes and mobile sculptures I could see hanging on the balconies. Some of the sculptures were interesting. Most were just trying too hard to be bizarre.

I imagined the artists crossing paths with the Swedes in the building's entryway. It was a toss-up which group would be more serious.

One of the artists came shuffling out, focused on her tablet. I caught the door on the backswing. There were mail cubbies just inside, with the tenant names stuck underneath each in block letters from a label maker. T. D. INNOVS was on the second floor. Trudy's cubby, like most of the others, had a few flyers stuffed inside of it advertising art events and performances, but no real mail.

I went up the stairs to look for her studio space. Passing by a couple of open doors to other studios, I got a glimpse into the little rooms. The wide building had been apartments once. Then someone with middling skill had cut new doors and torn out the kitchen fixtures and divided up the living areas into blocks. Some were like cells. Others featured large metal-framed windows. The T. D. INNOVS studio was on my right. It would have a window, I guessed, for that desirable western exposure Barrett had mentioned.

I knocked very gently. No answer, or sound of move-ment. I had the lockpicks ready, and opened the door before another artist poked their shaggy head out in the hallway.

Three things were instantly obvious. It was definitely Trudy's studio, the walls and easels adorned with her now-familiar compelling abstracts. She'd been hiding out here for days, from the blankets on the floor and the piles of prepackaged foodstuffs still in their Safeway bags, and the smell of recent cigarettes. And she wasn't here now.

I didn't see a purse. But I did find a phone charger on a little paint-spattered table, and more packs of American Spirits in one of the grocery sacks. She was coming back.

Wait for Trudy right here? There'd be no chance of her slipping away. It would sure as hell be a surprise for her.

And I could guess how that might play out. Trudy screams. Others come running to find a big, scarred man lurking in the studio of one of their own. I wouldn't get a chance to confront her, or con her, or even pull some citizen's-arrest bullshit. She'd probably vanish while the others were busy watching me and calling the cops. If she even bothered escaping. Trudy Dobbs wasn't even wanted for questioning yet, so far as I knew. I'd be more likely to leave here in handcuffs than she would.

Okay. So I'd stake out the building and watch, until she showed. If T. X. Broch was suspect number one, then Trudy Dobbs was a close second. And closing. Broch was a psychopath, but I knew Trudy had been at the cabin. Now she was on the run. And armed, if she carried the .25 from the shoe box at her house. Maybe there was a connection between the two of them. The loan shark and the artiste. An improbable pair, but Broch and Trudy had Kendrick Haymes in common, and he had held some dubious secrets himself.

I locked the door behind me and went down the back stairs. The door at the bottom was exit-only. Good. Trudy would have to come in through the front. Plenty of vantage points from the street. Or maybe I'd join the Brothers in their lodge. They could turn their doubtful glares to the window and help me keep watch.

Rounding the front corner, I saw the figure of a tall woman halfway up the block, walking quickly away from the building, her back to me. Dark brown hair under a white knit cap. Expensive-looking white leather jacket. Trudy?

I broke into a jog. The woman's long legs had already taken her across the street and I had to dash to beat the line of traffic accelerating from the stoplight.

She was the right height for Trudy, judging by the photograph of her and Barrett Yorke. Five foot ten to Barrett's five-four. The brown hair could be a match.

I didn't want to just run up on her. That might have the same outcome as surprising her in her studio. I kept jogging after her on the opposite side of the street, dodging pedestrians. At least I was dressed for it.

A quick glance sideways as I ran past didn't tell me if the woman was Trudy. That knit cap and a scarf and pair of sunglasses hid her face very effectively. I ran on for another block. Crossed the street to her side and stopped. I put my leg up on a hydrant to stretch my hamstring. And starting huffing and puffing like I'd just sprinted a mile.

As she strode toward me, I wavered and fell awkwardly on my ass, blocking her path.

She stopped. "Are you okay?"

I waved a hand vaguely, breathing so hard I couldn't get words out.

She took off her sunglasses to take a better look at the guy having a coronary.

Pointy chin. Snub nose. Not Trudy.

Shit.

"Sorry," I said, keeping up the heaving. "M'okay. Outta shape." I stood up.

"Take it slow, all right?" she said.

"Yeah, thanks. Jus' one more mile." I started running back toward Studio Oceania. I hoped I hadn't missed the real Ms. Dobbs.

The entrance to the building was held open by a leisurely stream of the lodge members trickling out onto the sidewalk.

Behind them, a tall brunette walked out of the building and got into a Volkswagen Jetta idling at the loading zone.

Damn it. Two possibles in as many minutes. I half-expected a bus full of lanky brunettes to pull up next. I cut through the street, running flat out. Maybe I could catch the Jetta at the first red light, and see if Trudy was inside.

An old Ford sedan lurched out of its parking space in front of me. I smacked against its front fender, my momentum almost hurling me right over the hood. I rolled off and loped unsteadily forward, eyes still on the retreating Jetta.

The Ford's driver yelled at me. A woman's voice. I glanced at her through the windshield as I crossed front of the car. An angry redhead, yelling an obscenity.

I stopped, one hand on the cold metal of the car's hood, almost suspended in flight.

Her face twisted from anger into something like terror. A face with high Slavic cheekbones, framing big jade-colored eyes. A face I'd known for years.

I was looking at a dead woman.

I was looking at Elana.

Age Seventeen

The footsteps stopped right outside the Gallison storage room. Two shadowy spots broke the long line of yellow fluorescent light shining under the door. That light was the only bit of extra color in the indigo dark of the room. Even the cutting rod had cooled enough that it no longer glowed.

Had someone spotted the carrying cases on their rope, as I'd lowered them down the side of the building? No. No, if we had been made, they would have gone after Dono first.

The rope suddenly jerked in my hand, five feet of it whipping silently off the coil and out of the window. Frayed threads floated into the air as it whispered over the edge of the cut glass.

Whoever was outside wasn't coming in. A guard? An employee? He was just standing outside the door. Maybe listening. Behind me, the night breeze moaned across the open hole in the window. Could he hear it? What the fuck was he *doing*?

I heard the squawk of a walkie-talkie again, muffled through the door. Then a man's voice, slightly more audible.

"—you call them? I don't have it." A pause, and another receiver squelch. "No, fourth floor. Just call the number on the damn sheet."

The code. He didn't have the entry code for the room. But he would get it. They'd call the designated contact for Gallison, probably a company exec, and that person would know.

He wasn't speaking quietly. Maybe they thought their burglar had already left. Checking the room just in case anything was missing. That was in my favor. I peered into the blue shadows. No way I could hide anywhere among the shelves. Yank the door open and run for it? That might be my only chance. Maybe I could even knock the guard on his ass, and give myself a head start.

The rope jerked and a few more feet played out the window. Dono. I could signal him and maybe he could get the guards to come down to the lobby. Somehow.

I stuck my head out of the hole, the whap of the night wind in my ears not quite loud enough to cover the sound of the little truck's engine starting, four floors below. As I watched, it pulled away from the building, quickly picking up speed.

Oh, shit. I hadn't replied to Dono's questions over the microphone. He'd loaded the last of the lenses. He probably thought I was on my way out of the building.

" 'Bout damn time." The guard outside.

"Hang on, this guy's got me on hold." A second voice. And more shadows under the door.

Two of them now. Shit shit shit. No way I could just dash right past and hope that they were slow on the draw. Draw. Dammit, did they have guns? I'd seen them in the lobby. Why didn't I remember that?

Okay. Calm down. You have to get out of here.

As if in answer, the night wind chilled my spine.

No time to think hard about it. The rope was there and I could fit through the hole. I tied the fastest bowline in the world around the nearest anchored shelf leg. Yanked it tight. Lay down on my stomach and shimmied my legs out of the window. I had a death grip on the quarter-inch cotton rope. It would hold. It had to.

My chest was against the edge of the hole, and the cut glass edge was slicing my T-shirt. I squirmed an inch farther before it slashed my skin. Another inch. Just my arms and head inside now, the rest of me dangling. The wind lapped eagerly at my clothes. As I cleared the window, I thought I heard the guards fiddling with the punch code.

Three stories up. The rope swayed, thumping me against the building like it had the cases. I couldn't feel my fingers. Climbing down hand over hand wasn't going to work. The rope was too slim to let either hand go for even an instant. I frantically found the dangling length with my foot, and wrapped my leg around it. There. I couldn't scramble down fast, but at least I could keep the rope from tearing all the skin of my palms.

I started down. Move the leg, then each hand. A couple of feet at a time. What if the guards found the hole, and looked out and saw me? What if they *shot* me?

Climb, dammit. Two stories up now. Maybe thirty feet to go.

And then I fell.

There was no feeling of descent, it was so fast. Just a leap in my gut and a crushing blow on my entire right side that brought blackness with it. The last feeling, far away, was of the long stretch of rope draping itself over my body, like a snake coming to rest.

*

I inhaled water and coughed. My face was on grass, and the grass was wet. I knew where I was instantly. Lying on the manicured yard of lawn between the office building and its parking lot.

They would be coming. I wasn't quite conscious of who *they* were, but I knew I had to get away. I pushed up, sat up, stood up. Just that fast. And fell down again.

Dammit. I crawled a few feet, just to feel the ground, then tried standing again. Better. Still in one piece, as Dono would say.

Walking now, lurching farther from the building and toward the street. Real thoughts eased slowly back into my brain.

Lucky. I'd been very lucky. Another foot and I'd have splattered my head on the parking lot curb. Were the guards after me? Had they finally gotten into the room? And why had I fallen? I hadn't lost my grip. The edge of the hole I'd cut in the window had been sharp. Maybe sharp enough to slice the rope until it snapped. One foot in front of the other. That was a song, right? From TV. Couldn't remember how it went.

Then I realized I was standing in the road. In the middle of the road, having walked to the dashed white line in the center. I looked back. The office building was three hundred yards behind me. And I'd even gone in the right direction, for our backup meeting place. Dono always set one, in case of emergencies. This qualified. The designated spot was a twenty-four-hour convenience store one mile east and one block north. Three hundred yards down, thirteen hundred to go. I limped to the side of the road and kept walking.

We'd made it. Dono had the lenses, and I had escaped. I'd be happy if I never cut it that close again. But there was—Crap, I was still wearing the surgical gloves. I stripped them off and stuffed them down the next sewer grate I passed.

Another hundred yards, and I was walking past a strip mall. I kept pace by marking the shops. Nail salon, hair salon, baby furniture, café. Everything closed and dark. There was a car coming around the corner one block up, turning toward me. A cop car. Sultan County Sheriff.

I kept walking. The cruiser closed the distance between us. It slowed and stopped. A muscled blond cop looked at me from the driver's window.

"Evening," he said. Expressionless.

"Hey," I said, smiling. Keep walking, or stop? A citizen would stop. I stopped.

"You all right?" he said. The cop's partner leaned forward to get a better look at me. Another youngish guy, Chicano instead of Nordic, with a buzz cut and glasses.

"Yeah, yeah. Just twisted my ankle in"—what month was it?—"football practice."

"Where are you going?"

I couldn't say home. He'd ask where it was, and I didn't have a good answer. "Bus station."

He stared. Pointed. "It's that way."

Shit. "Sorry. I lost my wallet. No money for a cab."

"You been drinking?"

"No. Not at all." Maybe if I passed a Breathalyzer, he'd let me go.

The cop looked up the road. Toward the Gallison building. "You came from that way?"

His partner said something quiet to him before I could answer. They both turned and looked at the readout on the onboard computer.

The driver stepped out of the car. Both of the cops had their eyes on me now.

"No ID, huh?" he said. "Hands on your head, please." He stepped around behind me. "Legs apart."

"What's wrong?"

"Hands."

The Chicano cop had gotten out and was coming around to us. The blond patted me down. My pockets were completely empty, I knew. I'd even lost the cell phone in the fall.

The blond cop finished, gave a nod to his partner. The partner opened the back door. "Inside," he said.

"Am I under *arrest*?" I tried to sound a little panicked, like a regular kid would be. Since I was pretty freaked out already, it wasn't hard.

"Call it a ride home. Get in."

I got in. The cop did the thing of making sure I didn't bang my head on the roof, accidentally or otherwise. He closed the door. The backseat was cramped. It felt like a dog kennel, with the bars on the windows and the mesh separating the front seat.

"What's the number?" the blond said to his partner after they'd climbed back in.

"Three-oh-four," said the Chicano, reading from the computer screen. He gave me a sideways glance over his glasses. The cruiser pulled forward, slowly, as the cops scanned the buildings for addresses. Or maybe for other suspects like me.

I tried to remember what I knew about Ford Taurus police cars. Nothing that could work any magic on the handleless doors of my cage.

What would Dono say? He'd tell me to stay put, play dumb, and wait for the lawyer. But I wasn't handcuffed. If I could peel back the door's interior shell somehow, and get to the lock mechanism . . .

A woman screamed. The scream was long, loud, and full of terror. It came from somewhere out behind the strip mall.

"Jesus," said the blond cop, as he hit the brakes hard. They were already opening their doors. The woman shrieked again, in pain maybe.

"Unit Ten, responding to distress, corner of Wilton—" the Chicano cop hollered into his shoulder mike. They ran across the street and toward the sound.

What could I use to pry at the door? I didn't even have a belt buckle.

Then, like I had willed it, the door swung open.

Dono was crouched at the rear fender. "Move your ass," he said.

I scrambled out and ran after him, limp and all. The nearest business was an outlet store for cheap leather goods—HALF OFF ALL DAY EVERY DAY—and I followed Dono's big silhouette around its corner and through the alley between it and a boarded-up travel store. We stopped in a trash-strewn lot behind the travel agent.

"That woman—" I said.

"Shut up." He was listening. I didn't hear anything, not even the sound of the cop car's engine. But I spotted our white pickup truck parked at the curb half a block away.

Dono was furious. Not just your everyday pissed off. That was common enough. I could gauge his black moods like a barometer, and right now the needle was pegged all the way to the left.

Shit, it wasn't my fault the guards had showed up at Gallison. If he hadn't have taken off so quick, maybe he could have *helped*.

"Come on," he said, and we jogged to the truck.

Instead of driving directly away from the cops, Dono turned and headed east, on a parallel street to the one on which I'd been walking. He drove very slowly. I almost asked why, but it was pretty damn clear he wasn't handing out answers tonight.

He stopped. Turned off the lights. We sat. Five silent and excruciatingly slow minutes passed.

Elana Coll, dressed all in black, dashed from around the corner of a consignment store and up to our truck.

"Scoot over," she said, pulling open the passenger door. I shifted sideways and Elana squeezed in next to me. Her dark hair was in one long braid, and it flapped against me as she yanked hard on the door to close it. Dono hit the gas and we were suddenly flying toward the freeway entrance.

Elana bounced around to face us. "Man, you owe me big," she said to me. "I saved your whole *life*."

Dono said nothing. Even his big hands on the wheel were relaxed. But I could feel the fury vibrating off of him. The remainder of my whole life might not be worth saving.

Elana caught the mood in the air and settled back in her seat. But pressed up against each other, I could feel each sidelong glance she sent my way. When I finally shifted my eyes to look, she gave me a grin that could have melted that window's glass all by itself.

Chapter Twenty-One

She was alive. The shock of it froze me in place.

Elana reacted first, stomping the gas. The Ford pitched forward, suspension squealing with the abrupt turn.

I shouted "Wait!" and chased her. She kept her foot on the pedal. An oncoming car braked so hard it skidded, fender missing both of us by inches. It honked wrathfully, but Elana was already half a block away and accelerating.

I was left standing in the street, staring at the Ford until it vanished.

One of the Brothers of Scandinavia hollered to ask if I was all right, and another mentioned it might be a good idea to get my butt off the road. The driver who had just missed us roared past.

She was alive.

So who was dead?

My phone browser was still on Trudy Dobb's Facebook account, with Trudy's shyly smiling headshot pulled up. I'd been looking for pictures of her face before. Not her body.

One of her online photos albums was named Trip to Baja. Lots of pictures on various beaches. The fifth picture in the album showed Trudy, almost in the background, turned toward a flight of blindingly white stone steps while the couple at the center smiled for the camera. She was caught in motion, her left foot up on the high step, weight forward and ready to push off, her leg extended behind.

Her right leg, with its tattoo of tumbling roses in faded red and black. The same tattoo I'd seen in the Jefferson County morgue.

Trudy Dobbs had died at the cabin, with Kend. Two bullets to the face. It had been her black wings of blood I'd been dreaming of, not Elana's. Elana had used her best friend's identity to hide.

But why? Had she been responsible for the murders at the cabin? The Elana I knew was gorgeous, and knew it. Used it. She would hustle or steal. But kill?

Willard. He had realized Elana wasn't the dead girl at the cabin, the moment he had seen that ink. He'd lied to the cops. To me.

Did he know if his niece had murdered her friends?

Christ, had Willard been in on their murders from the start?

It was noon. If Willard had held one of his traveling casinos last night, he was probably dismantling it somewhere right now. I wanted to see him in person, and watch his eyes as I asked him about his dear, sweet niece.

I called him. No answer. I looked up another number. It was a public business, technically, but nobody off the street just wandered into the North Asian Association for Trade. Their version of commerce benefited a narrow group.

One Russian family, specifically.

I let it ring. I was reasonably sure that someone would be at the NAAT offices around the clock, but less positive that the phones were working.

"Yes?" a voice answered after a dozen rings.

"Van Shaw. I want to talk to Reuben."

"No Reuben here."

"Take a message." I gave him my name again, and my cell number. "He wants to talk to me."

"Yeah." Unconvinced. He hung up.

Reuben K liked the card games. Liked the action, liked the girls. Mostly he liked feeling like a big shot. If there had been a game around Seattle last night, he would have been there, representing, letting Willard manage the tables while he preened for the players.

Elana had fled at the sight of me. Had she known who I was? It had been a lot of years, and God knew a good chunk of my face had been scrambled and pieced back together in that time.

But from my stunned expression, Elana would have known that I had recognized *her*. And that fact had been enough to spook her. If she wasn't afraid of me specifically, she was sure as hell afraid of someone.

She wouldn't be coming back to the studio space again, and she'd probably already trashed the Amex. Maybe she was out of the city altogether. I'd blown an excellent chance to corner her and figure out what the hell was going on. The hard truth was enough to turn my mouth bitter.

My phone rang.

"Up and at them, soldier! Time to squeeze this new day by the balls!" Reuben, still hyper from his Saturday night. Maybe with a little pharma help.

"It's afternoon, Reuben. And I called you, remember?"

"You did, you did, and it makes me very happy. You've thought about my offer."

I had forgotten about Reuben's proposal to have me work for him. Between the Kuznetsovs and Maurice Haymes, I had a world of career opportunities.

"That's not why I called," I said.

"No? Hang on." I heard a car door close. When he came back on, his voice echoed slightly in the smaller confines of the vehicle. "Van, my man. Really. Why would you call me so early and start my day with bad news? This is not what colleagues do."

"I need to find our other friend. The big man."

"He's such a friend, you don't have his number?" Reuben was petulant now. From manic to downcast in a heartbeat.

"I have his number. He might be where there's no reception." The cell phone jammers they used for the game.

"Huh. Maybe." Reuben exchanged a few words in Russian with someone next to him. "Our friend is working. Better if you talk to him later."

"I need him now."

"Now, always now. What if I want an answer from *you* now, Van? You thinking about the future or not?"

"Reuben—"

"Yes or no?"

I wanted to find Willard. But not enough to make promises I couldn't keep to a Bratva captain, however junior he was.

"No."

I heard the car's engine start, simultaneous with Reuben's exaggerated sigh. "Okay," he said. "I think it's the wrong decision, a man with your talent. But to show you no hard feelings, I'll let you talk to your big friend. You know Double-X Motorsports? In Tacoma?"

"I'll find it," I said.

"Better move your ass. He's got to have a thousand miles behind him by tomorrow night."

A thousand miles meant L.A., or maybe Vegas. Cities well out of the Kuznetsov territory, last I knew. Maybe Reuben wasn't bullshitting about his big plans.

I was on I-5 South in less than ten minutes. As I drove, the navigation app on my phone read off the directions to Double-X Motorsports in that female voice that always sounded to me like she was speaking to a mental patient. Chipper but soothing tones.

*

Double-X was part of a large two-story garage in the South End. Its sheet metal walls were painted a bright, clean ivory, while a sign above the big rolling door spelled out the name in purple and black, graffiti style, the X formed by crossed pistons. A good place for Willard's temporary casino. Nobody would think twice at seeing a parking lot full of tricked-out cars inside its heavy iron fence.

The lot was mostly empty now, the gate open. Coasting past, I saw a twenty-foot moving truck, backed up to the garage door. And Willard's Escalade, parked off to the side.

Gotcha, you big son of a bitch.

The industrial neighborhood was dead quiet on a Sunday afternoon. I parked half a block away, just as the moving truck turned out of the lot and passed by my pickup. Two men were in the cab of the truck. Neither of them was nearly large enough to be Willard.

I walked to the gate. Willard's black Escalade was still there. The two movers had left the rolling door open, the gap making a tall black rectangle in the stark exterior. A two-foot crowbar was wedged in the track under the door to hold it in place. I could hear the sound of movement and a radio playing be-bop jazz from far inside the open shop.

The music clicked off. I quietly picked up the crowbar and faded back to hide behind the Escalade.

Willard came out of the garage. He wore one of his usual brown suits with a green knit tie. The tie was loosened and his white shirt wrinkled. A long night. He set down a leather gym bag—the night's receipts, maybe— and turned to shut the garage door.

The steel door was twenty feet tall and fifteen wide. Even Willard had to tug hard at it with both hands to get it moving. He walked slowly backward, half in and half out of the garage, glancing behind him as he went.

I decided to give him a little help. Sprinting from behind the Escalade, I put all my weight into pushing the rolling door. It covered the last five feet in a rush. Too fast for Willard to get his suddenly stumbling bulk completely out of the way. He fell back against the doorjamb. The door's edge slammed on his right arm, just below the shoulder. He shouted and tried to get his feet back underneath him. I reached down and jammed the end of the crowbar into the crack between the door and its roller track, and pulled up. The door closed another inch. Willard yelled again, a higher pitch.

"Van, what the fuck?" he said. He yanked at his trapped arm, but he had no leverage. I hauled up on the crowbar, harder, until he stopped.

"You're breaking my arm," he said. His broad face was red and already sweating.

"Yeah," I said. "Tell me about Elana."

Willard started to push back against the door. His strength was massive. The sheet metal groaned. But even Willard wasn't stronger than high-carbon steel. This time I pulled on the crowbar for a slow count of thirty. There are a lot of sensitive nerve endings in the bicep muscle. The metal edge of the heavy door was pressing hard enough to stretch the fabric of Willard's suit jacket taut. When I stopped he looked like he might vomit.

"Next time I'll put my back into it," I said.

"What do you want?" he said between gasps. He saw me adjust my grip on the bar and changed tack quickly. "Okay, stop. I knew it wasn't her. The body, at the hospital."

"But you lied to the cops. And me."

Willard's breath hissed out of his teeth. "Ease off, for fuck's sake. Yes, I told everybody it was Elana. Even Hollis. I needed to buy some time. To find her."

"Did you know who the dead woman was?"

"No. But her body looked so fucking horrible, it gave me the idea. I figured playing stupid would buy me a day or two. If Elana was alive, maybe she'd get in touch. But she never did."

"Did she shoot Kend? And the woman?" I said.

"I don't know." His face was dripping, the usual stone expression replaced by a pain that might be more than physical.

"Bullshit."

"It's like I told you. She never showed for work, she didn't answer my calls. She still doesn't. I tried a hundred times. I even called the phone company and used a cop ID to get them to trace her phone. It's been off for days. Shit, my arm. I can't feel my fingers."

"Probably for the best."

"Did she call you? Did you see her?"

"I got a glimpse of her, before she rabbited. Why wouldn't she tell you if she was in danger?"

"I've been wondering that since I saw that girl on the slab."

What couldn't big, bad Uncle Willard handle?

Or maybe he was part of whatever had Elana on the run.

"She's not a killer," Willard said.

"You are."

"This isn't on me. I swear I don't know what happened."

I was angry enough with Willard to tear a few of his tendons, and enjoy doing it. But I'd seen his reaction to seeing Trudy. It hadn't been anguish after all. It had been relief.

"The cops, I don't give a damn about," I said. "You should have trusted me."

"I told you to let it go."

He slumped against the steel doorjamb. His shirt was soaked through so much that I could see the gray hairs on his chest, and his jowls sagged. He looked old. But he could still break my neck, if he got those dinner plate hands on me.

"Don't move." I hefted the crowbar to make my point. Willard stayed put as I walked a wide circle to come up behind him. I took the small carry piece over his right kidney out of its holster. A Kahr .38.

"Come on," he growled. "If I was gonna draw on you, I would have done it."

"Except that you're right-handed. Call me paranoid." I ejected the magazine and pocketed it, and did the same for the round in the chamber. The pistol I threw far into the garage, through the opening left by Willard's bulk.

"What now?" he said.

"Now you take your family drama and go fuck yourself," I said. "I'm done."

He pushed the door wider and gingerly lowered his arm, caveman brow crushed tight in pain. His hand was the same bleached color as the garage walls.

"I need to find her," he said.

"Tell it to the dead girl who's paying for her vacation." I started backing away toward the gate.

"Your grandfather would have helped." He turned around. His face was back to its usual stolid mask. Almost. "Dono understood family."

"My grandfather would have taken your money," I replied.

Chapter Twenty-Two

When the evening rush had finally subsided, Luce left the closing of the bar to Fye and her other employees, and she and Leo came to the house. I stacked wood on the hearth while breaking the news about Elana, and Willard.

"Thank God she's not dead," said Luce. "But that poor girl, Trudy. Didn't anyone go looking for her?"

"She lived alone. Elana knew that, and decided to buy herself some time with texts to Trudy's boss and posts on Facebook. It worked for a couple of days."

Luce sat in Dono's old wingback chair and stretched fiercely, like the topic of conversation demanded it.

"I should be happy," Luce said, "but using Trudy's money and things to run away just makes Elana look about as cold-hearted as anyone can get."

"She's desperate, maybe. It's hard to wrap my head around Elana as a killer. Maybe she saw it happen."

"Then why not call the police? Or Willard?"

"The cops, I can figure. Elana's family doesn't trust cops any more than Dono did. Why she didn't tell her uncle is anybody's guess. Maybe he's part of what happened, and she knows it."

Luce raised her eyebrows in surprise. "But he sent

you to the cabin himself." Then she sighed in exasperation. "Never mind. That could be an alibi, couldn't it? Pretending to be worried for Elana when she didn't show up for work."

"He was honestly surprised when it wasn't Elana's body in the morgue, I'm sure of that. That would lead me to believe he wasn't the one who pulled the trigger."

"Kend and Trudy, dead together," she said. "I wonder if there was something between them."

"Maybe. It would be a motive, if Kend were hooking up with somebody else. But I'll let that whole circle sort through their own trash. I don't give a damn anymore."

Leo jabbed at the fire with an andiron. He was still wearing his favorite gray hoodie, with a blue down vest zipped over it tonight, like armor. He hadn't said a word since halfway through my story. I signaled Luce with my eyes.

"I'm going to shower." She stood up and gave me a quick kiss. "Would you put on coffee?" Luce could drink coffee at any time, without it affecting her sleep one way or the other. Maybe it was a bartender thing.

Leo waited until Luce was upstairs. He sat on the hearth, the fire crackling into slow life as it ate the damp wood.

"You should have called me," he said. "When you went to have it out with Willard, you should've called."

"I wanted you on Luce."

He shook his head. "Luce had the whole lunchtime crowd around her. Or she could have stayed low while I was out. You were the priority, man."

"I handled it. I know Willard."

"You think you do. Now you're wondering if he might be killing people at cabins." His eyes flickered between me and the windows and the doorway.

"It was my risk," I said. "Maybe it was the wrong call, but it's done. Don't act like I crapped in your helmet."

"If he'd had another guy there to back him up, you would have been fucked."

"You're not some grunt that needs this explained, Leo."

He stared at me from under the gray hood. "Forget it." He got up and walked to the kitchen and out to the backyard.

I put another log on the fire and stoked the ashes to let the flames breathe. Leo was brittle. Maybe I should walk tiptoe on those eggshells. But tonight I wasn't in the goddamn mood.

Luce came downstairs, blond hair sleek as seal fur from the shower. She'd changed into my bleach-stained Mariners sweatshirt and her own yoga pants. If I'd owned yoga pants, she'd have probably have purloined those, too.

"Leo okay?" Luce said.

"Not yet," I said.

She hugged me. "Can you get him help?"

"I don't know what kind he needs. He's tried doctors, and pills."

"Maybe there are other ones."

Thousands. And programs and V.A. hospitals and volunteer organizations. Finding help wasn't the hard part.

I could hear Leo patrolling, coming up the porch out front. He was very quiet, but the old wooden slats creaked. I opened the front door to let him in.

"I'll make the coffee," I said.

I heard the kitchen door slam open with a splintering of wood. Leo, eyes wild, came flying through the kitchen. I grabbed for Luce but Leo was already digging his shoulder into her back at a full run, lifting her up like a football tackle and slamming her headlong into me. Glass shattered. I glimpsed a thick, whitish cylinder banded in duct tape hit the wingback chair, bouncing crazily, as I fell back and out through the open front door, Luce and Leo almost on top of me. We all tumbled off the porch. An instant before I hit the gravel, a clap-BANG of high explosive tore everything away from sight sound wall house Luce Leo

On fire. Leo was on fire. He was facedown and still. The back of his vest smoldered and glowed. I grabbed him and rolled him over to smother the sparks, before a hurricane of vertigo made me fall back again.

Leo was out cold, but breathing. Luce lay next to him, moving slowly, saying something to me. My ears were filled with a high insect whine. I tried to say her name, coughed, and was suddenly sick, vomiting through a mouthful of dust onto the gravel of the side lot.

Wisps of white smoke swirled around us. The other side of Luce's head was bloody. I crawled over Leo to check her. Her ear was cut, and as I bent to look closely at the pink wash, a spat of blood from my own head fell onto her cheek.

"—okay?" she asked. From six inches away I could make out her words. Her eyes weren't dilated. I peeled Leo's lids back to check his pupils. He thrashed a little, coming back to the world.

We had to move, my stunned brain told me. Whoever had thrown the bomb might still be near.

Movement, to my right. I had no gun. I fumbled to stand, and then Stanley bounded up to us. His anxious barks pierced through the ringing. He ran in mad dashes, to and fro. Addy Proctor walked slowly up the steps. Her round face was twisted with fear.

The smoke around us churned thicker now, blacker. And there was heat. I steadied myself and bent down to help Luce stand. Addy walked with her toward the street, as I got my arms under Leo and hefted his buck-sixty into a fireman's carry. I followed Addy, tottering under Leo's weight and my own unfamiliar legs.

We reached the sidewalk as the first fire engine came screaming onto the block. I could hear the siren just fine.

Chapter Twenty-Three

The paramedics bundled Leo off to the hospital, just as he regained full consciousness and started to ask me questions. They wanted to take Luce. She wouldn't go without me. They wanted to take me, too. They were very insistent. But we were both standing and answering their questions cogently, and eventually I told them to screw off.

One of them tossed us a handful of gauze pads as he left. I held one to the laceration on the side of my head, and Luce held one to her ear, and we watched the firefighters do what they could.

The explosion had shredded the side of the house and blown out every window in the front room. That was only the start. The flames in the fireplace hadn't been snuffed out by the concussion, and the old wood skeleton of the house made excellent fuel.

Two soaring arcs of water flew up and into the second story, the firefighters working the hoses back and forth. At this point their efforts were more about saving the nearby homes. The front of Dono's house was gutted. The back was invisible behind black smoke and spray. Whatever personal papers I had owned were ashes by now. Along with Dono's books. My mother's St. Christopher medal. Everything else.

A uniformed cop came over with his partner and questioned us. When he got to the part about whether I knew anyone who might have wanted to do this, I said no. I'd already told Guerin about T. X. Broch. Laying his name on the uniform would just lead to an entire night of repeating the same information, on the record this time.

Luce knew what I was leaving out, of course. Her face stayed neutral. But I could feel her vibe.

The cop told me detectives would be in touch. He was partly right. When people started throwing explosives around, the FBI took an interest, too. Maybe even Homeland, depending on who they thought was doing the throwing. It wouldn't escape anyone's notice that I'd received a lot of training in demolitions myself.

Local news vans had arrived five minutes after the fire engines. They had raced to get their people in the optimal spot to pose with the fire in the background. The photogenic part of the blaze was over. One shellacked mannequin hurried over with his cameraman the moment the cop was finished to ask us for an interview. I told him no, in much less polite language than I'd used with the medics.

Luce watched the firemen knock down a smoking wall to keep it from falling outward. "This wasn't Willard," she said.

227

I nodded agreement. "He may want to grind a couple of my bones to make his bread, but no. He wouldn't do this. It has to be Broch."

"Trying harder, after those two assholes yesterday."

I'd underestimated Broch. Fogh and Guerin had both warned me that the loan shark was violent beyond reason, and I'd still played defense. Dumb. Luce was right to be angry.

My phone rang, a 253 number.

"Mr. Shaw? Arthur Ostrander." Maurice Haymes's attorney.

"It's a bad time, Mr. Ostrander."

"I'm aware. You're on the television right now."

The news vans. Interview or no, their cameras would have at least filmed us from a distance. Luce was too good-looking not to wind up on the live feed.

"It's best that we talk immediately," he said. "I'm at my club downtown. May I send a car for you?"

"No," I said. I wanted to check on Leo.

"It's very urgent, Mr. Shaw. Or I wouldn't be calling at such a time."

Luce could hear what was being said. She gave me a puzzled look. I shrugged, almost as perplexed as she was. I had to give Ostrander credit for sparking our curiosity.

"If it's that important," I said. "Meet me at Swedish Hospital on First Hill in an hour. Emergency entrance." I hung up.

"That's Maurice Haymes's lawyer?" Luce said.

"And the family fixer, from what I can tell."

The flames in the house were slacking. We watched the firefighters work the hoses closer and tighter on the blaze. Luce reached out and took my arm with one hand. A temporary truce. The cut on her ear had clotted.

"Leo saved us both," I said.

"Yes."

"Because he was prepared."

Luce shook her head no. "That was just chance. Our good luck."

"Maybe it was good that Leo's brain is stuck in the suck. But I should have been ready."

"I'd say you can't fix this yourself," she said, "but those words would just wave a red flag in front of you. You *shouldn't*."

"Somebody tried to kill us tonight."

Luce laughed, without any mirth. "Uncle Albie used to tell me that laundering Dono's stolen cash through the bar was just to help us make ends meet. That we wouldn't survive without it. Maybe that was true. But Albie didn't do it just for the money."

She turned back to the house. The smoke coming from the smoldering walls was a translucent white, in the glare of the searchlights.

"He did it because he missed the thrill," Luce said.

Chapter Twenty-Four

Luce wanted to go home instead of the E.R. My protests only made her more adamant. I made sure she was safely in bed with her friend Marcie watching her before I sped to Swedish.

The admitting clerk asked if I was family. I told him I was Leo's brother.

"He's in 14C, an examining room," the clerk said, looking at the computer screen. "I'm missing a lot of details here. Does he have insurance?"

Leo didn't even have his backpack anymore. "Check with the V.A.," I said as I started down the hall.

The room had four padded examining tables with half-drawn curtains between each. Men in hospital gowns were asleep on two of the tables. Neither of them looked like they spent many nights indoors. Leo was sitting up in one of the far beds, bare-chested, while a young female R.N. examined the back of his neck.

"What's to report?" I said.

"Toasted and roasted. But nothing much else."

"His clothes saved him from a lot worse," said the nurse. She nodded to where Leo's vest and gray hoodie were thrown over one of the room's blocky wooden chairs. Only half of the vest was still blue. The back of it was crusted with black bits of scorched Gore-Tex. Tufts of whitish cotton showed through where the outer layer had been completely seared off.

That could have been Luce's skin.

"These burns on your neck and scalp are only first degree, Mr. Pak," the nurse said. "How is your hearing now?"

"Fine."

"Fine like totally clear, or fine like the ringing is less than before? Barry from the ambulance said you couldn't hear him talking to you when you were first brought in."

"Less," Leo admitted.

"Okay. The doctor will come and see you soon."

Leo frowned. "I'm ready to roll." He looked to me for confirmation.

"Mr. Pak," the nurse said. "You may have head trauma, or worse. You're here already. Let's make sure, okay?" She was a pretty girl, with wheat-colored hair and a dusting of freckles. She knew how to turn on the charm.

"There's nowhere else for us to crash right now anyway," I said to Leo.

He glanced quickly around at the windowless room. I asked the nurse to give us a minute. She took another glance at Leo, then nodded affirmatively and told us to stay put.

"Let the doc check you out," I said to Leo when it was just us and the sleeping homeless guys. "You might need an MRI. My head's barely screwed on, and you were between us and the blast."

231

"It was some kind of water gel, right?" Leo said. He hunched his shoulders, his compact body becoming even more coiled.

I nodded. "Not enough slam for plastic. Maybe some commercial brand."

That notion made the back of my brain itch. Something for me to talk to Ostrander about. He'd be arriving in a few minutes, if he kept our appointment.

"I don't want to stay here," Leo said.

His eyes were doing that flickering dance. There was only one entrance to the room, which meant only one exit.

"You saved our asses," I said. "Thanks."

"Luce is all right?"

"She is. And she's angry."

"I'm pretty pissed myself." Leo reached out to grab his vest from the chair. "Fuck, look at this."

"She isn't just mad at the bomber."

His eyes steadied on me. At least I had his attention. "At you?"

I leaned on the wall across from him. "Luce thinks I might be some kind of war junkie. Only really myself when things are tight." I shrugged. "Maybe she's not all the way wrong. Life seems damn real to me right now."

"And that's bad somehow."

"Bad or good. At least it's not wandering around at night like a ghost. I didn't tell you that part."

He picked at the charred vest, letting flakes of burnt fabric flutter to the tiled floor.

"You ever feel like that?" I asked. "Cut off?"

Leo shook his head no, and plucked another tiny black leaf. He rolled it between his fingers until it disintegrated to ash. "It's *too* real. I hear things."

"Hallucinations?" Speaking quietly enough that the nurse wouldn't hear, if she were just outside the door.

"Nah. Memories. My last rotation, the whole company was in Paktika province. We sat on our thumbs for a week at Sharana, eating the base chow and lifting weights and waiting on a green light for whatever the fuck they weren't telling us about. The rumor going around was that some Taliban chieftain had spilled everything under interrogation. He had told Intel about a training camp, way up in the mountains. Deserted during the winter."

I remembered Leo hesitantly asking me if my own bad dreams had started from a winter operation. Winter was dangerous as hell in Afghanistan. When we went out on a mission, we'd inevitably have less air support, or none at all. The weather might change from bright and clear to a full storm in minutes. Hiking through snow with seventy pounds on your back was like walking with anchors tied to each foot. And the enemy tended to dig into their shelters and fight hard, rather than retreat into the bitter cold.

"So if it was deserted . . ." I prompted.

"The chieftain had confessed that there were dead Americans buried at the camp. Guys that had been lost months before," Leo said.

233

I nodded. Given the option, Rangers wouldn't go hunting in the deep of winter. But sometimes there wasn't a choice.

"What they paid us for," I said. "To lead the way, and enjoy it when it sucks."

"Yeah. So the birds dropped our platoon off as close as the pilots could manage, but we still had a long night of up and more up. The elevation of the camp was somewhere around eleven thousand feet. Just a ghost town, really. Dry stone walls and plywood sheeting for doors and one iced-over well. No wonder the Taliban only used it in the summer."

"Did you find them?"

Leo looked at the wall. I wondered if he'd ever spoken this story out loud before, even during the in-patient program back in Utah. When he started again, his voice was fast and light, his words skipping over themselves.

"We had the K9 with us and she sniffed out the right spot fast enough. A patch about ten by ten. Obvious once we brushed the snow away. We started in at the edges with pickaxes. The sun was coming up but you could hardly tell with the fog and the cloud layer. Took us about three hours to clear the frozen top soil and the dirt underneath. It was a mass grave. Two of our infantry guys, and a bunch of locals. Families. Maybe people who'd refused to collaborate."

"Jesus."

"They were all stuck together. We had to cut them out of their clothes to pull them apart. Otherwise . . ."

I nodded. Otherwise the skin would peel off as readily as the clothing. I'd seen corpses left out in the cold, too.

"We'd brought bags but the bodies wouldn't fit inside. All their limbs were fixed in place, sticking out, and nobody wanted to try moving them. Too worried something would snap off. We just wrapped our boys with bags and tape as good as we could, re-buried the rest, and called for exfil."

Someone walked past the door, hurrying along to another room down the hall. Leo stopped.

"You said that you hear things," I said.

He shivered, like he was coming out of a trance. "I was in the Chinook on the way back. You know how it is inside a chopper. You can't hear shit, with the noise of the rotors and the wind and all of it. But I was right next to the bodies, where they were tied down to the floor, wrapped like Christmas presents. And I know I heard a sound. From under the plastic. Like teeth grinding on rocks. Every bump or drop of the bird, another something went crack in the bags. Muscle. Bones. I don't know what. But I could picture it. Those two guys, nothing left of them but icicles. Breaking apart from the inside out."

God. "That would screw with anybody's head, Leo."

"I didn't think on it like that, not right then. I just thought, *That's messed up*. But later on . . ." He faltered.

"Like scary movies as a kid. It doesn't bother you while you're watching. It's later, when you're thinking about it at night."

"That's right," Leo said. "Later. In the dark."

I waited. He didn't say more. He just looked at the burned remains of one of his only possessions. I knew Leo was twenty-five years old. But his face looked twice that, and his eyes in that moment were ancient.

"You brought them home," I said. "Whatever else, those men are where they should be because of you."

My leather jacket had been spared the fire, along with the few items I'd had in the truck, including one of Dono's burner phones. I programmed my number into it and handed it and my jacket to Leo.

"Phone's charged. Call me when they cut you loose."

He nodded, turning the little silver clamshell over and over in his hands.

"Leo."

I waited until he met my eyes.

"You're in the dark," I said. "But you aren't alone in it, brother. Clear?"

His skin was taut across the bones around his eyes.

"The dark's where we go to work," he said.

I grinned, almost a snarl. "Goddamn right."

Chapter Twenty-Five

It wasn't Ostrander waiting at the entrance. It was Rudy Rusk, leaning his stout mass against a Cadillac parked in a red zone. He wore the same blue blazer and gray trousers combo as the last time I'd seen him. The blazer needed to be let out. It puckered across his folded arms.

Rusk's angry face deepened another shade when I approached, smiling ear to ear.

"Rudy. How's your credit rating?" I said.

He reached behind him without looking to open the rear door. "Get in," he said, like it was a squad car.

"Yeah," I said. "Then we can go get milkshakes together. Isn't taxi service a little below your pay grade?"

Rusk's neck tensed. He wanted to swing at me. He'd probably enjoyed punching people when he was a cop, under the easy defense of resisting arrest. Retirement wasn't all it was cracked up to be.

I kept the smile in place. "Go ahead." After a day of getting tricked and lied to and nearly blown up, it would be a whole lot of fun to break a couple of Rudy Rusk's teeth for him.

He was smart enough not to take the bait. He opened the door a little wider, maybe hoping he'd get the opportunity to close it on my leg.

"I'll follow you," I said. "You remember my truck."

It might have been my imagination, but I was half sure I heard capillaries popping in Rusk's neck.

I shadowed his Cadillac to a building on Cherry Street, downtown. Rusk pulled into the valet stand outside. It was nearly two o'clock in the morning, but an attendant in a burgundy waistcoat popped out of the closest door immediately. I opted for the meter across the street.

The entrance to the white stone building was bookended by ornamental columns. Similar columns braced each fifteen-foot window on the first floor. Rusk waited for me in the doorway, at the top of a short flight of steps. A large calligraphic letter *A* was painted on the pebbled glass of the door. As I walked up, the door opened. The man behind it wore a suit coat in the same burgundy color as the valet's vest.

"Good evening, Mr. Rusk," the doorman said, and nodded to me. "Sir."

"What's the *A* stand for?" I asked him.

"The name of the club, sir. Aerie."

Of course it was. I could scoff at rich men naming their playhouse after the home of eagles. But my grandfather's bar had been named for a legend about a wicked woman and the Devil, so I supposed I shouldn't judge.

I let Rusk lead the way. The club's lobby was floored in marble and topped with a huge glass chandelier, and a small desk where the doorman sat. There was no other furniture. Each broad wooden door off the lobby was closed.

"Mr. Ostrander is in the lounge," the doorman said, leading us to the first door on the right. He knocked twice and slid the door open.

If the lobby was severe, the lounge was made to contrast it. Low leather chairs arranged in circles, a tawny wall-to-wall carpet and long bar at the far end. The décor looked early '60s, either as a retro nod to Seattle's jet-era boom times, or because it made the members feel young again. Most of the lights were dimmed and the room was cool. Ostrander occupied the brightest corner, near a hissing gas fireplace.

"Thank you for coming at such a difficult time," he said to me. "Please sit down. Can I offer you something?" He didn't acknowledge Rusk.

I shook my head no. There were two chairs, one opposite him and one closer to the fire. I'd had more than enough of flames for the night, but I chose that seat anyway. I didn't want my back to the open room. Rusk eased himself into one of the chairs in the next circle over.

"Let me start by apologizing for what must have seemed some odd behavior the other day," said Ostrander. He wore another three-piece, this one a glen plaid in muted brown. He looked tired, like gravity was pulling extra hard on his gaunt frame. "Rudy was acting in our interests, you must understand."

"I must."

"Beg pardon?"

"You were apologizing for your man," I prompted.

"Yes. Rudy explained to me what transpired in the Columbia parking garage, after our meeting. He overstepped his authority. I never asked him to search your vehicle, nor implied that he should do so." It was amazing how Ostrander could make any conversation sound like he was reading from a contract.

I looked at Rusk. "So what did plant the idea in your head?"

Ostrander leaned forward. "You've had a terrible night. From the newscast, I understand your home may be destroyed? Thank goodness you and your friend are unharmed."

I inhaled to speak and Ostrander held up a hand to stop me.

"I'm saying this because things may seem at their lowest," he said. "But there is opportunity here. Our offer still stands, if you allow Maurice and I to overcome the bad first impression we made."

I looked around at the lounge. A rosy glow from the dimmed overhead lamps caught facets on cut crystal glasses behind the bar. The bar itself looked like real walnut, and so did the wall paneling.

"Depends on the offer," I said.

Ostrander smiled his mortician's smile, the one that mimicked kindness without providing any warmth. "Before we go further, I must make something clear. I am not officially representing Haymes Development in this conversation. Everything we discuss is strictly hypothetical."

"Except the money."

"Excepting that, yes."

"Go on. If I think I can help you out, we'll talk price."

He nodded. "About two weeks ago, one of the sites under HDC suffered a burglary."

"Water gel explosives," I said.

Ostrander stared at me for an instant before firing an angry glance at Rusk.

"Rudy didn't tell me," I said. "You're looking for boxes, which you've already told me Kend had. HDC is a construction company, among other things. And tonight you called my number less than an hour after someone threw a bomb through my window. The bomb was made from a commercial explosive, very stable, like a building company would use for blasting rock or controlled demolitions."

Ostrander took a sip from his glass. Scotch neat, from the look of it. His knobby wristbones extended from sleeves closed with cufflinks shaped like Roman coins, with an emperor's laureled head in profile.

"I misjudged you, Mr. Shaw," he said.

"It happens."

He took a breath. "If—and I am only conjecturing here—if a large quantity of such explosive were found to be missing, it could be damaging to the company. Somewhat."

"Sure. A federal investigation could shovel a whole lot of Somewhat all over your building contracts with local and state governments."

He shifted in his seat. "Perhaps."

"I think I read about Maurice being touted as a candidate for governor, too. Tough to call for law and order with your son stealing bombs and killing girlfriends."

Ostrander looked like his Scotch had suddenly turned to vinegar, but inclined his head at the obvious implications.

"So you want your explosives back," I said. "Very quietly."

"We do. We have to."

I rolled my neck. My muscles were sore. The physiological hangover of a huge rush of adrenaline and endorphins after the explosion. Not to mention falling off the porch onto gravel with Luce and Leo on top of me.

"I'll take that drink now," I said, and stood up before Ostrander could tell Rusk to fetch it. At the walnut bar, the bottles were all out in the open, lined up against a frosted mirror on the back wall. With the member fees that the Aerie must charge, it would be considered déclassé to lock up the booze.

I picked the Scotch that was the same color as Ostrander's. Eighteen-year-old Laphroaig. I carried the bottle and a glass back to the chair, and poured myself a taste.

"Why do you think Kend wanted explosives?" I said.

"We don't know. At this point, that is immaterial. What matters—"

"—is retrieving it, I get that." I took a sip. The Laphroaig was like wood smoke and cinnamon scented from afar. "How much did he take?"

Ostrander looked at Rusk.

"All of it," said Rusk. "Two dozen cases of Tovex. Fifty pounds per. Plus blasting caps."

I knew what water gel explosive looked like, even before I'd seen the bomb wrapped in duct tape thrown through my window. Fat flexible tubes, like giant bratwurst. The tubes I'd seen were about eighteen inches long. Guess each tube at a kilogram. Two dozen tubes per case. I thought of Elana's Volvo and its big cargo space with the backseats folded down. Kend would have had to stack the cases all the way to the roof, but they would fit. There had been dents in the carpet from the weight. Over twelve hundred pounds of jellied destruction.

It must have been one hell of a nervous drive for Kend, down and around the Sound to the Peninsula and the cabin. One traffic stop by a curious state trooper and Kend would be in a supermax holding cell before he could take a breath. But it was better odds than boarding the ferry, where police dogs sniffed at every car in the terminal.

"The cases were gone by the time I got to the cabin," I said. "How do you know Kend had them?"

"Aside from the coincidence of their deaths on the same

243

night," Ostrander said, "there is some substantiation."

I made a keep-going gesture.

"Video," said Rusk. "The alarm and cameras at the storage site were disabled." He looked at Ostrander. "I've been telling you for months to get a better system."

Ostrander made a sound like a sigh.

Rusk tapped his smartphone. "But one camera for the company across the street caught him in action."

"It's nothing that could be held up as evidence," said Ostrander quickly. "Kend was masked, and only visible in the distance. But to anyone who knew him well, it's undoubtedly him."

"Let's see it," I said to Rusk.

He got the nod from Ostrander, pulled up the video on his phone, and handed it to me.

The clip was about thirty minutes long. For the first few seconds, it was only grainy color footage, at night, of an empty street with two small buildings across the way. A ten-foot-wide alley separated the buildings. The buildings were inside a large, aggressive-looking fence with barbed wire and signs warning of electric current.

Then a figure walked behind the buildings, from one side of the alley to the other. Perhaps sixty feet from the camera. His head was covered, in a ski mask or balaclava. He loped quickly past, gone in two seconds, dragging a hand truck behind him. Two minutes passed, and then he came slowly back across, pulling the hand truck, which was now loaded with three big and obviously very

244

heavy cases. The cases were unmarked. A minute later he ambled across once again.

I watched as the masked figure repeated the same process, as if the video were looped, seven more times. Rusk got up and fetched himself a vodka. Ostrander watched me watching the show. A few moments after Kend's last trip with the cases, the street in front of the camera momentarily grew brighter. Headlights, just off to the side of the frame. Then the clip ended.

He'd taken only one minute on each trip to drop the cases off at the Volvo. Kend was a lean guy. Too lean to load fifty-pound containers into a hatchback that fast.

"He had help," I said. Rusk nodded.

I handed the phone back to him. "And you thought it was me." I was at the cabin. I knew Willard, and Willard's niece was Kend's woman. A to B to C.

"We did. Until the attack on your home this evening," said Ostrander.

I had some incentive now, was what he meant. They had been half sure I was crooked before. Now they weren't certain if I was involved with the theft of the Tovex, but they were willing to bet that I was still dirty enough to steal it back from Willard, if he had it.

Ostrander steepled his skeletal fingers. "After Rudy found the security video, we hoped we could negotiate with Kend. Get him to return the explosives and avoid a felony charge, or worse. But he didn't answer Maurice's calls on Saturday."

"And then he turned up dead. And the Tovex is gone. And you're caught between the monster and the whirlpool."

"Scylla and Charybdis. Yes. It's too late to inform the authorities without repercussions. And we cannot sit by and simply hope the explosives are not used for—for other purposes."

They couldn't. Even if they gave half a shit about anybody else being blown up. If the Tovex were used again, after the leveling of my house, the assumption would be that the city had a mad bomber on the loose. Feds would descend like gray-suited raindrops. The explosives would eventually be traced back to HDC, no matter how Ostrander and Rusk tried to cover their tracks.

"I can get your toys back." I picked up the bottle of Laphroaig.

In my peripheral vision, they shared a look.

"You're certain?" said Ostrander.

"First, I need a number."

"Fifty thousand," Ostrander said.

I stopped pouring the Scotch. There was about a pinky finger's breadth in the bottom of the glass. "Fifty. For a governorship." I poured more. A lot more, until the liquor was the same finger width from the rim of the lowball glass.

"Two hundred," said Ostrander. "Thousand."

"Jesus," said Rusk disgustedly.

"Half now," I said.

Ostrander waved a finger idly. "That's absurd."

"You're not the one having bombs thrown their way," I said.

"Yeah, about that. Why the hell is someone trying to kill you?" Rusk said. He was back to risking his blood vessels. "Don't tell me you're an innocent fucking bystander in all this."

Ostrander looked peeved at Rusk's lack of decorum, but nodded. "You have to share how you're certain you can recover the cases. Give us some assurance that you can do what you say."

I took one very nice sip from the very full glass and set it back down. I'd had my fun with Ostrander and Rusk. I stood up from the chair.

"No need for dramatics," said Ostrander. "Half in advance."

I walked to the lounge door.

"If this is negotiation, it's pointless," he called.

I opened it and walked through.

"What is it you want?" Ostrander said, his voice strained taut as the door closed. I caught the start of another obscenity from Rusk. It startled the doorman.

I didn't know a lot of rich people. But I knew if you had a big hammer, every problem looked like a nail. Let them think I was angling for more money. They had told me all they were going to, and maybe all they could.

Which might just be enough.

Chapter Twenty-Six

At three a.m. on a Friday morning, the downtown streets were as close to deserted as they ever got. With the window open, I could hear the sound of my pickup's engine echoing off the glass monoliths, like the city was humming along to the tune. I drove the truck for a few blocks before pulling over about halfway between the Aerie Club and the Morgen. White shoes to blue collar, in under a mile.

I wasn't ready to talk to anyone else yet. Not even Luce. Instead I sat in the truck, and watched the stoplights cycle through their slow patterns. It had been a long day followed by a longer night. My head was reeling with everything that had happened.

I didn't trust Arthur Ostrander, Esq., farther than I could spit. But he had been right about one thing. I had incentive to find the explosives, and whoever took them. A hell of a lot. Stack up all the motivation and carve it into the rough form of my family home. Then put Luce's life, and Leo's and my own, as the mountains behind it.

Maurice Haymes could stick his money up his ass and set fire to it. None of us were safe until I found out who wanted me in tiny pieces. The person who had almost killed Luce. That was all that mattered.

Retrieving the explosives meant a lot to Maurice Haymes, too. Maybe his whole future. Ostrander had just proved to me that they were willing to pay a few thousand percent more than market value to get those cases back. Maybe Kend had figured out his dad's weak spot and had stolen the Tovex with the idea of ransoming it, to buy his way out of trouble with Broch. But Kend was killed before he could cut a deal with dear old Dad. Whoever had murdered Kend and Trudy had driven the Tovex away in the dually truck.

So who had helped Kend steal it? And who had it now?

Elana was the obvious first choice. She had a criminal record. She'd been at the cabin. She was even strong enough to load fifty-pound cases into the Volvo, if she had to.

But there was another individual I liked a lot better, for that kind of heavy lifting.

Barrett Yorke picked up on the third ring.

"You're awake," I said.

"Have you heard? About Trudy?" Her voice was thick.

I guessed what was coming, but had to play dumb. "Did she call you?"

"Trudy's dead."

"Dead."

"A relative had been trying to reach her, and they filed a missing persons report, and they found out it was her at the cabin all along. And nobody knows where Elana is. God."

The police would already be looking for Elana Coll. Once they compared the timings of Trudy's online posts against the times of death, that search would become very serious.

"I'm sorry," I said.

"Poor Tru." Barrett began crying, the quiet, smooth sobs of someone who has been crying for hours and is near exhaustion. Awake only because the grief wouldn't let her rest. "She was a really good person, you know?"

"She seemed like it. I liked her paintings."

Barrett wept through another two stoplight rounds. "You called me," she prompted, when the wave had passed.

"I did. I need to talk to your brother."

"God, get in line. What's going on?"

I sat up. "Somebody else has been asking about Parson?"

"*Asking* isn't the right word. That implies some kind of manners."

"Who?"

"Some jerk who said he was investigating Kend's death. He called last night and wanted to know if Parson was home, or where he was."

Investigating Kend, the guy had said. Implying he was a cop, without actually claiming to be. "Was his name Rusk?"

"He wouldn't say. He sounded all official, but he was a creep. Tell me this and tell me that. I figured he was a reporter. I told him where he could go, all right. He got so mad I thought he might just crawl through the phone."

"You were right not to talk to him. Where's Parson?"

"That's the thing. I don't know. I called Parson to tell him about the creep, and he just freaked. I explained that I didn't say anything, and so what? But he hung up. He hasn't been home all night."

Dammit. Rusk had Kend's computer. He was probably working his way through Kend's close friends, looking for anyone with enough heft to be Kend's accomplice. Maybe Barrett had diverted him to the next name on the list. Or maybe Rusk's cop instincts had told him he was on the right trail.

But the HDC security chief's questions had sent Parson running for cover. Which confirmed what I had only started suspecting about the big kid.

"Barrett," I said. "Is Parson—I don't know another way to put this—normal?"

She tsked. "Parson's fine. Everyone thinks that he's dumb, because he doesn't talk much and when he does, it's not complicated. But really, he's quite bright. He's brilliant with electrical things and engines and stuff. He just—he *feels* really hard. Loves me and our parents and his friends hugely. It nearly destroyed him, when he learned Kend and Elana—Trudy now, I guess—when he learned they were dead. He doesn't have a lot of defenses, you know?"

"Guileless."

"Yes. That's him. Van?"

"Yeah."

"Is Parson in trouble?" Her voice was small.

"I don't know, Barrett."

"I was really ticked at you, you know? Not just because you turned me down. I'm not *that* delicate. But I knew you weren't telling me everything, at Trudy's." She sighed knowingly, and it turned into a yawn. "You probably aren't telling me everything now. Men with secrets. Why are guys like you the ones I go for? You and Kend."

She had said it so quietly, I wasn't sure I'd heard her right. "Kend? Did you and he—?"

"Hmm? No, no. I just liked him a lot, is all. Nothing ever happened. Maybe if he and Elana . . ." She yawned again.

I was beginning to understand why all of the couple's love notes had been stuffed into a drawer in Kend's apartment. And maybe why the photo of Barrett and Trudy had been banished with them.

"If you hear from Parson, call me. I'll help."

"Sure." She sounded like she was falling asleep even as she hung up.

Parson Yorke had more devotion than a pack of Saint Bernards. Especially to his best buddy, Kendrick. Parson might have committed grand larceny with Kend. He was fervent in his belief that Kend hadn't killed Elana.

So do you think the rumors are true? Barrett had asked me on the rooftop bar. Parson had immediately answered

252

for me. *No.* A flat statement. No, Kend hadn't killed her. No, he wasn't a murderer. Parson might have meant both of those.

Or maybe the huge lump had unconsciously been saying, *No, Elana isn't dead.* Had he known?

I'd spooked Elana. She'd lost what little food and shelter she'd acquired by pretending to be Trudy. She might cut her losses and put a few thousand miles between herself and Seattle before ditching the Ford sedan.

But I didn't think so. She had stayed hidden in Seattle, after the horrors at the cabin. If she was still as stubborn as the Elana I'd once known, she'd stay in Seattle now. She would need money, and a place to stay, and she'd be desperate enough to ask someone for help. I could guess that good old Parson would be more than willing.

Unless Parson was the one that Elana had been running from all along.

Just a big naïve kid. Brilliant with electronic things. Like security systems. And maybe like bombs.

Chapter Twenty-Seven

Someone banged on Luce's door at nine in the morning. We had both been dead asleep, but the Smith & Wesson was in my hand before I knew it. I motioned Luce to get behind the bed.

Another three bangs. I was pretty sure I'd heard that knock before, but there was no point in taking chances.

"Yeah," I said.

"Guerin."

I put the gun in Luce's dresser, climbed into my jeans, and went to open the door.

Guerin stood in the hall with Kanellis, his partner. Kanellis was about my age, with longish brown hair and a whippet-like build. He had changed his look since the last time I'd seen him. A corduroy jacket and gray knit tie, over a hunting plaid shirt and tight trousers. Professorial.

"Morning," I said.

"I heard about your house. You two all right?" Guerin said.

"Yes, thank you," said Luce formally. She had slipped on a robe. Kanellis gave her a once-over that wasn't lost on any of us.

"You don't look otherwise occupied," Guerin said. "Let's take a ride."

I nodded and closed the door while I dressed.

"Are they looking into the bombing?" Luce said.

"They're looking into Broch. If we're lucky, it's the same thing."

She kissed me. I lingered, feeling the heat of her body through our clothes as strongly if we were naked again.

When I had returned from my meeting with Ostrander and Rusk the night before, Luce had been awake, waiting up with Marcie. As soon as we were alone, Luce had pulled me to her. The terror and pain of the night evaporated, and she clung to me with all of her strength and cried out for me to hold her back just as fiercely. At the end she gasped and bit into my shoulder, hard enough that later, when we were parted and damp with each other, we didn't know whether the blood spots left on the pillow were from love or from our earlier wounds.

I threw on my jacket, kissed her once more, and asked her to call Leo to tell him I'd come by Swedish as soon as the cops were done with me. Hoping to myself that it didn't turn out to be a long wait.

I followed the detectives to their car, a silver Lexus sedan. Guerin drove. Kanellis took the back, granting me the passenger's seat. Standard procedure, if a pair of cops had to escort a suspect without using the mobile jail cell that is the rear seat of a police cruiser. I was getting more uneasy by the minute.

"Your personal car?" I asked Guerin. He nodded. "Nice," I said.

"Better be. I commute from Everett."

"Where's our commute today?"

He made a gesture that I interpreted as *Wait and see.* He drove to the freeway entrance on Montlake and up to I-5 and north. We caught up to the clouds, and an occasional raindrop tapped on the windshield. Tap. Tap. Too heavy to ignore. Too light for even the slowest intermittent setting on the car's windshield wipers. Seattle water torture. Guerin satisfied himself with turning on the wipers for one beat every half mile.

He took the 85th Street exit. I could feel Kanellis's eyes on me from the backseat. When Guerin turned onto Highway 99, I suspected where they might be taking me. On this stretch you couldn't throw a pine-shaped air freshener without hitting a car for sale.

Guerin pulled into the lot of a business called Apex Auto. It was a very short climb to whatever summit the name aspired to. I counted eight cars on the lot with stickers in the windows. None of them were less than fifteen years old. Or washed. There were no colorful triangular flags or giant inflated gorillas around the lot as decoration. Just a cinder-block structure holding an office and two repair bays. The big metal bays were closed. The door to the office was open.

There were three official cars in the lot as well. Two pristine blue-and-white cruisers and an unmarked dark gray panel van. A man in a black and yellow CSI jacket was loading tackle boxes into the back of the van.

"This Broch's place?" I asked Guerin.

"Have you been here before?"

"No."

Guerin called to the man in the CSI jacket. "You set?"

The man nodded. "Harold's finishing now. You can go."

Kanellis popped a nugget of gum out of its foil packet and put it in his mouth. Very casual. "Let's take a look inside."

The two of them bookended me as we walked past the uniform minding the door. I knew what I was likely to see. Guerin and Kanellis knew that I knew it. But they wanted to watch my face when it happened.

We walked past the tiny reception area into the back. It was an ugly room. There was one large desk in the approximate center, with two chairs in front of it and four dented metal filing cabinets up against the wall. The drop ceiling was made of spongy white tiles, and the lumpy gray carpet was stained brown in places from years of coffee drips and spills.

Seated behind the desk was the body of a man. He was upright and only his balding head tilted forward, like he was glancing down for something he'd dropped some-thing on his lap. He had been middle-aged and burly, dressed in a tie and white shirt with the sleeves rolled up partway to show thick forearm muscles. An unhealthy percentage of the shirt was no longer white. Blood had stained it rust, from what looked like two high-caliber gunshot wounds in the center of his chest.

"You know him?" said Guerin.

"No. I assume he's Broch," I said.

"Torrance Xavier Broch," said Kanellis, like he was making an introduction.

"And this," said Guerin. I followed him through the open side door into the repair bays. The overhead lights were on full, and the contrast with the clammy office was startling. Guerin led me over to one of the oil pits and looked down.

Another corpse was lying seven feet down in the pit. The bodybuilder who had braced me at the Market. He was face down but his head was turned in profile, and I could see one very blackened eye and a yellowish bruise on the side of his head where I had clubbed him with my fists during our fight. He wore a skintight black tank top. His oversized biceps looked deflated. There was a small puddle of dried blood under his head.

"Best guess, until we have an official cause of death, is that the fellow in the pit was killed with that," Guerin said, pointing to a heavy socket wrench on the floor of the bay. One of the CSI team was picking fibers or other bits from the floor around it with tweezers. A large plastic bag was open next to him, ready for the wrench itself.

"The side door to the shop was forced," Kannelis said. "Maybe the killer broke in early and waited for Broch.

Or he busted the lock, and Mister Muscle came out to see what the noise was, and got himself clocked from behind. Then our guy went into the office and shot Broch at his desk."

"Broch had a gun in his desk drawer, which he didn't touch," said Guerin. "So the first killing might have been quiet enough not to alert him."

"You think it's a professional hit?" I asked.

"I'm not thinking anything out loud just yet," he said. From outside came the sound of a large vehicle pulling to a stop in front of the bay doors. "That'll be the M.E. Let's get out of the way."

"They haven't been dead long," said Guerin once we were back outside. "Sometime late last night or very early this morning. Nobody nearby heard any shots, so far as we know. A parts delivery guy found the bodies at six A.M. Where were you since about ten last night?"

"Besides ducking an explosion?"

"Besides that."

"I dropped Luce off at her apartment, with her friend Marcie. I visited my friend Leo Pak at Swedish. He saved us from the bomb. Then I went back."

"Luce is the blonde?" said Kanellis. He put a little spin of appreciation on the words that made me want to feed him his gray knit tie. He noticed, and smirked.

Guerin spoke sharply enough to yank our reins back. "You went straight to the hospital? Straight back?"

"I stopped downtown. Got my head clear."

"Downtown," Kanellis said, like I said I'd visited Neptune.

"Lemme toss a bomb in your direction. You can see how chipper you feel after."

"And you never saw Broch before just now," said Guerin.

"No. And if the killer broke in here to get to him, then he knew Broch by sight."

"Maybe," said Kanellis. "Of course, the business *is* registered to Broch. And he *is* the guy sitting at the big-ass desk inside. Not a tough mental jump."

"The guy lying in the pit had a tough week," Guerin said. "Somebody tuned him up pretty good a day or two ago, judging by his face. You know anything about that?"

"I told you what I knew about Broch. And what I could guess."

"While carefully avoiding any statements about your own actions during the past few days."

"You're not giving me a ton of credit. I wouldn't tell you about Kend Haymes and Broch one day and then rush right out to put bullets in Broch the next."

"Maybe you didn't have a choice," Kanellis said. "Maybe Broch was coming for you. A little preemptive strike. Who could blame you, a scumbag like that?"

I looked at Guerin. "Please tell me you're coaching him on interrogation soon."

"Hey," said Kanellis.

"I'll talk to Miss Boylan," said Guerin, "and your friend Leo."

"Are we done?"

"For now. But stay where I can find you, live and in person. I'm going to have more questions for you once we figure out who else had it in for Broch."

Great. If Guerin's call to Luce to confirm my alibi wasn't enough, now we wouldn't be going on that vacation I'd promised. I might talk her into going ahead without me. But I could predict how that far that conversation would get. Luce could be harder to budge than an Abrams tank once she set her mind to something.

Chapter Twenty-Eight

Leo was near collapse when I finally got to the hospital. The pretty freckled nurse said he hadn't slept all night, just sat and breathed and got out of bed to pace, when he thought he could get away with it.

I took him to Addy Proctor's. My phone had been ringing all morning. One of the calls had been from Addy, letting us know that her spare bedroom was made up and ready for Leo or me or whoever needed it, while we figured out what to do next. The second important call had been from the fire department, setting a time to meet an arson inspector at the house later in the day. All of the other calls were from reporters. The information that the fire had started from a bomb had leaked, and the press was ravenous for more information. I deleted their messages.

Stanley padded happily to snuffle at our hands as Leo and I entered Addy's home. No room in her house was any larger than twelve by twelve, all of them made bright by bleached wood flooring and pea-green flowers stenciled along the top of each wall. I felt too large and clumsy whenever I visited, although the confines didn't seem to bother Stanley.

Leo nodded mutely as Addy told him where he could

find things he might need. He lay down on the spare bed while she was in midsentence about the washer and dryer.

"You made it," I said to him. He was already asleep.

Addy and I came out to the living room.

"The doctors gave him clearance to leave?" Addy said. She sounded doubtful.

I nodded. "He just needs rest."

"Hmph. I suppose you'll tell me the same about you."

"I only need the number of a good housekeeper. My place is a mess."

"Funny." She sat down on an overstuffed brocade armchair, which half swallowed her. Stanley plopped down to lay his head on her small foot. "All right. You can be all Irish about it. But you'll pardon me if I show concern when houses begin exploding around people I care about. It scared me. I didn't like that feeling one bit."

Even Stanley looked reproachful.

"You're right," I said.

We sat for a moment.

"I can't even recall what it was like, the first time a bomb went off around me," I said. "It's been too long. So maybe I'm too much of a wiseass about how it might feel to a civilian."

"Which you are, technically. And so is Luce."

"Luce is double-tough."

"And she acts even tougher. I don't care. Take her and leave. That, in case you didn't know, is the civilian response to someone trying to murder you. The sensible response."

"I have to stay in Seattle." I told Addy the bare facts on the late T. X. Broch, and Guerin's insistence that I remain close.

She tapped her foot impatiently. "And when have you ever given a good goddamn what the police asked you to do?"

"When running would make me the prime suspect in a double homicide."

"Piffle."

"Piffle?" I laughed.

"Don't change the subject. You don't bother about being a suspect. You just want to feel your hands around the throat of the person who threw that bomb."

Her description was so on target I could feel my fingers clench a little at the idea.

"You do have a way of putting shit, Addy."

"My old advice-column expertise. Cutting through horsecrap is half the job."

"I thought you used to be a librarian."

"I've been working since I was fourteen. I've done a lot of things. And you're being slippery again," Addy said.

"Okay," I said. "I want to handle my problem myself. Not just trust the cops to do it."

"Is that satisfaction worth Luce?"

I knew the answer Addy wanted to hear. I just wasn't sure if that answer would be the whole truth.

"I'll talk to her," I said finally.

"That's something, at least."

I said my good-byes and left. I pointed the truck toward downtown, and Luce's.

Would she leave with me, knowing what it meant? Addy was right. The cops weren't the real problem. I could have Ephraim Ganz run interference with the law.

The problem was that I didn't want to go. Luce would recognize that about two seconds after I asked her.

I was on my way up Madison when a call came from Barrett Yorke.

"Van," she said. "Please." She spoke as if she was forcing each syllable out of herself.

"What's wrong?"

"It's Parson," she said. "He's in trouble."

"Where is he?"

"He's been hiding at a rental house our family owns. Van, he says that he's sure someone's following him. Driving past the house. He thinks they want to kill him."

"Who?"

"I don't *know*. I'm not even sure if Parson knows."

"Did he tell you exactly where he was? Over the phone?"

"Yes. God, was that bad?"

Rusk had pressured Barrett earlier. If he shared my suspicions about Parson, the ex-cop probably had her phone tapped.

"He needs to go to the cops, Barrett. Now."

"I told him that. He won't do it. He says he won't be safe, even with police. You should have heard him, Van.

He sounded like a little boy. He wanted me to come and get him. But if someone really is trying to kill him . . ."

"Tell me," I said. She gave me an address in the U District, north of the campus. I found a gap in the traffic and swung the truck through an intersection. An oncoming tanker-trailer hit its brakes and horn simultaneously, even though it had a full two yards left before it would have crushed me.

"Don't tell him I'm coming," I said. "I'll help him. But you call the cops. It's safer if Parson's in custody, no matter what he thinks."

"Why are they doing this?" Barrett asked. I wasn't sure if she meant the police, or whomever she believed was after Parson, or somebody else.

"Stay close to your phone," I said, and hung up.

I made it to the University District in ten minutes by pushing the truck to its limit down 23rd over the Montlake Bridge, and hammering through every yellow light and a couple of red ones up the grade toward campus.

The address Barrett had given me was two blocks from the UW's Greek Row. This close to the frats and sorority houses, the curbs were packed with cars. I left the truck in a random empty driveway.

The house was a bungalow, large for its type but still smaller than most of the houses around it. This neighborhood had scaled up a couple of notches since the last time I'd seen it. If it was a rental property, the Yorkes probably targeted visiting professors and other temporary university staff as tenants. I watched the house for a few moments. Nobody walked past the windows. The front porch was aggressively quaint. The door was painted a royal blue, with plants in terra-cotta tubs on either side of it, and a small garden hose to water them wound around a gnome. Bright and cheery.

The bungalow's yard was one big rock garden. Easier to maintain rocks than a lawn. I walked around and cut through the next-door neighbor's yard and jumped the low fence.

There was a heavy thump, from somewhere inside the house. I froze and listened. The noise didn't repeat.

No one in the backyard. I climbed up and over the porch railing to look into the window at a dining room and part of a living room space beyond. Still no movement inside.

I tested the back door. It was unlocked. A little unusual, for this part of town. I opened the door so slowly that a tortoise could have gotten out of its way. The hinges ticked ominously but made no creak.

When the door was just wide enough for me to slip inside, a man's voice spoke upstairs. Indistinct words, and not from a TV set. I closed the door just as slowly as I'd opened it, and as if in response, the voice spoke again. Just loud enough for me to make out the word *Where*.

Then another sound. A whap of impact against flesh, followed by a cry of muffled pain. A creak sounded from the room above me, and the smack of another blow.

Tell us, I caught this time.

Us. So whoever was doling out the punishment, there was more than one.

I took Dono's Smith & Wesson out from under my coat, and stepped cautiously toward the central hallway and the stairs. Looking up, I could see a small landing with three doors leading off it. One left, one right, and one center. A game show.

"Nobody knows you're here 'cept us," the man said, easier to hear without a ceiling between us. "This is just for starters, Yorke."

The first step didn't squeak under my weight.

I heard Rudy Rusk say, "Did you move it? Where?"

"We didn't. We didn't open the boxes." Parson Yorke said. I barely recognized his voice, it was lower-pitched and watery. The last two words came out as *tha bosses*.

"Fuck that," said Rusk. "You made bombs out of it. You threw one at Shaw. Is he working with you? Does he have the Tovex?"

"I didn't know what was in them—"

"Again," Rusk said. There was another whapping blow.

"Fuck, he's out," said the first voice.

"When he wakes up, use the knife on his eardrum," said Rusk.

I had taken advantage of their conversation to climb another three steps. They were in the room to the right of the landing. A shadow moved across one doorway and into the next, and I realized that the doors all led to one larger room, across most of the upper floor. There was the *tap-click* sound of a spring knife opening.

Parson Yorke wasn't my favorite person. But I couldn't leave him to get his ear swabbed with a switchblade. And I wasn't going to get a better opening.

I ran up the last steps in two bounds and came fast around the jamb of the right door, my gun leading the way.

The room was a master bedroom suite. Two men flanked Parson. The huge kid was slumped almost sideways in a plush linen chair, facing me. He wasn't tied to the chair, but I wasn't sure he would be capable of getting up. There was a lot of blood on his bruised face and triple-XL shirt. It stained the chair's ivory linen fabric. The men were ready for a corporate meeting, in light blue dress shirts and neckties. I didn't know the one holding the blade. He had brown feathery hair and there was more blood on his left hand.

"Hey Rude," I said, keeping my eyes on the man with the knife. I had the S&W pointed at his chest. "Throw it away."

He hesitated. I tightened my finger on the trigger and he quickly tossed the knife into the corner of the room. He glanced toward the bed, where their suit jackets were draped over the footboard.

"Don't," I said, and stepped into the room. It was a big enough space to allow me to stay well out of reach and keep a clear field of fire.

"We've got this, Shaw," said Rusk. "Stand down."

"You first."

"We beat you to Fat Boy, here. But you can still turn a profit out of this."

Parson moaned. One of his eyes was puffed shut and abraded.

"Move away," I said.

Rusk sneered. "You're helping him? This fucker tried to blow you up. He destroyed your house."

"Move." The knife man took a step back. Rusk stayed put.

"Twenty years minimum, for murder with a firearm," he said.

I aimed at his groin. "Doesn't have to be a kill shot."

There was the sound of footsteps downstairs. I moved sideways to get clear of the doorways.

"Vince," called the knife man. "Get backup."

Two guys, their guns within reach by the bed, two doorways, and at least one other player downstairs. And Parson was starting to wake up. Tactically speaking, this situation was going rapidly to shit.

Vince was not the brightest. He came charging up the stairs. I aimed at the top of the center doorway and fired, blowing a large chunk of the wooden frame to tooth-picks. Rusk and the knife man hit the floor. My ears buzzed with the sudden blast.

"Stay there, Vince," I shouted. The noise of the shot had revived Parson. He blinked and mumbled something, trying to press himself upright.

"Rudy?" called Vince from the stairs.

"Backup, goddamnit," said the knife man, rolling behind a chair. I pressed myself against the wall, where an armoire offered a small amount of cover. Rusk was up on his knees behind the linen chair and aiming a pocket derringer at Parson's temple.

"Drop the gun," he said to me.

"Nope."

The knife man edged toward the suit jackets on the bed and I fired another shot one foot in front of him that smashed a baseball-sized hole in the drywall. He ducked back behind the chair.

"We're leaving," said Rusk, "and he's coming with us." Parson numbly tried to pull away and Rusk yanked him back by the ear, using Parson's wide body as a shield.

"He can't tell you where the Tovex is if he's dead," I said.

"I'll chance it." Rusk angled his head toward the door. "Go," he said to his partner. The knife man ran out of the room and down the stairs without any more invitation.

Rusk hauled at Parson, pressing the derringer against the nape of Parson's neck. "You come with me, or I'll find your sister and cripple her," he hissed. "Get the fuck up."

Parson stood, wavering. Rusk kept his eyes on me. I could shoot him in the face. I was good enough to risk the shot, just past Parson's cheek. But that was my only option. Any chance to wound Rusk was gone. Maybe I'd have an angle when they made their way down the stairs.

Unless Vince and the gang were waiting to blow my head off the second I stepped out of the bedroom.

Rusk was almost out of the door, shuffling sideways with Parson between us. Parson looked at me, with his one sorrowful eye. He nodded.

And threw himself backward.

His huge mass bowled Rusk over and the two men toppled out onto the landing. Over six hundred pounds hit the slim railing and crashed through like it wasn't there at all. I ran forward as they fell twelve feet to land with a boom that shook plaster dust from the ceiling.

The front door was open. I didn't see the knife man, or anyone else. I dashed down the stairs, gun pointed. Still no one. A car screeched away from the curb in front of the house.

Parson and Rusk had landed on a slim hall table, completely smashing it and the decorative vase atop it. They were both on the floor, and moving. Rusk crawled dazedly toward the door. I smacked him on the back of his head with the barrel of the S&W. He slumped.

Parson made a gargling sound, hands clutching at the wall.

He was choking. Maybe he had hit the table wrong, or caught Rusk's arm in his throat. His face was all tones of crimson, flushed skin under the darker streaks of blood. I forced his head back and stuck my index finger down his throat. Air rushed into his lungs with a wet pop. He flailed at me and moaned.

"Lie still, damn it," I said. I felt his throat close again, down past my finger, and his thrashing became frantic. I didn't know the house. Was there a med kit anywhere? Parson's one visible eye bulged.

The garden hose. On the front porch. I jumped over Rusk's unconscious body and ran to where the hose was wound around the gnome. The blade on my knife was sharp. I sliced a foot of rubber tube from the middle of its length in less than ten seconds.

Parson's foot kicked a dent in the wall. I pinned his arms with my knees and yelled at him to stop thrashing. I didn't want to pistol-whip him, too, just to save his life. His huge body heaved, almost throwing me off. I grabbed his head and forced the tube down his throat and he coughed and gagged, just as air whistled into the tube. His body went almost limp as it focused completely on taking in oxygen.

We lay there, three large men collapsed in the shambles of the small hallway, like drunks in the grips of the world's worst hangover.

I gave Parson the okay sign. "You can breathe?"

He weakly returned the affirmative. From far away outside, I heard police sirens.

"You owe me, Parson," I said. "Help me save Elana. Have you seen her? Found her a place to hide?"

He hesitated. And nodded.

"Do you know where the Tovex is?"

He made a fractional head shake, and winced in pain against the hose.

273

"Thumbs-up or -down. And fast. Can you tell me where Elana is?"

Affirmative. He pointed at Rusk. Then again.

The sirens were definitely coming for us. Two cars at least and maybe a motorcycle. I checked Rusk's pockets and found an iPhone with a funky yellow-striped case.

"Yours?" I said to Parson. Thumbs-up. "You called her? Texted her?"

Negative. I turned the phone on, held it up for him. Parson tapped the Maps.

I looked at the list of recent addresses. The first was the bungalow, right here. The second was in the Ravenna neighborhood, just a mile north of us.

"Here?" I said. Affirmative. The sirens stopped outside and LED lights streaked the foyer of the house in whirling red and blue. I erased the address from Parson's phone.

When the cops stormed in, I had already tossed my gun away and had my hands raised in surrender. They didn't shoot me. Maybe my luck was on the rise.

Age Seventeen

Dono and Willard and Dono's lawyer, Ephraim Ganz, all turned to face me as I walked into the Morgen. In the middle of the bright afternoon, just enough sunlight fought through the grime on the high windows to allow Dono to keep the overhead lamps turned off, like he preferred.

The three men sat at the end of one of the long plank tables, where the illumination was marginally stronger.

Dono waited until the door had closed behind me.

"Elana's been arrested," he said.

I dropped my school backpack. "Why? For what?"

"Held on suspicion of grand larceny," said Ganz, "by Sultan County."

I looked at Ganz, then at Dono. He nodded confirmation. "We can talk here."

"She was arrested for Gallison?" I said. "She didn't have anything to do with it. Not really."

"The evidence says different, Van," Ganz said. "The Sheriff's Department found Elana's fingerprints on a tank of something like welding fuel left at the scene."

Fingerprints. But Elana hadn't touched the gear at all. She hadn't even seen it. I'd hidden the rod and the tank and everything in the locker in the back of the truck before we—

Before she and I had dropped off the truck together. Dammit. Elana had been pressing me for details about the Gallison job. She must have come back and opened the locker to find out what she could, just to satisfy her stupid curiosity. And she'd been careless in what she touched.

It wasn't hard to read Dono's face. *I told you, boy.* We'd fought that night about my recklessness, as he called it, in accepting a ride from Elana. I had argued that without Elana's help distracting the cops, I'd be in jail, so her poking around that night had worked out pretty darn well for us. Until now.

"That's just circumstantial, isn't it?" I said. "Her prints could have been on that tank for months."

Ganz shook his head. "The two patrol officers can place her near the Gallison office that night. She gave them a tale about coming home from a friend's and being assaulted, before giving them the slip. So right off the bat she looks suspicious. Yesterday the county detectives identified her prints and tracked her down at school."

"She called Willard from the sheriff's office," Dono said, "and Willard called me. That's why Ephraim is suddenly representing Elana, as of this morning."

Ganz glanced at his notes. "Before I got there, they pressed her to identify the friend she was visiting, and she couldn't. Add all that to the fact that a few hundred grand of optical lenses are missing from Gallison." He shrugged. "It's enough for them to work hard on unraveling her story. Right now, she's taking my advice and not saying one word more."

"Can they make a case?" Willard asked. It was the first time he'd spoken. He hadn't looked at me once since I'd first walked in. The three men were so varied in size they were like different breeds of canines. Ganz would be a Jack Russell terrier, Dono a muscular Doberman, and Willard—the big man would have to be one of those extinct dire wolves like the drawing I'd seen in the museum, the dog version of the saber-toothed tiger.

276

"With her priors," said Ganz, "I'd say they have a case and probably a conviction."

Holy shit. "Priors?"

"Elana's been arrested before," Willard said.

"Twice," Ganz chimed in. "Once for theft, and once for a fight with another girl that got out of hand and turned into a complaint of assault. Probation, both times."

There wouldn't be any probation this time. Not for a G.L. rap.

"We have to give the lenses up," I said. "That's what they want."

Dono looked at me.

"It was my job," I said. "It's my call."

"It was your field operation," Dono said, "because you wanted it, and I let you."

"If the lenses are sold, we can buy them back."

When my grandfather was at his angriest, he became very still. He hadn't moved a hair in the last minute. But now, as if recognizing that, he placed his palm lightly on the tabletop.

"If obtaining the lenses is even possible," he said, "what do you imagine the police will say when Elana changes her tune and hands them over?"

"They'll want a full confession," I said automatically. Then I realized what that meant. They would have Elana walk through every detail. Where the special thermal rod and other equipment had come from. How she got into the building. How she cut through the window.

And when she couldn't explain any of that, or demonstrate that she knew how to use the gear, the cops would know that she'd had at least one accomplice. Whom she would also have to give up, if she wanted to skate.

"I'm not an adult," I said. "I can take the heat."

Ganz whistled. Willard actually looked a little startled.

"Chivalrous," Dono said, in about the same way he'd sometimes call me *clever* when he thought I was anything but.

"You're seventeen, kid," said Ganz, "and I know the Sultan D.A. It's an election year and Gallison is big news there. He'll push to ignore your age. In trial *and* in sentencing."

"But if we give up the lenses—"

"Not an option," said Dono.

I looked at him. "So I'll owe you."

"It's not the money, God damn it."

"Jesus." I walked around the table. "You're worried about saving your own ass, right? If she tells the cops about me, then they'll turn around and look straight at you."

Dono was back to imitating a petrified tree again. "Be smarter than that, at least. A felony record would hang on you like an albatross for the rest of your life."

I didn't even know what the hell that meant, but I was too mad to care. Mad that whatever alibi Dono would invent for his whereabouts that night, it would be sure to hold up under scrutiny. It would be her word against his. And mine, if I played along.

Letting a fifteen-year-old girl get tossed into long-term juvie just because she made one dumb move sounded like the very definition of scum.

I looked at Willard. "Tell me you're not going to let Elana take this. There's got to be something we can do."

He grunted. "We can pass some money around. The youth center there is privatized. Somebody up top will have their hand out. If Elana keeps a good record, she'll be released before the max."

"One year," Ganz said, "with the right judge."

I stared. "A year in jail." How could they be so fucking casual?

"If Elana cooperates," Ganz amended.

Willard took a deep inhale. "I'll convince her."

He would. I had no doubt of it. God.

Ganz said some words about filing with the county for something, and scurried out the door. Willard didn't say anything at all as he left.

Dono and I were alone at the table. A minute passed, with him considering me, and me trying not to think about him.

"What would you do," he said at last, "if it had been you who left your prints on the tank?"

For once, I was ahead of my grandfather. I knew damn well that I would go to juvie rather than name names. But I wasn't Elana, and she wasn't me, and I could survive any place Sultan County put me.

"I'm going home," I said.

"It's nobody's fault, you know. Just damnable luck."

Easy to say, when you were on the right side of the coin flip.

I decided to take the long hike up onto the Hill instead of catching the Metro. On the steep slope of the Denny overpass, just as my legs were starting to get good and rubbery, a rattling Celica sped past and blasted its horn for no other reason than to scare the shit out of me. I should have been pissed off. But I didn't have anything left to give the Celica driver. My anger had steadily narrowed from Dono and Ganz and Willard and Gallison and the whole stupid world, to zero in right where it belonged. On me. I had let Elana give me a ride, so that she knew where the truck was. I was the one she had saved that night.

And when it was all said and done, I was going to be the one to let her take the fall.

Chapter Twenty-Nine

Ephraim Ganz and I walked out of the North Precinct of the SPD almost twenty-four hours after my arrest. He nodded to a younger man with a lawyer's satchel sitting in the lobby as we passed.

"Well," said Ganz, "you beat Rusk out of the door. But not by much."

"That was one of Ostrander's people?"

"Um-hmm. Not even a partner. If he's here, it's because the deal's already been cut and Rusk just needs a ride home."

"Rusk and his goons beat Parson Yorke half to death."

"Rusk says it was the other way around, that the big boy attacked them when they spotted his car and came to the house to question him."

"How'd that story fly?"

"About as well as you claiming to have found that Smith and Wesson just lying around at the scene. But Rusk stuck to his version, and so did you, and here we are. Everybody's too excited about finding Yorke."

The news about the explosives had broken. *Shattered* might be a better word. I'd told the cops that Barrett had called me about her brother, and that when I went to find the kid, I had overheard Rusk interrogating him about the missing explosives. It was true enough to hold up, and it got the cops very interested in the origins of the Tovex that had been flung through my window. A sewage storm of legendary proportions was building around HDC, with Maurice Haymes at its center.

The downside was that everyone had concluded that Parson must be my mad bomber. And there wasn't much evidence to indicate otherwise.

I picked up my pace to keep up with Ganz, who wove through the other pedestrians as easily as a mongoose through tall grass. "Parson told me he doesn't have the explosives. I believe him."

"But you're certain that he helped Kend Haymes steal them. Why wouldn't he be your guy?"

"I don't think Parson ever knew what he and Kend were taking. I saw the security video of the theft. The cases of Tovex were unmarked. And while Rusk was beating on him, Parson claimed that he and Kend never opened the cases."

Ganz looked skeptical. "The boy would steal dozens of heavy cases and never ask what it was?"

"Parson thought Kend was about the best guy who ever walked the Earth. Maybe Kend thought it would be safer for Parson if he kept the kid uninformed. He asked for help, and Parson jumped. But the next thing Parson knew, Kend was dead. Since then his life has gone straight to hell. He can't even barter the explosives with the cops."

"So who does have the repulsive things? The missing girl, what's her name?"

"Elana Coll. She might have helped with the theft. But I'm sure that whoever murdered Kend and Trudy at the cabin must have the Tovex now."

"The police are theorizing that Parson killed Kend and the Dobbs girl." Ganz pointed and we hurried to make the crosswalk. "They didn't say as much, but they have the look that all officers of the law get when they're about to close a big case. Like overfed cats."

"No. I'm guessing Kend stole the Tovex to ransom it to his dad and pay off his loan shark. But then Broch turned up dead, and the explosives are still missing."

"It gets better," Ganz said, smirking. "An inside source tells me police found a call record from Parson Yorke's cell phone to none other than the late T. X. Broch."

I stopped. Ganz kept walking and I rushed to catch up.

"You're kidding," I said.

"To the same rotten business where they found him dead. The kid knew Broch."

"Damn. Maybe Broch killed them after all, and Parson killed Broch, and the cops will find the cases in the trunks of Broch's crappy used cars."

Ganz handed his valet ticket to a parking garage attendant. "What kind of loan shark would want bombs?"

"One who doesn't care about money, maybe."

And that spun me off on another mental thread, as we waited silently for Ganz's car. It turned out to be a Tesla, as long and as shiny as a knife blade.

"Holy shit," I said. "I should have gone to law school."

"No good for you," Ganz said regally. "They won't let you shoot people to win arguments. Except in Small Claims. Drop you somewhere?"

"You can take me to the impound lot. I was in a hurry when I parked."

"Luxury car my ass," said Ganz. "It's a wonder they let you drive anything at all."

I didn't expect to be done breaking traffic laws yet. It had been a full day since Parson had shown me the address of Elana's new hiding place. If there were even a chance of finding her still there, I'd run every red light in town.

Chapter Thirty

I parked on the street and sprinted up the back stairs to Luce's apartment. After the fight with Rusk's men and a night spent in overheated interrogation rooms, I needed a change of clothes, and I needed another gun. I'd stashed Dono's Glock behind one of the baseboards in Luce's kitchen.

Luce had two locks on her apartment door. The spring lock on the knob, and the deadbolt, a heavy Medeco. It took separate keys to open the door, and I always unlocked the deadbolt first.

The key turned. With no resistance. If Luce were home, she'd have thrown the bolt. Habit. I'd seen her do it every time we walked in. If she were out, she'd have locked it behind her.

I stepped to the side. Put the other key in the spring lock, turned it. Pushed the door open.

"It's okay, Van." Luce's voice. "I'm here."

I didn't move. "You all right?"

"I'm fine. Just don't overreact, okay?"

I looked inside. The apartment door opened on a stubby hallway that separated the kitchen from the bedroom. I could see about half of the kitchen from the doorway. Luce was sitting very upright at one of the two dining chairs she owned, in her frayed Blue Moon Tavern T-shirt and tan jeans and bare feet. She nodded to me, and angled her head to indicate that someone was on the other side of the table from her. I came farther in, to where I could see.

It was Elana. She was standing, tall and stiff, one hand steadying herself on the three-burner stove and the other hand out of sight in a calfskin shoulder bag. She had dyed the scarlet out of her hair and chopped it even shorter, into a tufted black pixie cut.

She didn't say anything. Her eyes were big and her wide mouth parted. Jacked on fear or adrenaline or both.

"I promised her if she stayed, you wouldn't turn her in," Luce said.

I looked pointedly at the shoulder bag.

"You were chasing me," Elana said.

It was the first time I'd heard her voice in a dozen years. I had forgotten it. It wasn't low and warm like Luce's. Elana's pitch was higher, like she'd learned to talk girlishly and never stopped. Or maybe it was just tight with strain.

"I thought I was chasing Trudy," I said.

"Trudy's dead."

"I know. So do the cops. They'll be looking for you."

Those green eyes glanced behind me at the open door. "Who are you working for?" Elana said. "Willard?"

Luce shook her head. "No one, El. I told you."

"Willard told me to stay out of it," I said.

Elana nodded. "He was right."

"What happened to you?" said Luce.

"You should keep away," Elana said to me as if she hadn't heard.

"The hell I will." I said. "Someone tried to blow us up. Where's the Tovex?"

Luce shot me a look that meant *Rein it in*.

"You're here," Luce said to Elana, placing her palms flat on the table. "Tell us what's going on."

Elana looked at me. "You first."

"I found the bodies at the cabin. I thought that somebody ought to give a shit about what happened to you."

"Why? You think that you owe me something?"

"Elana, please," said Luce. "We're your friends."

"Her friends end up dead," I said. "Or damn close. You should see what Parson looks like now. You're out of options, Elana. Haymes and his goon squad will run you into the ground, if the cops don't."

She stared. "That's insane. I didn't kill Kend."

"What Haymes really cares about is getting his explosives back, before somebody uses them to take down a building. Where are they?"

Elana didn't answer. Just looked at me, and then at Luce.

"You don't have to be afraid of Broch now," Luce said. "He's dead."

"Dead?" Her green eyes darted to me. "You did that?"

"I was about to ask you the same thing."

Elana's face twisted. For a moment I thought she was about to burst into tears. Then another emotion broke through to the surface. Something like satisfaction.

"Move away from the door," she said.

"They'll find you, Elana."

"I won't give them the chance." Her hand shifted inside the bag. "Move."

I backed up, through the stub of a hall and into the bedroom. Elana walked forward, keeping her distance from me, and with half an eye on Luce as well. She stepped sideways and out of the door.

"El," Luce called, but she was already gone.

I closed the door.

"Damn you," Luce said. "Why did you push at her? I could have talked her into giving up."

"No. She was making a point."

"She wasn't here to threaten me. She wanted help."

"Money. Parson can't be her personal cash machine anymore."

"And someone to talk to, most of all. Didn't you see her? She's terrified."

"She should be. She's got the cops and Rudy Rusk after her. And somebody else."

"Who?"

"The person who helped her and Kend and Parson steal the explosives from Kend's father. That's the only way I can make sense of it. Kend wasn't a thief. Parson might be able to figure out an alarm schematic, he had

288

some kind of savant gift for that. But somebody wanted the Tovex, and probably got the schematic for Kend by bribing some HDC employee. I thought that it was Broch, putting the squeeze on Kend Haymes. Now Broch is dead, and people are throwing bombs at us, and Elana still looks ready to shoot anything that gets in her damn way. So there's got to be somebody else. Somebody who betrayed Elana and Kend."

"Then why wouldn't she go to Willard? If anyone could protect her, it would be him."

"She doesn't trust him."

"That's crazy. He'd never hurt her."

"Probably. But that doesn't mean he'll help her, either."
Like before.

"God." Luce stood and instead of coming to me she stepped to the fridge and opened the cabinet that hung above it, where she kept the liquor. She took down a new bottle of Walker Red and cracked the seal.

When she reached for the second glass I said, "Not for me." She set it back and poured herself a shot and downed half of it.

Addy had asked what Luce was worth.

I pulled the same chair that Luce had been in closer, and sat down. "Albie missed the thrill, you said."

She squinted at me over the glass. "Changing the subject?"

"Only halfway. I'm not chasing Elana to get some high off it."

She took a taste of the Scotch, less a sip than touching the liquid to her lips while she thought. "If you want us safe, all we have to do is leave."

"Maybe."

"If what you want is payback for your house, or for people threatening me—"

"For you."

Luce made a strained smile at my rapid answer. "Then you know what I think about that. Revenge makes everybody pay double."

I folded my hands. The fingers on my left were a fraction tighter, from the last time I'd been wounded and the Landstuhl surgeons had to do some delicate work on the soft bits in my forearm.

"You know I'm not sleeping much," I said.

She looked at me for a moment, and then set her glass on the stove and came to sit across from me. "I do. I wake up and you pretend to be waking up with me." Her eyes flickered to the scars on my face. That happened so rarely with Luce now that I noticed it more when she did it. "Are there dreams? Nightmares?"

"Sometimes. But those are just reminders." I thought about the words I needed. "In combat, everything can be confusing. Chaotic. That's what all the training is for. So that when you can't see and you can't hear and nobody's telling you what to do and you're scared all to shit, you'll still do the thing that's likely to keep you alive."

Luce nodded. Waited.

"That's how it was for me, lots of times. Sometimes even when we were the guys making the enemy piss their pants. And then one time, it wasn't. There wasn't any fear or uncertainty then. Just action and reaction."

Luce had a dreamcatcher in her kitchen window. A wooden circle containing a spiderweb pattern of threads and colored beads, with a crystal at the center that tossed shards of the spectrum around the room when the sun touched it.

"It wasn't a thrill," I said. "It was clarity. So clear that sometimes the world after that day seemed like something I was looking at through the wrong end of a telescope."

"Is that how you feel now?"

"No. I haven't felt like that for a long time." I tapped a splash of orange on the table. "But the dreams. They sometimes come before. And I've been dreaming."

Luce reached out. She didn't take my hand, just rested her arm on the table and touched my knuckles with her fingertip, like I was touching the bit of orange light.

"Like Dono," she said.

I looked up at her.

"After a job. His dark moods. You know."

"I don't."

"Jesus, you don't. I forget how young you were when you left. You never got to know him as an adult." She ran a hand from her forehead back through her marigold hair. "It was hugely obvious whenever Dono had something going, even though he wouldn't say a word about it, of course. He'd be bright-eyed and laugh more and be superfocused on everything. Like caffeine or cocaine without the jittery parts."

"I remember. His accent would come out when we worked."

"Right, that too. Then there was afterward. He'd crash. Practically in mourning, except that he'd snarl instead of weep. The first time I noticed, I thought the job had gone terribly wrong."

"It probably didn't matter how it went."

"Just that it was over," she said, nodding.

"I'm not my grandfather."

"You're not a crook, no. But you both—" She hesitated. "You both need something more than you can get from a regular life. It was crime for him, and for you when you were a kid. Maybe it was the Army later. The chance to live intensely. With different rules. I don't know what exactly."

"Dono always wanted to be a pirate. Maybe I'm a different kind of throwback." I forced a grin.

She made a joke of considering the question seriously. "I could see you as a samurai. All swords and rituals and battle. You'd have thrived then."

Not so much today, was the implication. Great in the moment. Fuck-all at planning for any kind of future.

I exhaled. "All that is learned behavior. It can be unlearned."

Luce's face was impassive. My phone rang.

"Elana's here," Leo said on the other end. I knew exactly where here was, because I'd given Leo the location. He was parked in Addy Proctor's ancient Saab wagon, outside the Ravenna address I had found on Parson Yorke's phone. Elana's new hiding place.

Luce could hear Leo's voice across the tiny table, and stared at me.

"I'm on my way," I said.

"You're going after her," said Luce.

I put the phone to my chest. "She might turn herself in, like we hope. Finally tell the cops who her partner was. Or she could be looking to skip town with the explosives, now that the heat's on."

"Jesus, Van."

"If the same asshole who tried to kill us goes after her, she'll need help."

"So now you're protecting her?"

"She's on the move," Leo said.

"Leave the line open," I said to him. I reached down and popped the baseboard and removed the Glock.

Luce went white. "How long has that been there?"

"You weren't here when I had to hide it."

"Go."

"I don't have time to explain. I'm sorry."

"I'm sure I'll manage. Get out."

Leo's voice popped through the air. "She's going east on 65th. In a green Audi."

Luce shut the door behind me, and threw the bolt. It made a very decisive sound.

"Stay on her," I said to Leo, as I raced for the exit.

Chapter Thirty-One

Leo followed Elana, and I crossed the city to connect with Leo. She stayed off the freeway. They wound down through Ravenna and across the Cut, through my neighborhood—or what had been, my house now being what it wasn't—and farther south into the Central district, where I joined the loose parade.

We drove past the large campus of Garfield High School, where Elana had once planted a kiss on me. It seemed impossibly long ago.

Leo came back on the line. "She turned left on—shit—Fir, I think it is. Where the hell are the street signs in this town?"

"We do that to mess with the tourists. Give her some room. She might be watching for a tail."

All three of us drifted farther down into the Central district, which was like a patchwork quilt of Seattle's gentrification. Abandoned houses sagged next to shiny townhomes that looked as though the construction crews had just finished smoothing the cement. Rows of residences gave way to industry.

Elana led us on a long path south on Rainier and finally turned onto Cloverdale. My stomach muscles started to tighten. Was she going where I thought she might be? The feeling intensified over the next few blocks.

"She stopped," said Leo. "Corner of Volpe Street."

I knew exactly where it was.

"Don't park," I said. "Keep going past and circle around. I'll meet you one block north."

Leo was standing outside the Saab when I pulled in behind him. We walked back to the block where Elana had finally stopped. There was a liquor store at the corner, with a dumpster against its wall. The dumpster made good cover as Leo and I peered around the edge of the building.

"She went in there," Leo said.

The place had no sign. It looked barrel-bottom. Years of exhaust soot had etched the mortar and bricks. The windows were smoked so that no one could see in. A black Lincoln Town Car was parked in front. In contrast to the building, the Lincoln was pristine.

Leo grunted. "Great neighborhood. You know this place?"

I nodded. "The North Asian Association for Trade."

"North Asian?" said Leo. "Like North Korea?"

"Like Siberia."

A metallic-blue BMW came fast up the street and stopped with a hiss of antilock brakes half a foot behind the Lincoln. Two men got out.

The driver was a hard case. He didn't look like anything else. His hands and forearms were veiny and corded with muscle, outside the pushed-up sleeves of his shiny black tracksuit. His face was long and Asiatic around the eyes, and his cheekbones and brow ridge stuck out like knuckles in a clenched fist. The blue edge of Bratva tattoos showed at his collarbone. A hitter, no question.

His passenger I knew very well, from his high forehead right down to the tips of his pointed thousand-dollar shoes.

"And that there," I said softly, "is Reuben Kuznetsov."

Chapter Thirty-Two

The Russian mob?" Leo asked.

"*A* Russian mob. It's less organized than you might think."

"Still bad news, I gotta assume."

"Yeah." What the hell was Elana into?

We watched the front of the North Asian Association for Trade. Reuben and the hard case had gone inside. Nothing was visible, behind the smoked windows.

"So the girl is what, a gangster?" said Leo.

"I don't know."

"How do the North Siberia Whatevers tie to her boyfriend getting dead?"

"I don't know that, either."

Leo nodded. "Good to have quality intel."

The front door of the NAAT building opened. The brutal-looking hard case in the black tracksuit came out first. Two other men in athletic wear followed him. Lower-level Bratva thugs, both short, both burly.

Reuben K came out.

Elana was holding his hand.

She had changed clothes, probably back at her new hiding place. A blue wraparound blouse cut low, and trim gray pants that made the most of her already impressive legs. Reuben held the passenger door of the BMW open for her and she stepped in. The three heavies started to climb into the Lincoln.

"Come on," I said. Leo and I ran the length of the block back to the Saab. He tossed me the keys on the fly. I took three left turns very fast and there was an anxious half minute before we spotted the Beemer and the Lincoln cresting a hill two blocks away, heading for Rainier.

"Doesn't look like the girl's a hostage," said Leo.

"No."

"So why are we following them?"

"Because she still might lead us to the explosives."

"And because you're pissed off."

"That too." I was a fucking embarrassment, is what I was. I'd been played by Elana Coll. Worse yet, I wasn't even sure why.

We followed them south and then west to Columbian Way and the West Seattle freeway, and up onto the tall bridge fifty yards above the Duwamish River. Down on Harbor Island, cranes the heights of office buildings loomed over freighters. Steel shipping containers swung with surprising speed and grace through the air to settle onto railroad cars. The same train tracks extended north through the acres of petroleum fields, with their white tanks looking like a colony of massive barnacles stuck to the island.

The shiny blue BMW and the Lincoln stayed to the

right and took the exit that led to a long, slow slope down onto the opposite side of the island. It was the middle of the afternoon. There was enough road traffic to offer us cover. Still, I let Reuben stretch his lead out an extra hundred yards. Leo looked at me quizzically.

"We won't lose them," I said. "The island doesn't have a lot of roads."

The BMW took point in circling around to follow the shore of the western waterway. A quarter mile along, they turned into a shipping yard. The yard looked like a small prison. Eight-foot chain-link topped with razor wire, and a rolling gate made of iron slats with a heavy alloy lock on one side.

Across the avenue from the yard was a parking lot. I pulled into the lot and stopped where we could watch.

"BerPac Imports," Leo said, reading the sign on the building. "*Ber* for 'Bering Sea,' I guess, with your Siberian buddies."

Reuben and Elana and the thugs went inside as we watched. Elana leaned against Reuben's tall frame, huddling together in the chill air.

The BerPac building was two stories high and maybe fifty feet wide, with wood siding painted navy blue. An open dock stretched across the back of the yard, with room enough for a semi-trailer to pull up alongside the waterway. BerPac had an articulated crane, a small one by island standards, fixed in place at the edge of the dock.

The BMW and the Lincoln weren't the only vehicles parked in front of the building. There was also a GMC truck, silver with the BerPac name stenciled in red on its sides and tailgate. The GMC had four tires on the rear axle.

I pointed that out to Leo. "Those tires look brand-new to you?"

"Pretty clean."

"Uh-huh." If I thought my tire prints might be at the scene of a murder, I'd prioritize some shopping at Goodyear, too.

"BerPac is the place," I said after a moment. "I don't know if the explosives are inside, or what Reuben would want with them. But if that dually isn't the same one that was at the cabin when Kend and Trudy were killed, I'll eat its new radials."

"Which means the limp dick driving the Beemer killed them."

"Or he had it done. Best guess is that Reuben sent that mean-looking mother in the black running togs."

Leo looked at me. "And."

I nodded. "And Elana knows all about it. Maybe she even set them up."

"If all they wanted was the raw explosives, why kill two people?"

"I don't know. Kend's death would cover their tracks. That makes a kind of sense. Trudy might have just been collateral damage."

"That takes a serious kind of cold, Van."

We sat for a moment. One of the Bratva thugs came to the rolling gate and pulled it shut. The lock closed with a clank we could hear inside the car.

"So the explosives could be in the building over there," said Leo. "Or maybe they used to be, and now they're gone. I don't know a shit-ton about mob guys, but if they steal something, it's to sell it, right?"

"This is a hell of a lot of trouble and risk just to fence some commercial water gel for twenty cents on the dollar. Reuben is crazy, but it's a different kind of crazy." I drummed my fingers on the steering wheel. "He wants the Tovex. He's got some reason for needing over half a ton of explosives."

"Well, that's fucking alarming."

"Yeah." Reuben wasn't a terrorist of any stripe, so far as I knew. Like most crime families, the Bratva's politics started and ended with themselves. It always came down to money, or power, or both.

Reuben had the explosives that Kend had stolen. T. X. Broch had held the paper on Kend's gambling debt. Most loan sharks had bigger fish backing them up with ready cash and protection.

Maybe Reuben's family had been backing Broch. Which meant Reuben could have thrown Broch some pocket change, and owned Kend from tip to toe. Broch wouldn't have been stupid enough to protest.

I could easily imagine Reuben dangling the offer of freedom in front of Kend. *One night's work, steal a few boxes from your father, and all debts are forgiven. Easy as sin, my friend. Elana, bring your man another drink.*

Had Elana been playing Kend from the very beginning? She could have introduced Kend to Reuben at Willard's card game. Made sure Kend learned about Broch's ghost book. Let him run, set the hook in deep, and let Reuben reel him in.

And now she was dressed to show off every asset, holding hands with Reuben K and smiling ear to god-damn ear.

"If there's a race for stupid," I said, "I'm in the lead."

"They were your friends, brother," Leo said, eyes still on the far-off gantries and shipyards and looming walls of stacked containers. "I'd have trusted them, too."

"It's not like the Regiment. I trusted our guys. I trust you. With these people I should know better."

He shrugged. "Do we call the cops?"

"There's nothing to hand them. Nothing that would permit a search warrant. If we can get a line of sight on where the explosives are, I know a detective who might be able to make things happen." I thought about it. "The girl's our best angle. If I threaten her with what we already know about Reuben, maybe she'll turn on him to save herself."

"That means talking to her when her new boyfriend's not around." Leo looked back at the BerPac building. "Or are you thinking extraction?"

I grinned. "Let's not storm the castle just yet. Even if

we managed to magic her out of there without our asses getting shot off, a kidnapping beef isn't going to help our case with the cops."

"Kind of exposed here, Sarge," said Leo, looking around.

He was right. The parking lot was for a private business. It wouldn't be much longer before someone came out to ask us what we were doing there.

Leo nodded to the overpass. "We get some field glasses, and we could watch the place easy from under there."

"And follow her when they leave, and wait for a better opportunity. Works for me."

"Hold up," Leo said. He pointed. "By the dock."

Through the chain-link I could make out the black tracksuit of Reuben's lieutenant and another thug in red walking out of the side of the BerPac building. As we watched, they climbed down a ladder at the edge of the dock, and out of sight.

"Shit," I said. "They have a boat." If they left by water, we couldn't follow.

In ten minutes the two men climbed back up the ladder and went back inside. We waited. No one came out.

"What now?" said Leo.

I figured we had another hour before the sun dipped below the landmass of West Seattle. Already the shaded spots were stretching their fingers toward the east. If Reuben and Elana left by boat when it was full dark, we might not see them at all.

I fished my phone out of my back pocket.

"Calling for pizza, I hope," said Leo.

Food wasn't a bad idea. But there was something else we needed more.

Chapter Thirty-Three

Lad, I'm starting to dread your voice on the phone."

I had heard Hollis over the speedboat's engine before I could really see him. It was dusk now, the shadows melting together to blend water and land. He pulled alongside a dock at the southern tip of Harbor Island, and I jumped onto the bow.

The speedboat was a twenty-two-foot Stingray that looked as common as concrete but could pierce the waves like a javelin. When I'd been home for my short visit last year, I had found moorage for the boat in Hollis's marina, where he could give it the occasional glance, and keep the salt air from eating through the engine hoses.

"You made good time," I said, climbing into the cockpit.

"Said you were in an all-fired rush, didn't you? Wait, now!"

I had taken the helm and pushed the throttle forward. Hollis sat down heavily, his fleece pants sliding him treacherously sideways on the bench seat. I swung us to port and we sped across the narrow waterway.

"You didn't say anything about abduction," Hollis said. His face was pinker than usual with the wind and cold, and his ears were nearly white. Over the fleece he wore a cherry-red anorak.

"There's a blanket in the cabin," I said. "Wrap it around yourself."

"Christ, you're a pushy bastard. I'm fine."

"For cover, not cold. You look like a marking buoy."

He sighed, but acquiesced. I slowed the speedboat as we neared BerPac. Its dock was on the opposite side of the water, about a tenth of a mile away. Reuben's boat was still there, tied up at the ladder. It was a glossy Cobalt powerboat, thirty or so feet long with a high black profile. Not quite a cigarette boat, but close. It had a small hoist installed on the rear transom, maybe for winching a dinghy out of the water. A boat ideal for fast runs to the islands and trolling for salmon close to the coast. I didn't imagine Reuben had fish dinner in mind.

A couple of the businesses on this side of the water had the lost look of abandonment. I picked one that looked especially ramshackle, and shifted into reverse to tie the speedboat to its vacant floating dock. This close to land, the odor of rotting milfoil pushed away the smells of the engine's exhaust and the clean salted air.

"So that's BerPac," Hollis said, peering over the bow. "What can you tell me?"

"I called my man at the Port. BerPac there has two standard twenty-foot containers scheduled for delivery in the wee hours tomorrow night, on the feeder ship MV *Osprey*. The *Osprey* will take delivery of the containers

306

from a Maersk Panamax, which is out in the Sound right this very minute."

"Containers of what?"

"Ah." I could feel gleeful energy radiating off Hollis. "It's a regular delivery, apparently, three or four times a year. BerPac does nearly all its business with Norilsk. You know what that is?"

"A town in Siberia."

"A *mine* in Siberia. One of the biggest in the whole fucking world." Hollis was talking like he hadn't learned this himself in the past half hour. I let him. It was faster than interrupting. "They mine for metal. Nickel and copper, but they extract platinum, too."

"So it's two containers of metal?"

"Don't think of it as two containers, lad. Think of it as forty-two million dollars. That's the insured value."

Jesus. No wonder Hollis looked delighted.

"But Reuben owns the damned metal already," Hollis said. "Or his family does, which amounts to the same thing. BerPac places a wholesale order with Norilsk for whatever the stateside buyers want. Customs signs off on the containers. It's all legit."

I thought about it. The navy blue of the BerPac building looked as black as the channel water at night. Lights blazed upstairs and down in the building. I didn't see anyone pass the windows. Four men and one woman inside the little fortress, and the place was as quiet as an orthodox church.

"Why does BerPac import metal in the first place?" I said, mostly to myself. "Scratch that. Why does the Bratva Brotherhood?"

"A front?" Hollis guessed. "It's useful to have an authentic business."

"Could something else be in the containers?"

Hollis waggled a hand. "Odds are Customs would open them up and have a look-see before letting them come ashore. You know how careful they are these days."

A few tons of metal. Two twenty-foot containers that could be hauled by a couple of semi-trailers. Too much weight for anything smaller. How much weight?

"Do they weigh the containers?" I said. "On the freighter, do they put them on a scale?"

"No. The weight's recorded on the manifest of the port of origin."

"Which is in Siberia."

"Of course."

"Where Reuben's father can make up whatever rules he wants."

Hollis's face went slack with surprise. "You think the manifest is false."

"I think if I were a Bratva boss with Old Lev's pull, and I wanted to get money into the States, I'd make sure that the manifest had everything just perfect, except for about fifteen percent less on the weight. Bribe or threaten a handful of people, and it's done. Customs opens it up on this end and sees metal, like they expect to, and let it go.

Reuben's job is to remove the extra platinum or copper before handing off the metal to the legitimate buyers."

"Skimming from themselves," Hollis said. "I like it."

I did, too. Except that the BerPac shipment would be business as usual for Reuben and his family. It didn't explain his need for the explosives. If he even had them.

"Why the sudden interest in the Kuznetsovs?" Hollis said. "There's something profitable, I hope?"

"Elana's with Reuben K."

I felt Hollis lean towards me. "*With*, as in *in bed with*?"

"I assume."

"You didn't mention that on the phone."

"She wasn't a question. BerPac was."

"And Willard?"

"I don't know."

"So he could be part of whatever you're poking your nose into. Were you planning on telling me any of this? Or just waiting until I stepped smack onto the bear trap?"

I looked at Hollis's wide outline. "They might have killed me, Hollis. They might have killed Luce."

"You don't believe that. Not Elana."

"I believe Reuben could. And if Elana's shacking up with him, then maybe she and Willard aren't what I thought."

"Listen to yourself. Willard's not your enemy, lad. Next you'll be thinking I want you dead."

Out on the water a flock of gulls screeched a stuttering exchange as they winged just above the surface. I turned back to BerPac. The same lights were on. Still no movement.

"Thanks for bringing the boat," I said.

"That's all you have to say?"

"I get it. You want to stay neutral. I won't ask any more favors."

"Jesus, boyo." Hollis shook his head and climbed out of the cockpit onto the dock. In the deep black of the unlit shore, it looked like he had vanished.

His voice came out of nothing. "I loved your grand-dad. He was a fine friend," he said. "But he was also the loneliest bastard it's ever been my fortune to meet."

"And I'm just like him. I've heard this song."

"No, lad," said Hollis. "Even Dono knew he had to trust somebody. Else what's the fucking point?"

Age Eighteen

"You unnerstand the rules?" the corrections officer said to me in a bored and rapid voice, as she unlocked the door leading to the exercise yard. "No touching. No walking around. Stay seated. No foul language or aggressive behavior. No passing anything. You pass anything at all, we got to do the whole search thing again, and that means full search for her. You unnerstand?"

I did. Cavity. I wasn't sure what they were so afraid I might hand to Elana. They'd already taken my jacket and checked my shoes and socks and patted me down and given me a swipe with the metal detector wand. She wasn't a damn serial killer. I also understood the rest of the rules. The guards had run through them twice already, pointing to a plastic board with the same instructions printed on it in big red letters, like the NO RUNNING NO SPLASHING NO DIVING rules at public swimming pools. I guessed Sultan County Detention was used to dealing with morons on both sides of the fence.

The exercise yard was smaller than I had expected. Just a rectangle, half cement and half mangy grass, inside the twelve-foot chain-link. Picnic tables with benches on either side took up the part of the cement ground nearest the door. Some of the tables were already occupied with inmates and their families.

"There," the C.O. said, pointing to an empty table. I sat. The table and benches were made of the same hard plastic as playground equipment, molded and painted to mimic wood. All the pieces were bolted to the cement.

The guard left, but other C.O.s stood around the tables, not quite out of earshot. The families talked low. Very low. If I tried, I could hear a girl, maybe the inmate's younger sister, weeping at the next table over.

A different door opened, farther down the windowless wall of the center, and the guard came out, leading Elana. Not every juvie institution made their inmates wear standard issue, but Sultan did. Elana wore a white T-shirt and rust-colored scrub pants. The day was too warm for her to need the matching long-sleeved V-neck I saw on other inmates, with SCD JUVENILE RESIDENT emblazoned on the back.

She looked around, spotted me, and walked toward the table without being prompted. Her brown hair hung loose to her shoulders. No headbands allowed in detention. They hindered searches.

Elana looked pretty much the same as the last time I'd seen her, except for the shorter hair. Same high cheekbones and slightly tilted eyes. Her wide mouth was set in a straight line.

She sat down and looked at me.

"I thought you would be Willard," she said. "The guards just say there's a visitor."

"I'm your stepbrother, today."

"Why?"

I spread my hands. "To see how you're doing. They wouldn't let other people except Willard come here for a long time."

"No visitors except primary care, first six months," she said, like a recitation. "It's a privilege. Which I lost before I even had it, so that added another three months."

There had been problems, I knew that much, even if Willard was close-mouthed with Dono, and Dono similarly curt with me where Elana was concerned.

"What happened?" I said.

"Fights. You have to fight here. There are gangs."

"Three months to just get the privilege back, or—?"

"Three months added time for the fighting. Plus for some other things." She didn't elaborate.

I asked, even though I dreaded the answer. "How much time?"

Elana scowled at me. "I'm not mad at you. Don't get all guilty."

I realized what it was about her that looked a little different. Motion. She didn't fidget anymore.

"I should have stepped up," I said. "Told the cops what happened."

"Then you'd be an idiot. I'd still be here, and you'd be on the other side of this building with the boys. Or maybe doing time in Monroe."

"You'd have gotten a lighter sentence. Maybe none at all if I could've convinced them you weren't in on it."

"And you would have had to give up Dono. Uncle Willard explained everything." Her voice was bitter.

At the next table, the family with the weeping young girl was led away by one of the guards. The inmate had already left, but the girl kept crying anyway. Nobody paid any attention.

"I'm sorry," I said.

Elana shrugged. "It's done. Another fourteen months and I'll be out. I'll have my GED by then. I can get my driver's license in here, too."

Fourteen months. Christ. Almost two years in all. That was more time than Dono had served in County when I was a kid.

"You're okay? You're safe?"

"Tell me about Watson instead," she said. "It's boring without news."

So I told her some of the stories from senior year. Mostly tests I had muffed and parties that had been lame, trying not to make anything sound like too much fun. Elana listened and made a few of the right expressions in the right places. When there was three minutes left in our allotted half hour, I stopped right in the middle of a tale about Rob Firmino and his buddies filling lockers with water balloons. We were silent for a moment.

"What do you need?" I said. "When you get out?"

"When I get out, I'm going to pick a direction and drive away. For a while, at least." Her feline eyes looked at me. "You can resist the urge to visit me here. That's what you can do."

"The County says you get an allowance to spend. I could—"

"I don't want to see you again," she said. She stood up and the C.O. started to walk over to our table.

"Elana."

"All done?" said the guard.

"Done," Elana answered. The guard nodded and headed for the exterior door. Elana took a step or two backward in the same direction.

"Call it my present," she said to me, before she turned and followed. "I just had a birthday."

Chapter Thirty-Four

Shortly after noon, the hard case with the clenched face came out of the BerPac building and climbed down into the Cobalt powerboat. He started the engine and cast off the lines and drove the boat north, up the channel and out of sight.

There was no sign of anyone else around the building. Not Reuben, nor Elana. They had been inside BerPac for twenty hours. She had walked in on his arm. Practically with a spring in her step.

So why did I feel so uneasy about her?

I dialed Leo, in the Saab. "Any movement?"

"I'd have called."

"The big son of a bitch just drove the boat away."

"You going to follow him?"

"We want the Tovex. Or the girl."

"Better decide on which," Leo said. "We can't stay here forever."

No we couldn't.

"Hold position," I said. "I'll bring the boat across."

Clouds had been slowly rolling in from the west all morning, black and heavy with intent. The temperature at noon was colder than it had been at midnight.

February was determined to go out fighting.

I met Leo at the car. He sat in the driver's seat, watching the front of the BerPac yard. He didn't look fatigued, or bored. He looked positively sharp. I realized I felt the same.

"They're waiting," I said. "For the feeder ship to deliver the metal late tonight. I don't know why they're waiting. Or why they had to be here for so long beforehand. But they're here, and it's coming."

Swallows nested in the unconquerable thickets of blackberry bushes that grew alongside the roads and between the towering columns of the overpass. The dropping air pressure had them on edge. They swooped in and out of the brambles at top speed, never losing a feather.

"When it's dark," I said, "I'm going in."

Leo was very still. "I got faith, man, but—"

"No fireworks. I just want a closer look. The Tovex takes up a lot of space. If it's in the building, I'll spy it through a window, or at least figure out where it could be stashed. If I get eyes on it, we call Guerin and he brings the whole damn world down on BerPac."

"What about Elana?"

"What about her?"

"Come on. I've seen the girl. Guys would belly-crawl naked through scorpions for less."

"We weren't like that."

"Then what?"

I thought about it. "Our childhoods were both pretty

316

twisted, in similar ways. I always figured she and I were more alike."

"And you're hanging on to that."

I looked at him. He shrugged.

"If this was just about retaliation, what would we do, Sarge? We'd set up in one of those old shacks across the water, wait for the Russian dude to walk by a window, and *bam*. Simple. But we aren't doing that."

"That's a line I don't want to cross. Unless I have to."

"So obviously there's something else you want."

There was. I wanted Elana to tell me how. How she'd gotten so tangled with the Kuznetsovs that she could see her friends dead. How we had gotten our lives so fucked up.

But I wasn't going to get that chance. The best I could hope for was visiting her in prison. Again.

"If you're going in there tonight," Leo said, "you'll want spare magazines. And some darker clothes."

He was right, the workout gear I was wearing wouldn't cut it. I had some black jeans and a jacket as spare clothes in the speedboat. The right costume for the job. If Elana Coll could dress to kill, so could I.

Oh.

A realization, so stark and solid that it trapped my breath in my throat.

Damn.

"Leo," I said. "I think I've made one king-sized hell of a mistake."

He turned.

"Elana isn't a killer. But she's aiming to become one," I said. "She's going to kill Reuben."

*

Elana had run from the murder scene, and Willard had lied to me. Those two facts added together had poisoned my thinking about the whole situation from the start. Every move that Elana made, I had been working on the assumption that she had helped to steal the explosives, and was trying to stay one jump ahead of whoever was after her. The cops. Rusk. T. X. Broch. But none of them even knew Elana was part of the equation. I was the only one who had been chasing her.

She had gone to ground, after fleeing from the cabin. She had used Trudy's credit cards for money and Trudy's studio to hide in because it was better if everyone thought that Elana Coll was dead, for as long as she could pull it off.

Camouflage. Concealment. While she tried to find out who had murdered her friends.

Elana had been surprised when Luce and I had told her that Broch was dead. She knew Kend was a compulsive gambler. She had been looking for his loan shark. When she found out he was already dead, her first impulse had been anger, at me, thinking I had stolen her revenge.

Luce and I had told Elana something else, too. We'd

told her about Haymes, and the Tovex. She'd been confused about why Haymes and his attack dog Rusk would be trying to find her. I'd said the word *explosives*, and she'd replied with a blank stare. Perplexed. She hadn't known about the theft at all.

But she'd put some pieces together, right there in Luce's kitchen. A dead loan shark plus explosives, and a mental lightbulb had switched on. Elana had left immediately. Gotten herself looking fine. And ventured out to find Reuben K.

"If she wants him dead," Leo said, "should we leave her be? Let her do it?"

I looked at BerPac. In the gloom of the overcast sky, it looked isolated and forsaken.

"She been in there for a full day," I said. "Something's wrong."

"Back to Plan A." He looked at the low ceiling of clouds. "Weather's for shit."

"Snow, or rain, or both. Maybe winter works in our favor for once. It wouldn't be the worst thing to have everyone huddled inside that building."

He grunted. "Gotta love your optimism, man."

I turned to Leo. "I'll be breaking laws. If this goes sideways, maybe I'll have to break some big ones. You're not an accessory, not yet. And you don't have to be."

There was bright amusement in the tightening of skin across his cheekbones. "Kinda forgetting they tried to blow me up, too."

"That is a fact."

The wind pressed harder outside, making the swallows launch into another frenzy of loops and spirals.

"We're at the party," Leo said, "so we might as well dance."

Chapter Thirty-Five

Leo steered the speedboat in tight to the concrete pilings, ten feet under the docks. The outboard under its rubber cowl burbled gently as it pushed us forward through the darkness at a half knot. The cloud cover was so low I could have spiked it like a volleyball.

We'd agreed that the open dock was the best insertion point for the heavily fenced BerPac yard. I stood up on the starboard bow. When we were ten yards shy I held up a hand. Leo eased off on the throttle. Before the boat could drift I jumped high and grabbed the support beam with gloved fingers.

Under me I heard the outboard's growl deepen as Leo nudged it into reverse. I began to make my way in the opposite direction, toward BerPac. Left hand, right hand, left hand. Like the obstacle course at Benning, only with more splinters and the possibility of getting shot at the end.

The fence between the yard next door and BerPac extended out from the concrete dock over the water. I had to hook the toe of my boot through the chain-link, and reach to get my fingers on it. Very slowly. The metal rattled softly with my weight, and the fence pipes creaked.

At least there was no razor wire. I climbed around the fence edge, biceps stretched to the limit with the strain of moving like a sloth.

On the other side now. I got hold of the concrete lip of BerPac's dock, took a big inhale, and hauled myself up, behind the stunted pyramid of the articulated crane's base. I lay on the concrete and looked around.

Nothing and no one on the dock. No cameras on this side. No motion sensors on the exterior lights. Just three lamps along the building wall and a whole lot of lovely shadows. I hunched low in one of the pools of black.

The boat was tied back in its place, down at the bottom of the dock ladder. Through the dim, I could see something at the rear of its cockpit that hadn't been there before. A long rectangular crate, six feet by three by three, like a casket for an especially fat corpse. Too small to hold the Tovex cases, unless they had unpacked and repacked all of the water gel tubes into the crate. I didn't have the tools or the time to open it and find out.

And I had a different priority now. Where was she?

Light shone weakly from two windows in the building. One upstairs, one down. The windows were placed high, intended to maximize sunlight more than allow any view of the outdoors. Nothing moved inside to interrupt the light.

I took the Glock from my jacket pocket and ran along the chain-link to the corner of the building. The room revealed itself through the window degree by degree as I edged closer. It was an office area with messy desks and filing cabinets and no people at all. The opposite door was open to the far room.

I could see the side of a chair through the door. And a woman's leg, a long calf in gray pants and short black pumps.

There was a second window farther along the near side of the building, light beaming out onto the fence. I went around the corner toward it. A stubby length of dowel rod propped the window open an inch. I waited. No sound came from inside.

I peered through the glass panes. Elana lay slumped in the chair, her back to me, with only a patch of dyed black hair visible. The chair was tall and upholstered in brown leather, out of place in the empty, crude space of what looked like BerPac's garage. Elana's head lolled to the side. I watched her for a few heartbeats. She might have been breathing. But her hand hung slackly from one wooden arm of the chair, and her legs were splayed without grace. A painful sprawl. She would wake bruised and sprained in half a dozen places. If she woke at all.

Drugged. Or so exhausted she might as well be.

A rustle-thump of movement. Upstairs. Were all of the men up there?

I waited. No one came into the room.

Could I get her out? There was the door to the office area I'd seen. The big garage door to the front was closed and locked. One more open passage out into what looked like a hallway, where the stairs must be. I tested the window. It swung easily on its hinges with only a tiny tick of sound.

I hoisted myself up and gently set a boot on the windowsill. Listened again. I sat on the sill and dropped into the room.

Elana had not stirred. There was another brush-step of sound from the floor above. Then only the lengthy, even wave-beat of Elana's breath.

In three steps I was beside the chair. Her face was so relaxed that her jaw hung loose, with her wide bottom lip half an inch off center. I checked her eyes. Her pupils were a fraction too wide to be normal. I could sling her over my shoulder and go out the back to the dock. Signal Leo, or swim with her limp body to the opposite shore, if I had to.

Motion behind me, reflected in her unseeing jade iris.

I spun, raising the Glock. Made it halfway before the Taser barbs hit me.

Every muscle from my scalp to my toes seized in anguish. It was like being simultaneously crushed in a vise and torn apart by horses. My lungs were desperate to scream but unable. My last clear vision was of the hard case's brutal face, twisted in triumph, in the hallway door. In the next instant I was slammed to the cement floor so hard that the world went very far away.

The worst effects of a heavy electrical shock wear off quickly, if you survive. I was just rounding the moon and coming back to Earth when I heard Reuben K's merry laugh.

"Hit him again," he said.

And I was long, long gone on a rocket of agony.

Chapter Thirty-Six

Terror woke me. Not all the way. Not the way that banishes a nightmare almost instantly. I was very tired. My mouth tasted foul. We rose up and dipped down, and then the *We* suddenly resolved into me and Elana, lying next to each other on the coarse non-skid floor of a boat's deck. My jacket was gone, and I could feel the spiky surface through my T-shirt. It was still nighttime.

The up-and-down motion was lulling. I didn't want to fall backward into sleep again. Couldn't help it.

Then I snapped to, as hands grabbed my shoulders and ankles and I was lifted very rapidly. When they dropped me I was just alert enough to expect it, and tucked my chin to my chest for the big *whump* of impact. My teeth clenched on a wad of cloth in my mouth.

"Awake?" asked Reuben from somewhere. I tried to look. My wrists and elbows were bound tight behind my back. Same with knees and ankles. I could writhe, a little, but not turn.

The hard case in his black tracksuit came into my line of sight, blurred and tilted on the diagonal from my point of view. He stood feet planted, staring at me. I had a moment of clarity that told me he was about to stomp on my head.

"Kasym," said Reuben.

The hard case looked up.

"Turn him over so he can see," Reuben said. Then something in Russian, maybe repeating the order.

Kasym put his boot on my shoulder and kicked so that I rolled to the other side and onto my face. I squirmed to get back upright.

Reuben walked over, leaned down to look at my face from a foot away, like he was peering into a fish tank. His high forehead and snub nose came into startling focus.

"Hey, you look lively," he said. He grinned at Kasym. "See, you gave the bitch too much. A half dose is just about right."

I tried to spit the rag out, but couldn't seem to get my mouth and tongue to coordinate. Reuben tapped my cheek.

"Party time, my friend," he said. "A little Z blend."

That explained why I was so out of focus. They'd doped me. The same stuff used for severe insomnia. Or date rape.

Reuben plucked the cloth from my mouth with his long fingers. I coughed through shuddering breaths, as Reuben strode away to sit on a stool by a broad work-table. Kasym joined him. He glared at me for another moment and then picked up a tool and bent over to adjust something on the table.

The drugs they'd given me weren't so different from Ambien or other sleep meds. Shake it off, Shaw.

Reuben smirked. "Kasym's pissed because you almost killed him, did you know? He gave you the big zap with the stun gun back there, but fuck if you didn't get a shot off." He leaned back on the stool to look at Kasym, who wouldn't meet his eyes. "Right past your ugly head, eh?"

My vision was clearing. I could see farther away now. Beyond Reuben and Kasym at the worktable there was a large window, and through its panes I could see the shiny white curve of a petroleum tank, looming in the near distance. A roof arched thirty feet over our heads, made of wooden beams and aluminum sheeting. Despite the roof, it felt and sounded like we were outside. The Cobalt bobbed gently nearby. My mind assembled these facts groggily and came up with the conclusion that we were in a large boathouse next to the petroleum farm.

Where was Elana? I twisted and was half surprised when my body cooperated. Elana and another man lay against the wall of the boathouse. Elana was facing me, bound like I was, with thick plastic zip ties around her arms and legs. A strip of tape across her mouth held in a lump of rag. She moved weakly against her bonds. The man was dressed in paint-stained coveralls. He was not tied and gagged. He might be dead.

"Come here." Reuben's voice. "You'll appreciate this."

He grabbed the zip tie that was around my elbows like a handle, and dragged me across the floor. He was strong enough to make it a fast journey. The sharp plastic of the zip tie bit into my skin, and the blessed pain whisked away the last of my dizziness.

Reuben propped me up at the corner of the workbench. "Look," he said, striding over to the boathouse wall. A dozen large black duffel bags were stacked near the door. Reuben lifted one with a grunt of effort and unzipped it as he brought it over to me. "I brought the party."

There were three steel boxes inside the duffel, each about a foot square and half an inch thick. Each box was open at the top, revealing the inside packed with gluey, cream-colored Tovex depressed into a *V*.

Shaped charges. Closed on all sides to direct all the kinetic force of the detonation into that *V*. The blast wave would slice through just about anything. They used charges like them to demolish buildings.

"We made fifty of these in the last two days," Reuben said.

The two squat Bratva thugs came into the boathouse. They were wearing blue pants and matching coats. JUR-LEE PETRO was in white across their backs. Kasym barked something at them in Russian, and they each picked up two of the large duffels and shuffled out the door as quickly as they could manage under the weight.

Reuben yanked the stool around, where he could sit in front of me. His eyes looked electric, despite the bags of fatigue underneath. Cranking himself up with coke or meth or maybe both.

"It takes some hours to set all these in place. Like dominoes. But oh, it will be worth the wait." He winked at me. "You'll see."

"What will I see?" I asked, slurring the words.

"The *culmination*," he said. "I like that word. It's a new one, for me. You have been one stinging pain in my ass, but now I understand why. It was destiny. Because you were supposed to be here."

"Where?" There were tools on the worktable. Maybe something that could cut through my zip ties. If I could convince Kasym and Reuben that I was still out of it.

"Don't play stupid," Reuben said, as if he'd heard my thoughts. "I know you've been watching, you and your *uzko glaziye* friend. He's the same little shit who was at your house when Kasym threw our message through your front window, yeah?"

A message. The bomb had just about killed all three of us, and it had most definitely killed the house.

Leo. He'd have been watching BerPac. He would have called the cops.

"No, no," said Reuben, giggling as he read my mind again. "No help from him. We thought you might come poking in, little rat. After he put you on the dock, I called some soldiers of my own. They waited for him to come back to shore. Bye-bye, slant-eye."

Oh, Christ.

Kasym walked away from the worktable to the boat. He pulled a wheeled trolley over next to the dock's edge, and then jumped down agilely into the cockpit and disappeared into the cabin.

"I don't understand," I said. *I dunn unnerstan.*

Reuben sighed. "Maybe we inject a quarter dose, next time. Okay. No point in bringing you here if I don't explain."

That's right. I'm too stoned. Go away and let me see what's on the table before your killer, Kasym, gets back.

Instead Reuben reached up to the table, took a roll of duct tape, and wound a long strip of it around and around me and the four-by-four workbench leg. Stuck. Very. I tried hard not to let the comprehending fear show in my eyes.

Reuben grabbed a bucket off the floor and marched over to dip it into the water, on the end of a slim rope tied around its handle. He came back and tossed the water into my face. The icy salted jolt across head and chest felt like a baby brother to the Taser. I gasped.

"Good," said Reuben. "Not much time, and I want you to know everything I've done for you. Fucking ingrateful shit."

He was angry. Happy, too, because Reuben was always the happiest of psychopaths. Anger was new.

"I tried to bring you in," he said. "I told you the world was changing. That it was my time. Didn't I?" He pointed at the remaining duffel bags. "That's my proof, right there. Kasym dials his phone and all the little bangs go off like firecrackers. They destroy the retaining wall at the waterline. They cut holes in those fat tanks, and let the pressure inside spray the jet fuel and diesel for a hundred meters. A tsunami of one million barrels all over that corner of the island and all the water around it. And then—"

He gestured with his thumb at Kasym, who was using the Cobalt's hoist to lift something large and heavy off of the powerboat, out of the crate I'd seen in its cockpit. It was bluish-white and shaped like a stretched barrel. I'd seen some like it, on airfields in Iraq.

An MK-77 incendiary bomb. Kerosene and white phosphorus and God knew what else. Over seven hundred pounds of Hell.

Reuben gave me a huge smile. "And then we light the match."

*

There was no point in pretending any longer. I was stuck tight. "You'll kill thousands," I said.

"Oh, hundreds only. Maybe less. Not the point, really. I'm not a fucking anarchist." He said it like I'd offended him.

"Then why?"

"Magic, Van my man." He was excited now. A kid looking forward to Christmas morning. "The biggest trick in the world, with everyone looking the other direction. Police. Fire. Every-fucking-one of them. Can you imagine?"

I could. I could imagine a fire that was unquenchable, so hot that it burned right through the concrete island itself to the water. Millions of gallons floating and ablaze in the Sound. A bonfire higher than the gantry cranes, devouring the huge freighters. Crossing the eighth of a mile to the Seattle shore, where it would find a new feast in the piers and boats and buildings.

"You're going to steal the metal shipment. All of it," I said to Reuben. My voice sounded hollow.

"That's right! Very good, Van. But the metal is just money. A means to an end." He spread his arms wide, as if to embrace the world. "Right now there's more than seventy million dollars at our dock on the other side of the island, just waiting for me. We'll load it as soon as we hear the first bang, and be gone before the cops shut the island down."

"Lev will bury you. Even if you are his son."

"Papa will be dead before anyone unravels what happened." Reuben said. "Right now he's in the air, coming in from Irkutsk. By the time his Gulfstream lands here, his money will be my money. Lev will not see Russia again."

He got off the metal stool, picked it up, and calmly threw it twenty feet across the boathouse. It landed with a crash and I heard Elana cry out in muffled alarm from behind me. Kasym barely paused in loading the incendiary bomb onto the wheeled trolley.

Reuben sat down cross-legged next to me. Two buddies having a heart-to-heart.

"Lev is ancient. He didn't even question why the BerPac orders had spiked so much. I created fake companies, to buy lots and lots for this shipment. I told you. It's *my time*. And the seventy million is my war chest. The Brotherhood captains who aren't already on my side will be gone, just like him. We are *ready*."

His face distorted. The jollity and even the anger cracking like dry clay, so that the madness showed through. "I wanted you to be my friend, Van. You got the skills, the smarts. When that insect Broch came to me and said you were poking your nose into Kend Haymes, that you'd busted up his gambling place *and* his men, I laughed. Of course you were too much for him. I told him I'd take care of it."

There was a tiny bubble of saliva at the corner of Reuben's mouth. The bomb was tied to the trolley now. Kasym wheeled it slowly toward the doorway.

"And I did. I did right for you. Kasym ended them both, so no more problems from Broch." He waved a finger at me, chiding. "But you'd keep fishing. I knew you would. Right then was a very risky time for you to get too close. So we gave you a distraction. Sorry about your house, but you know. You shouldn't be attached to things."

Things like Luce, and Leo. "You're fucking bughouse, Reuben."

His slap came so fast that there was no pain at first, just a snap of my head to the left and a flash of light.

"I did you a *favor*. And you repay me by what? Trying

to skull-fuck the best day of my life?" His voice cracked. As he looked at me a new mask slowly formed, this one of sadness. "You could have been rich."

He stood and began loading the last of the duffels with the shaped charges onto the trolley, next to the incendiary bomb. Kasym stepped onto the boat and shouldered a full rucksack onto his back. He adjusted the straps as he spoke Russian to his chief.

Reuben picked up a red packet made of soft plastic from the table. The packet was about half the size of a shoe box. He and Kasym walked over to the incendiary bomb on the trolley, and began conversing. The red packet had what looked like a digital timer on the side. Wires led from the timer into the packet. As I watched, Reuben twisted the dial on the timer and red numerals appeared.

I didn't speak Russian, but I got the gist. Firebombs rupture and explode on impact. The red packet was a small bomb, probably crafted from the Tovex. It would provide the kick that would set off the much much bigger and hotter bang of the Mark 77, once there was a lake of refined fuel surrounding it. Reuben slapped Kasym on the shoulder and put the packet bomb into the top of the hard case's rucksack.

Kasym heaved his weight into moving the laden trolley out the door, just as the two thugs in their Jurlee Petro costumes came back. The duffels were gone. Most of the shaped charges, excepting the few Kasym had on the trolley, would be in place now.

One of the squat bruisers pointed at Elana and said something to Reuben.

"Yeah," Reuben agreed. He pointed to me. "Here."

The thugs walked over and picked up Elana and set her gently down in front of me. Her eyes were wild and she was drenched in sweat. They yanked the strip of tape off her mouth and she spat out the wad of rag.

The three men got into the Cobalt. Reuben started the engines and began backing out of the boathouse. He looked over and gave me a blissful smile.

"You know what the very best part is? Why I decided I needed you both to be here at the end?" he said. "When the cops eventually ID your bodies, they'll tie her to Kend and the stolen explosives. They might even think that you, hero soldier man, were working with them, building the bombs. Cable news will eat it up. Terrorist plots. Beautiful girl. Rich family."

The boat was clear of the dock. Reuben shifted into forward and the engines rumbled with power. He raised his voice over their growl.

"It's all very romantic."

Chapter Thirty-Seven

Oh God," said Elana. She was curled up, still hoarse from the cloth gag. "God."

"Elana," I said. "Elana, look at me. Get up on your knees. Now." She started moving, but I wasn't sure if she'd really heard. I bent my legs and planted my boots on the cement floor. The zip-tie bands squeezed into my thighs.

She focused on me. Her eyes seemed clear of the effects of the drug, but there were bags of exhaustion underneath.

I tilted my head toward the man on the ground. "Is he dead?"

"N-No." She'd gotten herself onto one side, but it was too precarious and she fell back. "They gave him a shot. I saw it."

"Wake him up. Hurt him, if you have to." She started squirming his way, like a worm.

I pushed hard with my feet. Harder. My boots had traction, and the leg of the worktable ground into my spine as I pushed with all my strength. I could leg-press a thousand pounds. Sprint like a motherfucker. Maybe I could tip the table. Break the four-by-four leg off. Anything.

Nothing. The table might have been bolted to the wall, for all it moved.

Elana made it to the man in the coveralls. She shouted in his ear. Bit him on the cheek.

"He's too far gone," she called.

"Then you'll have to get on your feet. Find something on the table that can cut me loose."

"He's got a little screwdriver. In his chest pocket."

"Grab it."

She went to work with her nose and chin. No whining. No delay. A smart girl in a tight situation. She worked a tiny Phillips head out of the boathouse worker's pocket, got its yellow plastic handle in her teeth, and started worming her way back.

Elana used my legs as a step to get onto her knees, her back toward me. Her hands were close to my chest. She dropped the screwdriver onto my stomach and got it into her hands.

"Start punching holes in the tape," I said. "Don't worry about aiming. As many as you can, as fast as you can."

It took a bunch of attempts before she got into a rhythm. The screwdriver's point jabbed my bicep and chest muscles a dozen times, and a dozen more, the pain welcome as each tiny dot appeared in the tape.

I leaned forward, hard as I could, like I was trying to hoist the entire table onto my back. I felt a strand of the tape pop. Another.

"Keep going," I tried to say, and all at once the tape tore and I fell clumsily on my side.

I twisted up onto my forehead and got my knees

338

underneath me. I took one practice bounce, kneecaps banging hard into the floor, and with the next one jumped up onto my feet. I leaned against the table to stay upright and see what it held.

A claw hammer, with two more screwdrivers and a bunch of painting supplies. Blunt pliers and bits of wire left over from Reuben making the packet bomb. Nothing that would cut the thick plastic of the zip ties. There was a metal toolbox, closed but lid unlatched. I craned way over and used my head to knock it to the floor. It spilled its contents with a jangling crash.

Just tubes and soldering bits and pieces and a small propane torch with pistol grip and blue fuel cylinder, probably for tiny welding jobs on portholes and copper pipes. No utility knives or box cutters.

Oh, shit.

I knew what I had to do.

I fell to my knees and worked my way over to the torch. Got the nozzle between my fingers and hopped awkwardly back to Elana.

"What are you doing?" she said.

"Stay right there," I said. "Lean against the table."

I worked the fuel cylinder of the torch in between her lower legs, just above her bound ankles. The brass nozzle pointed outward. It looked like a snout of a cartoon character, puckered up for a kiss.

"Hold very still. And don't look," I said. "Jesus."

"Are you laughing?" said Elana.

"Nervous response." I turned and felt blindly until I got the pistol grip handle between my hands. It was clumsy. The trigger was under my ring finger and pinky. I had to squeeze as hard as I could. Squeeze *click*. Squeeze *click*. *Click Whump* as the flame started, singeing the hairs on my forearm. It settled into a steady, sibilant breath.

I took two long, slow breaths of my own. Made my mind go somewhere else, where what was about to happen was just a picture on a television screen seen from far away.

This was really going to hurt.

I leaned backward. My wrists dipped toward the torch. Its flame licked my hand and I matched the torch's hiss as I got the thick plastic of the zip tie into the right spot. Was it melting? It was all by feel, I couldn't see behind me. The heat on my wrists went from bearable to the instant horror of someone sawing my hands off with hacksaws. I pulled against the zip tie, muscles popping, away from the flame. Burning plastic dripped down onto my fingers. I might have screamed. Fall backward, tip over the torch, and Elana or I or both of us could be ablaze in an instant.

Then my hands flew apart, just as far as the strap around my elbows would allow. I gasped and choked with the immediate respite. I wanted to throw myself into the cold water of the boathouse. Drowning would be an afterthought.

"Van," Elana was saying. I nodded shakily. We weren't safe yet.

With my hands unbound, I picked up the torch and began to cut Elana's hands and elbows free. She got singed, even with me keeping the flame away from her skin, but she only showed it in clenched teeth and the occasional curse. After that, the rest of the cursed plastic ties were easy.

There was no phone in the boathouse, and the only boat in the wide slip was a dinghy with oars. Not even an outboard.

"Can you row?" I said to Elana.

"I guess. But you—"

"No." There wasn't time for help to get here. Kasym might be preparing to set off the shaped charges right now. The big blast would follow moments later. Uncontained, with the winds in the worst possible direction, I could even envision the blaze reaching the skyscrapers of downtown. There weren't enough firefighters in the state to stop it, once it got momentum.

The boathouse worker was still out cold. I picked him up and set him in the dinghy.

Elana climbed in and began fumbling with the oars. "Van, you don't have to stay."

I untied the lines and pulled the dinghy to the mouth of the boathouse and pointed its bow towards the Seattle skyline.

"Get to the opposite shore. You go to the first person you see. Forget explaining the truth. Tell them this guy's your dad and he's had a heart attack. Get their phone, and call 911 and say the words *bomb* and *Jurlee Petroleum* as quick as you can. Fill in the rest after. Understand?"

She did. Her face was pale and stricken and fierce around the cat-green eyes.

Before I ran out of the boathouse, I grabbed the claw hammer off the worktable. Better than nothing.

Chapter Thirty-Eight

The ominous clouds finally opened. Splotches of icy rain began to patter onto the ground. Sleet dripped thickly from the chain fence of the petroleum farm. Reuben's men had cut a large, square hole in the fence to wheel the trolley with its deadly payload onto the property.

In the dark, the tanks looked like a pagan holy site, a twenty-first-century Easter Island. Some reservoirs were lean like grain siloes, some fat like small stadiums. Each perfectly rounded and glistening in the gentle yellow lights that shone from the top. Even the patchwork bits of light and shadow on the ground were curved.

At the base of the tank closest to me, I saw the dark boxes of shaped charges stuck to the side. Black tumors marring pristine skin. Glued in place with instant epoxy, maybe.

Pipelines cris-crossed the farm. The small pipes were a foot in diameter and low to the ground, the largest one a yard wide and up on supports. I stayed low and close to it for cover as I ran. The farm smelled cloyingly of gasoline fumes, thick enough that the freezing rain couldn't completely push them aside. Even the air was flammable here.

I didn't know where Kasym was, among the acres of tanks. If they were blowing holes in all of the bigger containers, he would push the incendiary bomb on its trolley near to the center of the farm, for maximum effect.

He'd have a gun. I had a claw hammer. It would be a surprise attack, or nothing.

I ran for a hundred yards, like a rodent scuttling alongside the big pipe. The sleet coated my hair and my back.

Then I saw it. The Mark 77, on its trolley, halfway between two gigantic tanks. No Kasym. And no packet bomb visible on the long blue-white tube of the Mark 77, either. Good. Better than good. Kasym must still be off setting the last of the shaped charges.

I found a guardhouse, a glassed five-foot-square shack for the petro farm security to stay out of the weather. It was empty. The phone lines had been torn away from the wall and the receiver.

As I turned back toward the pipeline, I felt the whip of a bullet passing the bridge of my nose. It splintered the glass behind me.

I ran.

On the second shot I heard the little crack of a suppressor, like a clap heard from far away. Handgun. Sixty or seventy feet off. Kasym was taking the time to aim. I rolled under the pipeline. A third round dinged a metal support strut only a foot from my knee.

Taking cover would be pointless. He knew I wasn't armed. He would just walk up and blow me away. I needed distance. The ground was becoming slick with rain and ice granules. I heard Kasym's footsteps, running after. My legs pumped as I sprinted hard for the shadows between the tanks.

No more shots whipped past. He was concentrating on catching me, or at least keeping me in sight. A lethal game of tag. I rounded one tank, then another, skidding on the wet pavement. I glanced back and saw him, dressed for the exercise in his tracksuit but hampered by the pack on his back, which still looked half full. I was winning, stretching the yards between us.

But Kasym didn't need to catch me. Just attach the packet bomb to the incendiary, get clear of the blast zone, and set off the charges. How many minutes did we have, until the firestorm?

He wasn't following anymore, I realized. A muffled thump came from back near the big pipe, a hundred feet away. Was he moving away from me? Or circling around, to put one between my eyes?

I had stopped next to a set of narrow stairs that wound up and around the side of the nearest tank. Being on top would give me a better vantage. Staying down would give me room to run.

I went up. Slush wept from the thin steel grate of the steps. I took big, low strides while holding on to the railing, three stairs at a time.

On my tenth step, maybe thirty feet up from the pavement, I saw Kasym. And froze.

He was making his way very quietly around the curve of the next tank over, his automatic leveled in two hands. Maybe he didn't have the big bomb ready and didn't want to risk any interruptions. Or maybe he just really wanted to kill me.

I couldn't move. Any sound, and he'd look up and have four shots in my center mass before I could complete a step. The sleet spun through the air in tiny cyclones, in and out of the light, lending everything around us a diamond sparkle.

Kasym kept advancing. Halfway around the curve now and almost directly in front of me. I played rabbit, waiting until the fox padded away into the tall grass.

He passed. And felt my presence, high above. I knew it an instant before he did, and even as he started to turn and raise the gun I was following through on a fastball throw of the hammer. It whirled and glanced off his head. I heard the gun clatter on the ground as I bounded down the stairs.

The hammer had dazed him, but he was not down. He reeled after the fallen gun. I tackled him. We rolled through shallow puddles of ice water. He clocked me hard across the cheek with his elbow. I kneed him in the stomach. On my second kick he got a forearm under my chin and shoved until I gagged. He was very strong. I heaved and yanked and got him off me. His other hand dipped toward his waist as we stood and I hit him one hard straight right before jumping back. The blade of his knife sizzled the air in front of me.

He lunged. If he hadn't been stunned he might have put the knife hilt deep in my heart. But he overextended, and I grabbed him by the wrist and chopped my hand down on his elbow. The knife fell from his numb fingers. I tried to twist his wrist behind him, around the backpack. Rip his arm off at the shoulder. He drove me into the side of the steel tank. My arm holding his was trapped between us. He hit me with his big fist under the ribs. Pain. My whole body shook with the force of it. I spun away from the next punch but he had me now where I couldn't dodge. And his head was clearing.

Instead of trying to push away, I clinched with him. I couldn't take another paralyzing hook to my kidney. Kasym pushed harder, trying to mash me right into the paint of the tank. He stank of old sweat and grease. My hand clawed at him, trying to get a hold. The fabric top of his rucksack was open. He drove the bone of his shoulder under my chin. Pressed into my windpipe. Over his back, I saw the little red packet bomb with its timer. I couldn't breathe. My fingers closed almost robotically on the dial. Red numerals appeared, bright in the shadows both real and in my brain. 01:00. And then 00:59. The timer beeped as its numbers counted down.

Kasym heard it. Knew what it meant. His eyes went wide in panic. He shoved at me, but now I was the one holding tight. He thrashed like a shark, trying to head-butt, to claw, anything. I hung on. The timer beeped, almost happily.

347

It wouldn't be bad to go out like this. With an enemy. With purpose.

I'd miss Luce.

And there was still Reuben.

Kasym stepped back and shoved frantically again, and this time I let him go. The weight of the rucksack stumbled him backward. I punched one-two-three one-two-three, all head hunting, not caring if I broke my hands on his skull. He fell to a knee and I kicked him so hard in the ear that he flew sideways to the ground.

Then I was running, a lurching monster's gait. How far away did I need to be? Twenty yards. Thirty. I fell more than dived behind the curve of the next tank and looked back.

Kasym was still, incredibly, conscious. He was up on his knees. He'd gotten the rucksack unbuckled around his chest and was removing the strap from his shoulder when the bomb went off.

I have seen it before. I wish that I could say I was still amazed by the effect of high explosives in very tight proximity to the human body. But suicide bombers are as much a fact of modern warfare as mustard gas was a century ago. And there is not much variance, not with a bomb that close. The middle of the body vaporizes. The extremities often remain.

Chapter Thirty-Nine

Half-blinded, ears ringing, I staggered my way through the gore to retrieve Kasym's gun. An FNP-45 with a chunky rectangular suppressor. Ten rounds left in the magazine, and one in the chamber. Enough. I also snatched up the claw hammer, which was slick with blood. Black smoke swirled and danced, thrown this way and that by the whirling sleet.

Some part of me realized that I was running on very efficient autopilot. Fury and training combining to shut out any pain, any distraction from the objective. The objective being Reuben K. The rage said *Go*. The preparation said *This Way*.

By the front guardhouse was a flatbed diesel Ford, empty of any load. I climbed up and smashed the window with the hammer, and used it again to crack the steering column so I could reach its ignition wires.

Even in first gear, the moving truck snapped the padlock and chain on the gate of the petroleum farm like they were licorice ropes. I swung the truck onto the road, tires skidding on the wet asphalt, and let all eight pistons eat as much fuel as they could handle. It was a little over a mile to the BerPac yard on the opposite corner of the island. I had the flatbed in fifth gear before I had to brake and turn wide to the right. I wanted as much of a running start as possible.

The gate at BerPac was a lot tougher than a chain-link on hinges. The flatbed truck weighed about five tons. Its speedometer was cresting forty miles per hour when I hit the gate.

It wasn't even a contest. The gate crumpled like tin foil and exploded backward, flying wildly through the air to chop like a giant's cleaver into the BerPac building. The truck bucked and slowed but didn't stall.

I saw the scene through the cracked windshield in tableau. The loading dock's crane in motion, with a huge steel shipping container suspended in midair on fragile-looking lines. One thug behind it. The second man to the side by a waiting semi-trailer, gawking at the oncoming flatbed. I pointed the wheels at the big target of the container box, letting the truck coast as I jumped from the cab and rolled twice on the pavement.

Two seconds later the flatbed walloped the container and the massive box spun madly, rainwater spraying off it. Cables snapped with high-pitched bangs. I was up and running. A scream sounded somewhere under the crash. Then came an almighty kettledrum boom as the corner of the steel container, loaded with seventy million in precious metal, fell to the dock.

One of the thugs had ducked beneath the semi-trailer. He saw me advancing, the gun in my hand, and he took three big running steps and jumped off the dock into the Sound.

Reuben ran out of the BerPac building, holding a cell phone. Maybe he had been trying to reach Kasym to figure out why they'd only heard one pop, when they'd been expecting a whole fireworks show.

He gaped. The sight of me had to be a hell of a shock, even without my looking like I'd been tenderized and broiled. He dropped the phone to fumble at the small of his back. I smacked him in the forehead with Kasym's pistol. He flailed and I hit him again. I grabbed my Glock from his belt and tossed it aside.

Reuben was still standing, that big head surprisingly tough, but too disoriented to do more than keep his balance. Blood was starting to run down his face. One of his hands moved thoughtlessly to touch it. I frisked him, found his car keys in the pocket of his leather jacket and took away a knife and his wallet. He was starting to fight back again when I wrenched his arm and frog-marched him over to his electric-blue BMW. I bounced his face off the bumper twice before stuffing him into the trunk.

Tires screeched behind me, where the gate had once been. I wheeled around to see Addy Proctor's old Saab clattering its way across the yard. Leo was driving. As he came to a stop, I saw that his face was a mask of dried blood, from a deep cut on his forehead.

"Jesus Christ," I said, stepping up to the car. "Reuben said you were dead. I was about to go hunting for your body."

"I'm a little surprised, too," he said. He opened the door and shakily lowered one leg to the ground. The Mossberg shotgun was resting in his lap.

"What the hell happened?"

"I got antsy waiting in the car. We'd been parked there all day long, you know? Risky. So I went to ground in the bushes nearby. Two of those assholes"—he nodded at the BerPac building—"came sneaking up in the dark, making so much noise I could have heard them if I'd been playing drums. Idiots."

"Are they dead?"

"They wish." He lifted the Mossberg. "Your granddaddy's rubber shells. I figure I broke a few of their bones, shooting that close. I tied them up and gagged them with some of your neighbor's yarn from the backseat and left them in the sticker bushes."

Addy's knitting securing two Bratva killers. That was a mental picture.

From high up on the bridge, I heard sirens. And many more coming, somewhere in the distance.

"What about your face?" The flesh around his forehead cut had swelled. A last few drops of falling sleet did what they could to wash the blood from his cheek.

Leo looked sheepish. "I slipped. Smacked my head on the concrete." He closed his eyes and winced.

"Don't go to sleep," I said. "We'll get you to a hospital."

"Yeah. That might be a smart idea. I got to the car and drove off to find you, but I passed out somewhere off the road. Lucky I didn't drive right into the water."

I couldn't see the emergency vehicles coming down the long overpass onto the island, but I could see a river of lights, flashing off the low, dark clouds and making prisms of the rain.

"We both had some good fortune today," I said. "Let's get the hell out of here while it lasts."

Chapter Forty

A few hours later, I was sitting in a gravel lot two miles off the North Satellite terminal of Sea-Tac airport. The lot was empty, waiting for a construction project that might never come. Reuben's BMW was about the only thing in a hundred yards, any direction. The BMW, and me, and Reuben, still in the trunk.

He had made a lot of noise for the first half hour after I'd stopped. Threats and promises and pleas like a play-list on repeat. I heard him continually trying the interior trunk release, which I had broken before closing him in. When his raving stopped amusing me, I told him that if he said another word I would run a hose from the exhaust pipe into the trunk and let the carbon monoxide calm him down. He held his tongue for another hour, when he'd asked for water. My answer was to start the engine and rev it once. There was no more chatter after that.

I had not minded the wait. I spent most of the time in the driver's seat, slipping in and out of sleep. The pain of my burned wrists, and too many contusions to count, kicked rapid eye movement in the ass every time it got near. Finally I was rested enough to get out and walk around the parking lot. The cold felt good. A few

354

laps and my steps were a lot more reliable than when I started.

Around six in the morning my phone rang. I told an unfamiliar male voice at the other end where I was. He hung up without another word.

Twenty minutes after, two black limousines pulled into the lot. I stood beside the open BMW. My Glock was visible in the front of my waistband. The dead Kasym's FNP was at the small of my back.

The limousines stopped abreast of each other, twenty feet in front of the BMW. Two large men in rumpled dark suits and white shirts with no ties got out of the front of the left limo. Another similarly dressed man got out of the driver's seat of the second car. They all left their doors open.

The men looked around the lot. Looked at me.

"Throw the gun away," said the one who had been driving the second car. He had a heavy Eastern Bloc accent.

I smiled and shook my head.

Couldn't really blame them for being cautious. Besides the hardware, I was filthy and scarred and looked like a rabid dog who would enjoy passing along the sickness.

I heard the whir of a window rolling down. The man who'd spoken to me leaned in to hold a conversation in very quiet Russian. The other two men and I watched one another.

Finally the driver opened the back door of the limousine, and Lev Kuznetsov stepped out.

There was no question he was Reuben's father. Same height, stretched much thinner and slightly stooped on Lev, and the same big forehead. Where Reuben was balding, Lev was completely hairless. His eyebrows were so pale as to be invisible. Lev was older than I'd imagined. He must have been near fifty when Reuben had been born. He wore a black double-breasted suit with wide lapels and a tie the color of late-summer corn. His black knee-length coat might have been sable. If so, it had cost more than his son's Beemer.

Most of all, Lev looked immaculate, despite the long flights. Maybe that was the secret to power. Kings stayed elegant while soldiers got dirty.

If my gun caused him any concern, he didn't deign to show it. He walked up to stand ten feet from me.

"You are Shaw," he said.

"Yeah."

"Willard has said that my son has caused you troubles." Lev's accent was very thick and he spoke crisply, as if testing the proper pronunciation.

"Not just me." And I was sure that by now, it wasn't only Willard who had fed Lev information about what had happened in Seattle. The old king may know more about Reuben's schemes than I did.

"I am here," Lev said. Meaning, *Hand him over.*

I nodded and didn't say anything.

"Yes. The deal. Willard said of your concerns, your—" He made a please-fill-in-the-blank gesture.

"Conditions."

Lev nodded shortly. "I would like to hear these from you. Your words."

His voice was spiced with anger. I knew I was following a new map through a minefield. You trust that the path is safe. But not one hundred percent. Lev Kuznetsov had avoided a very bad situation, by luck rather than by his own intrigues. He might feel indebted, and pissed off about that unfamiliar emotion. He might be offended that I had laid a hand on his son, no matter what the cause. Ego was unpredictable.

"I'll give you Reuben, relatively intact," I said. "You get to stop a coup. Reuben will know all the Bratva captains who were ready to back him. In return, your Brotherhood forgets about me and my people. And I get your promise that Reuben won't ever be a threat."

"That condition, I can give the promise. Your people?"

"Reuben tried to kill my woman, and my friend."

Lev made a small hum of acknowledgment. "And you have him alive."

"Because he's worth something."

"Not money?"

"Not money."

Lev nodded. "You are not fearing, meeting me—us—like this?" He dipped his head toward the empty lot.

"Willard respects you," I said.

Lev made that same little hum. He looked over the hillside that bordered the lot, still grassy and lush even in

357

winter. A moment passed as he thought about whatever he was thinking about. I didn't have to think. My options were very limited, if this went sour. But I was willing to bet large.

"Willard has talked of you with the same regard," Lev said. "This deal can happen."

I leaned into the BMW's driver's side and popped the trunk.

I had expected Reuben to call out once he knew his father was near. He had not. When I saw him in the trunk, matted with stink and trickles of crusted blood on his face, I understood why. His eyes had the bright, unadulterated terror of a child who is certain that the boogeyman lives in his closet. And who has just seen the closet door move.

The two men from the other limo hustled Reuben almost gently into the backseat. One sat next to him. The other waited by the driver's door.

Lev had not looked directly at his son during the whole exchange.

"I will have some—adjustments—to make," he said. "There will be opportunities. We would welcome a man who earns respect."

"No. Thank you."

He nodded and walked back to the limousine. His driver held the door for him and they all got in their cars and drove away, headed back toward the airport. By this time his private plane would be refueled and checked and ready to return to Siberia.

A few minutes passed. I sat on the hood, taking deep breaths.

Willard finished walking down the hillside and crossed the wide parking lot to meet me. He wore a trenchcoat over his suit, and the coat and his pants were wet where he'd been lying in the grass. The Merkel .30-06 with its telescopic sight was slung over his shoulder. It looked like a BB gun in his hands.

"Everything good?" he asked.

"I don't think Lev and I will be sharing vodka shots soon, but yeah."

He put the rifle into the BMW's open trunk and shut it.

If I had drawn the Glock, the plan was that I would start shooting Lev's men working from my right inward. Willard would start with the men to my left. I didn't plan beyond that. My odds of survival wouldn't rate it.

"Thanks," I said.

Willard shrugged. "It took a lot for you to trust me."

While I had been negotiating with Lev Kuzetnov, I had also been very aware that Willard could have changed his allegiance just by changing his aim by about half a degree.

"Don't suppose Elana would have forgiven me," Willard said.

"Your niece isn't someone to piss off. When Kend and Trudy were killed, she went hunting for the murderers herself."

Willard showed surprise about as much as he showed any other emotion. His eyebrow twitched. "To kill them?"

"She loved Kend. And she's got a lot of steel. When things got very bad with Reuben, she didn't crack."

He took a long inhale. "I'll be damned."

"Won't we all."

He looked over Reuben's BMW. "Nice ride. Is it yours now?"

"I miss my truck. If you can fit into it, I'll give you a lift back to your car."

He managed, with his head denting the roof fabric and his shoulder pressing me off center from the steering wheel.

Chapter Forty-One

Addy Proctor and I were sitting at a circular table on her narrow front porch, taking advantage of a sudden spell of bright sunshine in between the winter drizzles. I was rewiring one of her table lamps. Addy was reading a novel by Pat Barker and diligently eating oatmeal cookies.

Sunlight or not, it was still cold. Addy had encased herself in a couple of thick blue sweaters and a black cloak, of all things. Even Stanley, lying at her feet, had a wool plaid blanket over him. The blanket had many gnawed patches. He kept his eyes open just in case a cookie rolled off the table.

Guerin's silver Lexus turned onto the block and pulled up in front of Addy's house. Stanley noted my attention and a growl started somewhere down around his pelvis. I put the toolbox on my lap and put the tools on the table away in its plastic tray. While the open lid concealed my hands, I slipped the Smith & Wesson from under my coat and into the bottom of the box and covered it with the tray as Guerin got out of the car.

"I'll put your tools in the coat closet," Addy said. She hadn't missed my little sleight of hand. "If we're away when you come back for them, you use your key." Stanley stayed with her as they went inside.

"You should have called," I said to Guerin. "What if I'd gone to Rio for Carnival?"

"Then I would have assumed you'd fled the country," he said, without any levity.

He sat down in the chair Addy had just vacated. There was something in Guerin I hadn't seen before. He looked as shipshape as ever. But he carried an unseen weight underneath the spotless glasses and starched collar. Like the detective had gotten plenty of sleep, but no real rest.

"This isn't official," he said.

I nodded. He wasn't holding cuffs. I wasn't calling Ganz. That was the only way an official visit could go, right now.

"Got something new on Broch?" I said.

"Broch," he said, like I'd asked whether the cops were working on who shot President McKinley. "We got other things than Broch. We have a suspected terrorist, identity as yet unknown, who blew himself up so completely I'm glad there's any DNA left. We have the manager of a boathouse next door, who was meeting a client he knew as Mr. Algin. That's about the last thing he remembers. The poor prick was so doped up that night that even if he fingers Algin someday, which I doubt will ever happen, any defense attorney can blow holes in it like—well, like the dead fool who left his size twelve boots as his suicide note. And we have one very large firebomb which, from the whispers, has been missing from an Air Force base

362

for over a year. Not that the Pentagon will confirm that."

"Where'd this happen?" I said.

He ignored me. "We also have a stolen truck from the petro site, which crashed into a Russkie shipping company on the other side of the island. Another dead body there, looking like Godzilla stepped on him. The stiff is clearly Russian, based on his dental work, but damned if anybody will ID him, either. The Feds and Customs agents are going over BerPac splinter by splinter." He pointed at me. "And of course, there's your buddy Leo, who happened to be wounded that same night."

"Injured. He was injured. Fell down the steps over there at the house."

Guerin glared at me. "You are too fucking cute by half. You think you can't get nailed? Usable prints are on something, somewhere. Or we'll find a camera somewhere that wasn't knocked out that night, with your very identifiable mug right there on high-def."

I took a sip of Addy's lemon tea. "Let's say any of that happens. Nail me for what?"

He kept up the cop stare for another moment before leaning back in his chair. A fire engine drove down the block, probably on its way back to the Madison Park station. We both watched it pass.

"Yeah," Guerin said, still looking at the street. "Everybody knows we dodged something really goddamn nasty. One of the Feds couldn't even stand to be in the middle of the petro tanks while they were dismantling all the bombs and checking for booby traps. Said it was like being in the middle of an inhale, with the scream about to happen."

I raised my eyebrows. That was how it had felt to me, too. I didn't share the thought. But maybe I understood why Guerin looked the way he did.

He turned back to me. "So all this crap goes public and it takes six months to get your ass into court. Maybe you wind up visiting Gitmo for a while. Maybe you're a fucking national treasure, for as long as the news cycle lasts."

Guerin stood up.

"Or maybe it's a sleeping dog," he said. "We haven't decided yet. But keep Rio out of your plans. You don't want people getting the wrong idea."

"I'll be right here," I said. "I got a house to build."

Chapter Forty-Two

Barrett and Parson Yorke brought Elana to the cemetery on Crown Hill to visit their friends' graves. They had all missed Kend's funeral the week before. Elana had been in hiding during the ceremony. Barrett had stayed with her distraught brother.

Even now, Parson looked shaky. The bruises from Rusk's beating had healed, but his hurt went deeper than that. He was out on bail, after a lot of legal legerdemain by the Yorke family. They were playing him up as a big, dumb kid who trusted the wrong people. It wasn't bullshit. But his passport had been confiscated by the Feds, just in case.

The cemetery still allowed upright grave markers, which were scattered in familial patches through the grass and trees and flat stones. Kend's was a small wedge of granite, with his full name and birth and death years on a plaque. Other Haymes graves were nearby. On the oldest, the dates were so smooth that I could only make out that the stone had been carved in the nineteenth century. Kend's marker was the smallest.

Barrett read a poem. Parson stood and stared blankly at the marker. Elana wept, silently.

In the days after Harbor Island, Elana had told me her story of the long, horrible night at the cabin. Kend's gambling and his evasiveness had been driving a wedge between the two lovers. Barrett had been a focal point of that tension. Elana had been convinced that she and Kend were having an affair.

When Kend had called Elana and said he was leaving for the cabin, she suspected the worst.

"I thought about how weird that was for him to just leave, and I kept obsessing about Kend and Barrett, together." Elana had told me. "Then I called Trudy and ragged to her about all of that same crap for half the evening. Finally I figured, screw them both. I might as well catch them in the act."

"You and Trudy drove out together. In her convertible," I had said.

"Kend had taken my car, since he didn't have one anymore. I was so mad. That was just twisting the knife, right? Taking off for the weekend with Barrett in my own car."

"What happened?"

"Trudy and I got to the cabin. It was really late, almost morning. No Barrett anywhere. Kend was still awake. And angry. He said we had to leave, but he wouldn't tell me why. He kept looking up the road."

"Waiting for Reuben to come and buy the Tovex." But it had been Kasym who had made the witching-hour visit instead.

"Finally I was so furious with Kend that I had to leave, to go up to the main house, and cool off. Our fighting had exhausted Trudy. She stayed. In case Barrett really did show up, but also because she didn't want to drive anymore."

Elana had returned an hour later, to find a nightmare.

"I hardly remember seeing them," she had said to me. "Isn't that strange? It was so—"

"I understand." I remembered the cabin a little too well. When the images came back, Elana would need help dealing.

"I just remember running. Running for help. Running away. Maybe whoever had killed them was after me. I drove as fast as I could. It wasn't until I got to the ferry that I realized my purse was back at the cabin. Trudy's purse was still in the car. So I paid for the ferry with her cash, and that gave me the idea."

"Hide out as Trudy," I said, "until you were safe."

"By that time I knew—or thought I knew—why someone had killed them. Kend had been honest with me, about the gambling at least. He was in way too deep. We'd argued about asking his father for help, but he wouldn't. I was sure I could find his bookie. I risked telling Parson I was alive. He tried to help me by placing bets around town, asking who knew Kend. Broch's name rose to the top of the list."

Which was why Parson had called Broch's place of business, and made himself a prime suspect in Broch's murder. For all Reuben's boasting of doing me a favor by eliminating Broch, the loan shark's death had also snipped a loose end that might have led back to the Russians, after all the bombs went off and Kend was linked to their theft.

Elana and Barrett had cried a lot together during the past week, and reconciled. Their circle had become smaller, and tighter.

They didn't leave a rectangle of bare earth on graves anymore. Too bleak, probably. Strips of fresh grass sod made an emerald patchwork in front of Kend's marker. Elana bent down and placed the bouquet and touched Kend's name for a long moment.

"Thanks for coming," she said to me, rising. "Walk with us to Trudy?" Trudy had been cremated. Her urn was in a columbarium on the cemetery grounds.

Elana was unsteady on the dirt path on her heels. She took my arm as we walked down the gentle grade toward the enclosed mausoleum.

As we made our way through the cemetery, I finally shared the whole story of what I had done with Reuben Kuznetzov. Her mouth was set in a firm line of approval at hearing how Old Lev's men had hustled him into the limousine.

"I knew it had to be Reuben, when you talked about Kend stealing cases from his dad's company," she said. "Reuben oozed up to me at Willard's card game a few months ago. He pretended he was just making conversation. Did Kend work for his dad? Was he treating me right, spending money on me, shit like that."

"Digging for info, and hitting on you at the same time. Efficient," I said.

"Later on I found him getting all chummy with Kend. I thought Reuben was just looking for another sucker to bet big at the card game. But he was setting Kend up the whole time, wasn't he?"

"He was probably already imagining ways to steal the metal from his father. He wanted a big diversion. And Reuben knew how to work with explosives."

"I was ready to murder him," she said. "I *wanted* to do it. Not have Willard step in and handle things. If my uncle never learned about my troubles, that would have been fine with me."

The last time Willard had tried to help, he'd convinced Elana to stay silent about our theft at Gallison Engineering. I still felt shameful about that. And I couldn't fault Elana for being wary of her uncle's priorities. Kend and Trudy hadn't meant anything to him.

Elana and I hung back, as Parson and Barrett stopped to admire some of the older stones. Elana shook her head. "I tried to play Reuben, to get close enough. Told him that Kend's loan shark must have killed Kend and Trudy at the cabin, and that I had run away and hidden for a few days, thinking Broch would come looking for me next. I said I was so relieved to hear Broch was dead, and could I just hang with big, tough Reuben for a while until

I felt safer?" She mimed batting her eyelashes and fanning her face.

"He wasn't fooled."

"Stupid me. I put on the terrified girl act and he said, 'It's okay, baby, I'll protect you.'"

"Reuben wasn't a bad actor himself. And maybe he suspected you already."

"The second we walked in the door at the shipping company, that pet maniac of his stuck me in the neck with a syringe. I knew I was dead. I was so surprised when I woke up in the boathouse. With you."

"I was pretty glad to wake up there myself."

It had been a very, very close thing. I was still pushing the details of that night away with a mental broom handle. I would look at them more closely when some time had passed, and marvel at the nearness of it.

"Willard's asked me to take over the card game," Elana said.

I looked up, jolted out of my musings. "Do you want to?"

"It's a possibility," she said. "I might try being a straight citizen instead. The path not taken."

"What will Willard do?"

She smiled. "I'm not sure even he knows that. But he's gotten edgy. He might need more action than he admits to."

Willard *had* looked happy, with the rifle in his hands after the meeting with Old Lev.

The granite plaque for Trudy's niche was understated and elegant. Elana was pleased. It read TRUDY instead of Gertrude, which Elana said she would have hated.

We walked back to the parking lot. The path was smooth, but Elana took my arm anyway.

"I'm glad that you didn't kill Reuben," I said.

"I was certain that I could, at first." She shook her head. "I'm not sure now."

"It changes you. After."

She looked at me. Her jade eyes traversed the line of each scar in the left side of my face, without haste or shame, and came back to meet mine.

"I wish you could have known them," she said.

I looked across at the verdant lawn, the rows of markers, and thought about that ghostly separation from reality that had plagued me, after the focus of danger. I didn't feel that remove now. I didn't feel any longing to be at war, either.

Mostly, I felt relief that I wasn't occupying one of those graves.

It was enough.

Chapter Forty-Three

Luce and I stood on the orphaned stone steps, looking at the charred wreckage of the house. The bits and pieces had fallen where they had first burned, and the rain in the days since had steadily driven the ash and smaller chunks down into the hollow of the old stone foundation, creating a pit of wet charcoal sludge. What remained standing looked like a piece of theater scenery.

"What's the opposite of *façade*?" I said, stepping down to walk around the edge of the heap. "Is there a word for just the back of a house?"

She smiled, tucking a strand of gilded hair behind her ear. "I wonder sometimes if you've always had gallows humor, or if that's an Army thing."

"Yes and yes."

Two days of sunshine had grudgingly allowed some warmth, and neither of us wore coats. Luce's green blouse replaced a fraction of the color from the trees that were now gone. I wore a plaid flannel shirt with long sleeves, although the temperature didn't require it. The bandages on my burned wrists made too many people look at me with mixed parts embarrassment and pity.

I pushed a small pile of slag and timber out of the way

with my foot. "I'll need a rake and a shovel. Maybe a few things survived."

"One of the gang at the bar will have lawn tools. We'll come out and make a day of it," Luce said, a fraction too cheerfully.

"You don't need to," I said.

"I don't mind." Then she looked at me sidelong. "You don't just mean the salvage work."

"You've been wanting to talk to me," I said. "Waiting until things calmed down."

Luce looked down at the porch slats. The fire had left a piecrust of wood at the far corner. It started three paces from the steps and curved around for fifteen feet before its burned-match end. "You had to keep yourself safe. And me."

"So here we are."

She nodded. I waited.

"We aren't right for each other," she said. "These past weeks, even before this"—she motioned to the house— "I've been in knots. It wasn't about Willard, or even Broch and his goons."

A crow landed on the back fence, looked us over, decided against whatever it had in mind and flapped off.

"We were trying to make a fling more than it was, maybe," I said.

"Please don't. Don't mark us down like that," she said. Her eyes were wet, which added an extra dimension to their stormy color. "When you were here last year, that time was so short and intense. I thought that when you came back home and you stayed, it could go two ways. Either what I felt was all a ball of infatuation and new energy and it would fade and I'd be fine with that ending. Or we'd develop into something more."

"But neither happened."

"No. And you know it, too, I can tell. I'm wanting you more. And you're pulling away. This nightmare with Kend and the Russians, for God's sake. That wasn't why. That just gave you a direction to go."

"I don't mean to."

"If you did, this might be easier. You seemed—*happy* isn't right. Resolute. More than with me."

"I don't need thrills to be happy, Luce."

She thought it over. "Maybe not. But it doesn't change the fact that you're bred to it. That kind of excitement. After all the grief of the last week, could you say you would have preferred to stay out of it? If Elana and all those people hadn't needed saving, would you still have gotten involved?"

I didn't know how to answer conjectures like that. I hadn't jumped in looking to play hero. Or even because I wanted to see Reuben K hang. If the bombs had gone off and the city had burned, I would never stop wondering if I could have stopped it. I couldn't have lived with the question. Not if I stayed in Seattle. Maybe not anywhere.

None of which mattered to me and Luce, together. The answer wouldn't fix us.

"Our lives," I said. I had thought I was going to say more, but whatever words were next didn't arrive. We both just stood.

"I like running things. I'll probably find something else to manage, after I sell the Morgen someday," she said.

"I'm not blaming the bar. Or you."

She stood at the edge of the highest step. The kind of woman the Norsemen had in mind when they dreamed up Valkyries, high on the wing over the battlefield.

"I really do—" Luce said, and I was shaking my head to stop her almost before she'd started.

It was probably true. All the more reason not to hear it.

Chapter Forty-Four

It didn't take long for the winter rains to return. A soft, icy patter had driven the most of the world indoors while Leo and I ran on the two-lane road of the Arboretum. We wore waterproof gear with hoods and baseball caps. Our feet, mine in my broken-in ASICS and Leo's in a pair of New Balances we'd bought earlier in the morning, were wet. Seattle socks.

Each time a car would approach, we'd jump the tiny, rushing river along the curb and wait for the car to hiss past. We could have run through the mud alongside the road. Or taken a longer route to loop back to the house. But the slower pace was better. Leo was still healing. And although the bandages were off my wrists, every once in a while a joint or muscle would twinge to remind me that it was less than happy.

"You ever been through here before?" I said, nodding at the dogwood trees.

"No," Leo said between breaths.

"It's bare-looking now, with the leaves gone. When spring comes, it's a hell of a place."

We waited for one minivan to ease past. Leo watched the tree line, scanning it in the same way he'd had eyes on every street and car we'd passed.

"You sleeping?" he said.

"Mostly," I said. "I had that old dream just last night, with the rifle fire. But I could sleep after. You?"

"Off and on," he said. "But the days are better."

We came to the end of the park and wound our way around to Montlake. I stopped to stretch out my Achilles. Leo stood, shoulders back, exhalations making white bursts in the air.

"V.A. gave me a start date," he said. "Last week of March."

"The inpatient program?" I asked. He nodded. "How long?"

"Two weeks, they think. Out-care afterward."

"Not too long."

"Not too long," he agreed. "And it's in the city."

"So I can visit."

"Yeah."

"Maybe your nurse can, too," I said.

He glanced sideways at me. "You know about that?"

"She blushed a little when I picked you up at the hospital last week. And her blouse wasn't all the way zipped."

Leo might have smiled. It was hard to tell sometimes with Leo.

He wasn't the only one making plans. With the paltry insurance on the house, I had just enough to afford a new foundation and to buy the lumber for the framing. I'd figure out the rest as I went.

A future, one piece at a time. Luce wouldn't be part of it. I'd have to take that in steps, too.

"How far?" said Leo, looking up the hill of 24th Avenue.

"To my street? Over a mile, all up. It's a meat grinder."

"We could catch the bus," he said. "If you want."

"I'm not the guy with stitches in his head."

"Screw that. Bet a steak dinner that I can beat you." His grin was obvious now. Baiting me. Trying to take my mind off my troubles.

I came out of the stretch. Bounced twice on my toes, loose and springy, and looked up the long, steep incline.

"Shut up and run," I said.

Acknowledgments

I would like to thank the following people for making *Hard Cold Winter* a warm season:

First, to my editors Lyssa Keusch at William Morrow, and Angus Cargill at Faber & Faber. They have been tremendous collaborators in shaping the novel and adding depth to its characters, and they make a tough job look positively elegant. I am especially grateful for their encouragement and enthusiasm through the challenges of writing a book to deadline, which may be the most unnerving part of any writer's sophomore effort.

The teams at both houses are the best any author could want. Sincere appreciation and admiration to Danielle Bartlett, Kaitlin Harri, Richard Aquan, Mark Steven Long, and Rebecca Lucash at Morrow, and to Sophie Portas, Luke Bird, and Katherine Armstrong at Faber.

My agent is Lisa Erbach Vance, at the Aaron Priest Literary Agency. Lisa navigates waters for which I not only have no charts, sometimes I'm not even sure I have a boat. Her expertise and understanding keep me afloat, and it's my great fortune to work with her. Caspian Dennis of the Abner Stein Agency carries the flag superbly for us on the opposite shore; thank you, Caspian.

This novel is fiction, and I occasionally play fast and loose with jurisdictions, geography, methods, or anything else that will keep the story moving, keep the legal teams happy, and keep classified or dangerous information where and with whom it belongs. That said, I have aimed for accuracy wherever possible. I am deeply indebted to the professionals, both named and anonymous, who have lent their hard-won knowledge and experience to the work. From the veterans of the United States Army, those include Christian Hockman, Bco 1/75 Ranger Regiment, and Matt Holmes, 82nd Airborne, 1st Brigade combat team. From law enforcement and emergency services, my thanks to Officer David Jacus and District Ranger Dean Yoshina, both of the U.S. Forest Service, and to Fire Chief Matt Cowan. As always, the really cool stuff is theirs, and any mistakes are mine.

I belong to a writing group led by the amazing teacher and author Jerrilyn Farmer. Her contributions and those from the rest of the Saturday Morning Gang—Beverly Graf, Eachan Holloway, Alexandra Jamison, and John McMahon—can't be overstated. An extremely talented bunch.

A belated thanks and love to friend Áine Kelly of Galway, Ireland, for providing the Irish Gaelic phrases for my first novel *Past Crimes*. I messed up and left Áine out of the acknowledgments in that book, but hope to make it up to her by stealing even more of her time to help with the next work. We'll negotiate over pints.

To my family, immediate and extended: I love you. Could never do it without you. Would never want to.

And finally: A piece of every book belongs to those who make time for it. Thank You, Dear Reader.

Now available in paperback

ff

Past Crimes

COME HOME IF YOU CAN . . .

Answering voices from his past, Van Shaw – soldier and former thief – returns to Seattle after a decade's exile, only to find a whole heap of trouble, and himself the prime suspect in a brutal attack on his grandfather, Dono.

Plunged back into the dangerous underworld he had vowed never return to, Van finds that the secrets held by those closest to him may be the deadliest of all.

'This guy has got what it takes.' Lee Child

'Lee Child's hero, Jack Reacher, may just have a fresh rival . . . The flashbacks to his past, and the dark characters he encounters along the way to this personal epiphany, make Hamilton's first Van Shaw novel and his formidable protagonist hard to resist. There will be more; Shaw is too taut and smart a hero for there not to be.' *Daily Mail*

'A zipline ride of a thriller . . . Hamilton has crafted a compelling new hero in Van Shaw.' Gregg Hurwitz, *New York Times bestseller*